To my two favorite women in my life:

Connie, my wife,
Without you these books when have never
seen the light of day. Thank for your endless
support and limitless cuddles!

Carol,
It's been one hell of an adventure. Thank you
for being such a significant part of it and
caring so much what happens to these
characters.

SHADOWS OF THE EVER-AFTER

* * * * * *

BOOK TEN

* * * * * *

D.W. Neuman

ALSO BY D.W. NEUMAN

FICTION

SHADOWS OF THE EVER-AFTER
Copyright © 2016 by D.W. Neuman

ISBN (978-0-9907247-8-0)

Nothing's forgotten,
Nothing's ever forgotten.

-Robin of Sherwood

1
Saturday November 17, 2001

When we last left our heroes, Thomas, Sam and Bill and their families, were being held in Building 42, an underground facility deep within Area-51 while the world, and millions of its citizens, succumbed to Dr. Matsushita's deadly plague. And then things got worse when Dr. Matsushita used Emily's ability to regain his powers, imparted a heart attack unto the President of the United States and commanded Gavin to open his portal, which released dark creatures from the Other Place into the world.

* * *

Fire alarms emanated throughout Building 42. Seconds later an automated voice instructed the facility's inhabitants to evacuate in an orderly manner.

"Let's move," Robert told his wife, Hobbes and Gabbi. "But stay close."

The four of them hurried down the corridor as doctors, scientists, support staff and off duty guards opened their own room doors and joined them as everyone headed towards the large elevator. Once there they stepped inside and moved to the rear as it filled up. As soon as the elevator reached capacity the doors closed and it shot to the surface and dispensed everyone aboard into the hanger. The doors closed and the elevator descended to retrieve the next group. Armed guards were stationed across the hanger entrance to prevent anyone from leaving.

"Now what?" Emma whispered.

"Follow me," Robert told them, "and look confident."

With Robert in the lead the four approached one of the guards.

"Halt," the soldier ordered.

"Take it easy Sergeant. I'm the Director of Central Intelligence."

"Yes, sir, I know who you are, but we have orders to keep Building Forty-Two on complete lockdown."

"I'm countermanding those orders, Sergeant. I've been given instructions to escort these two scientists, along with my wife, to a top secret location to further develop the cure."

"On whose authority, sir?"

"The President of the United States. Now get out of my way, these two have millions of people to save and every second I stand here arguing with you means the loss of additional innocent lives."

The soldier stood fast, his eyes searching the ex-DCI's face for a hint of deception. After an excruciating long six seconds he finally acquiesced.

"Very good, sir. Be careful out there."

"Thank you Sergeant, we will."

The four strode out of the hanger towards an enclosed aviation fence off in the distance.

"Don't look back," Robert told them, "and keep moving. We're almost there."

When they reached the fence Robert scanned his badge. The gate beeped open and they pushed through.

"That one," Robert said and pointed to a mid-sized helicopter.

"I didn't know you were a pilot," Hobbes said.

"Neither did I," Gabbi added.

"He's full of surprises," Emma, Robert's wife, told them as they climbed onboard.

Robert pulled his right door shut and began the startup process as Emma closed the front left door. Hobbes and Gabbi piled into the rear seat.

"Get your seatbelts on." Robert looked over and saw a few of the guards pointing at them. "I think this is going to get bumpy."

As the propellers began to spin up six guards sprinted towards them.

"Oh shit, they're coming," Gabbi informed them.

"I see them," Robert replied. "But I still need twenty more seconds."

"They'll be here before that!" Hobbes exclaimed.

"I know! I know!"

The guards made it to the fence, badged themselves in and raised their weapons at the occupants inside the helicopter thirty feet away.

"Fifteen seconds. Come on you piece of shit."

"Get out of the helicopter!" one of the guards yelled and made a motion with his arm that indicated the same intent. The six men fanned out in a semicircle, their rifles up and ready to fire.

"Ten seconds."

"Exit now or you will be fired upon!"

"Fuck, they're going to kill us," Hobbes uttered.

Emma turned her head towards her husband. "I love you."

Robert never had a chance to reply as Emma disengaged her seatbelt and burst out of the helicopter, her door left wide open.

"NOOO!" he screamed after his wife.

Emma ran straight at one of the guards, screaming at the top of her lungs. The guard depressed his trigger and shot her three times. Blood, from the exit wound, sprayed into the cockpit and splashed across the console and Robert's face as her body pitched backwards from the bullet impacts and crumpled to the pavement.

"NOOOOOO!" Robert screamed as a beep sounded from the console that indicated the propellers were at speed.

The other guards turned to reacquire their targets in the helicopter.

"GOGOGOGOGO!" Gabbi shouted. "GETUSINTHEFUCKINGAIR!"

Robert, knowing his wife sacrificed herself for their freedom, pulled hard on the throttle and stomped down hard on the right rudder. The helicopter lifted off the ground and pivoted to the right, bullets impacting its side rather than the windshield. As the rudder spun in their direction the guards had no choice than to dive out of the way or become paste. In that moment Robert centered the rudder and pushed forward on the cyclic stick. The craft shot forward, soared over the fence and flew just feet off the ground as they made their escape across the enormous desert complex known as Area-51.

"What the fuck just happened?!" Hobbes yelled from the backseat of the helicopter as Building 42 grew smaller behind them. "What the fuck just happened?! I don't understand! Why would they do that?!"

Gabbi was just as hysterical and emotional as Hobbes was, but she tried to calm him down anyway while tears ran down her own cheeks. "I don't know Hobbes. Just try and breathe. It's going to be okay."

"It's not going to be okay!" he insisted. "Look Gabbi," Hobbes said as he pointed to the helicopter console. "Emma's blood is all over it!"

"SHUT THE FUCK UP ALREADY!" Robert Duncan, the former Director of the CIA, roared from the front seat as he wiped his face. His fingers came back with some of his wife's blood on it and for a few moments he couldn't tear his eyes away.

Hobbes and Gabbi closed their mouths and began to internalize the horrific event they'd just been subjected to as

4

Robert continued to pilot their stolen, and now damaged, aircraft towards Las Vegas. He checked the instruments and noticed that both the oil pressure and fuel gauge were steadily dropping. He strained his neck to his right and checked the tail of the helicopter looking for any damage. Nothing.

"Look out the left side window," Robert instructed, "and tell me what you see."

Hobbes didn't move so Gabbi leaned over him and peered out the window. She didn't like what she saw.

"Shit. It looks like we're leaking some sort of liquid; fuel maybe from some bullet holes."

"Any smoke?" Robert asked.

"No, sir."

"Okay, good." Robert kept the helicopter low and steady as they rocketed across the desert floor, staying low in hopes of evading the radar.

"Are we going to make it to Vegas?" Gabbi asked, somewhat alarmed.

"As long as the oil pressure doesn't drop too much more I think we'll make it in one piece."

Hobbes lifted his head. "What happens if we lose oil pressure?"

Gabbi answered. "Oh nothing; well other than the fact that the engine would seize up and we'd crash."

Hobbes eyes widened. "I don't like the sound of that."

"Well it's not going to happen," Robert told them. "If anything we should be worried about a fighter jet blowing us out of the air."

"Wait, what?" Hobbes anxiously looked out the window at the surrounding sky.

"We just escaped from Area Fifty-One of all places and on top of that I threatened the President."

"Threatened him?" Gabbi inquired.

Robert nodded as he concentrated on the fast moving terrain in front of them. "Yes. I informed the President that I'd tell the world he was the one responsible for the plague that's ravaging our world."

"That's ballsy."

"Let's just say he didn't take it particularly well which is only part of the reason why we needed to get out of there."

"What's the other?" Gabbi asked.

"The other is that I made a promise to Thomas, and his family, that I'd protect them. We all know how much that's been skewed ever since Nikolay Dmitriev emerged from the portal. Thomas, because of me, was exposed and hunted down like an animal, then delivered right to the doorstep of the sonofabitch Dr. Matsushita."

"I hate that guy," Hobbes uttered. "He gives me the creeps."

"Not to mention he's responsible for the deaths of millions of people. I should have put a bullet in him when I had the chance."

Gabbi spoke up. "Dr. Matsushita knew but no one could kill him because he was the only one that could manufacture the cure before it was too late."

"Exactly."

Robert changed course slightly to avoid navigating into one of the mountains that surrounded the perimeter of Groom Lake. He gently tilted the helicopter's nose up to gain some altitude.

"Come on girl," he coaxed the flying deathtrap, "you can do it."

Hobbes and Gabbi watched as the side of the mountain filled the cockpit's view. And then, just as quickly, they were over it.

Robert descended as low as he could as the lights of Vegas appeared in the far distance.

"I think we're going to make it," he told his passengers, "but I'm pretty sure we were picked up on radar coming over those mountains."

"What's that mean?" Hobbes asked. "Are they going to come for us?"

"Most assuredly. But we can lay low in Vegas for a few days and try to avoid anyone coming after us."

"I sure hope so."

The helicopter zipped low over the bleak landscape towards the city.

"Sir," Gabbi started, "I...um...I just wanted to say I'm sorry about your wife, Emma."

Robert could feel his wife's dried blood on his face and, out of his peripheral vision, could see it splattered across the console. He winced as his brain continuously replayed her death in his head over and over, her body pitching backwards as the bullets hit her. Her final words she spoke before she exited were etched in his memory. *I love you.*

"I don't want to talk about it."

"Of course. Sorry."

Robert rechecked the gauges again, as he'd been doing since their escape, and realized they were going to make it. He carefully redirected the helicopter towards McCarran International Airport and began to watch for powerlines they could run in to.

"Where are we headed?" Hobbes asked.

"An annex of McCarran airport," Robert replied.

"Annex?"

"More specifically we're going to land at JANET."

"What's that?"

"JANET. It stands for Just Another Non-Existent Terminal. The CIA, and other divisions of the government, fly their employees out of JANET to Area Fifty-One and back every day. The planes are non-descript and access to it is highly regulated and restricted."

"That's how they get to work? Why didn't I know that, since I worked for the CIA at one point?"

"It's not something that is discussed," Gabbi explained, "unless you work in Area Fifty-One."

Hobbes gave her a strange look. "So you've..."

"If I told you I'd have to kill you," she said in an attempt to lighten the mood.

"Oh, ha ha."

Robert began to scan the radio for any tower traffic but all he heard was static. He scanned the sky for any other airplanes or helicopters but it was clear. Hobbes and Gabbi also peered out the windows as the airport came in to visual range.

"It's like a ghost town," Gabbi muttered.

"No shit," Hobbes said in agreement.

"We're about to enter JANET annex," Robert informed them.

The helicopter, on its last leg, flew over the fence line and touched down in a designated landing zone.

"Hold on, don't get out yet," Robert said as he scanned the surrounding area for any signs of threats. Seeing nothing out of the ordinary he disengaged the helicopter's power and shut it down. The propellers took a minute to spin to a halt as they continued to watch for any signs of life. There was no reaction to their landing whatsoever; nothing.

Gabbi broke the silence. "I don't know whether to be happy or creeped out that no one's paying attention to us."

Robert looked over his shoulder at the two of them, part of his face still speckled in dried blood. "When we get out I want you both right on my tail. Don't talk, just stay with me. We're not out of the woods yet, understood?"

Gabbi and Hobbes nodded.

"Good. Let's go."

The three exited the aircraft and followed the former DCI towards the security checkpoint, which would give them access to the outside world. As they opened the doors to the small terminal they weren't prepared for what they encountered. Bodies, in various stages of twisted anguish and decomposition, littered the floor. The three of them had never really seen what Dr. Matsushita's virus was capable of first hand until now.

"Holy shit," Gabbi muttered as she placed her hand over her nose and mouth in an attempt to stifle the putrid smell.

Hobbes turned to one of the potted plants that flanked the doors and puked into it.

Robert, not sensing any movement from any of the bodies, twisted towards the two behind him.

"Are you both going to be able to handle this because I can tell you right now, it's not going to get any easier. If this terminal is any indication of what lies ahead then you're in for a real awakening." He paused. Listen, don't forget the cure's already been injected into our systems so we're going to be fine."

Gabbi nodded. "I'll be okay, sir."

Hobbes wiped his mouth and stood up. "Me too."

"You sure?"

"Sorry. I guess I've gotten more used to seeing the damage that weapons inflict. This…," he said as he surveyed the room, "…this is something else entirely."

9

"Yes," Robert replied. "Yes it is. But we have to keep moving. There's no telling when they're coming for us."

Robert, without waiting for a reply, turned and headed towards the secure exit. Gabbi and Hobbes shared a glance and then followed behind, stepping over and around the corpses on their way to the exit. Robert, as he approached a downed security guard, stooped down and retrieved the man's firearm from his hand; the same hand he'd used to end his own life as the virus ravaged his body. Robert quickly extracted the magazine, saw that it was only missing one round, and reinserted it back in the sidearm. He placed the weapon in the small of his back, took the dead man's two extra magazines and motioned them forward.

"Come on."

* * *

If they drove any vehicle, they quickly determined, would have been next to impossible due to the roads and sidewalks that were clogged with the dead. Thousands upon thousands of bodies filled the streets, haphazardly sprawled out in some chaotic pattern. Undaunted, but sickened, the trio eventually made their way to the doors of the MGM Grand an hour later and pushed open the lobby doors. Inside the same gruesome scene mirrored the outside that they'd just escaped from. The hotel lobby was filled with dead tourists and staff, all in morbid poses and various death thralls. However, the smell wasn't nearly as bad due to the hotel's frigid temperature provided by the air conditioners and purifiers that continued to operate.

Weapon out and ready, Robert motioned for Gabbi and Hobbes to remain where they were as he inspected the area. Satisfied that they were the only living ones around Robert walked around the extensive front desk area and up to an empty check-in terminal. Once there he waved them over.

"What's the plan?" Gabbi asked as they approached.

Robert kept typing on the keypad as he answered. "Getting us a room."

"A room?" Hobbes questioned.

Robert nodded. "We need to lay low until the cure is dispersed into the atmosphere a few days from now. Until then it's too risky to be outside, let alone on the road."

"The road? The road to where?" Gabbi inquired.

Robert inserted a blank door-card into the machine and waited for it to be encoded. He repeated the process two more times and then handed one to each of them.

"Palm Springs. Thomas and I agreed on a location there for us to meet up once he and his family escape Building Forty-Two."

"In Palm Springs?"

"That's correct. My plan is to utilize whatever resources I can get my hands on to make sure his family maintains their freedom for the rest of their lives."

"And us?" Hobbes asked.

"You are part of their family and that plan. The choice, of course, is up to you since neither of you have any abilities, but they want you both to be protected. However, in the meantime, I have to leave you."

"What?" Gabbi exclaimed. "What do you mean leave us?"

"Don't worry, I'll be back. I just need to gather supplies and weapons. Besides, it'll give me some time to collect my thoughts. I know the President will be sending a team after me so we need to be prepared for when they arrive."

"And what are we supposed to do while you're gone?" Hobbes asked.

Robert motioned at the keycards in their hands. "I wouldn't recommend the buffet at this point, but you should empty out the snack shack on your way up to your room where I highly suggest you take a shower and try to relax. My guess is that the majority of the hotel rooms are either empty or abandoned at this point, especially after the panic hit. There are too many bodies on the ground level, and outside, to indicate anything else."

"Alright. Then what room are we headed to?' Gabbi tested.

Robert finally cracked the smallest of grins. "One of the penthouses of course."

"Seriously?" Hobbes asked.

Robert pulled the handgun from his waistband, and the additional magazines, and handed them to Hobbes. "Sweep the penthouse thoroughly and then barricade the door. When I return I'll knock so you'll know it's me, but don't expect me for at least six hours."

"Thank you."

"Yes, thank you, sir."

"You're both going to be just fine," Robert told them. "Stay safe. I'll see you later."

They watched the former DCI leave through the same doors they'd come through.

"I guess what happens in Vegas doesn't stay in Vegas," Gabbi said offhandedly.

"You can say that again," Hobbes replied as he looked around the lobby and shuddered. Off in the distance the sound of slot machines filtered into the lobby. "So, you think we have time to gamble or should we just head up to the room?"

2
Saturday November 17, 2001

Later that same morning the President, from the depths and safety of NORAD, made a televised announcement.

"My fellow Americans, I send this message of hope out to those that are huddled in your houses and afraid to venture outside. I send this message to those that have experienced the horror that this plague has bestowed upon our world and have lost all hope. And I send this message out to the other countries we share this planet with. America has the cure.

"We're currently mass-producing this cure and forty-eight hours from now we will distribute it throughout the United States in one fell swoop. The cure will be loaded onto rockets, launched into the atmosphere and then detonated. The cure, heavier than air, will float down to the surface to be breathed in. From that moment on you will become immune to this outbreak. Until then, stay indoors and ride this out.

"I know the United States was brought to the brink of disaster, and millions of lives have been lost, but we are strong. We will survive and rebuild as a nation, and we will do it together. With that said I need each and every one of you to help me with this endeavor. America isn't the only country that's suffered and unfortunately our planet will continue to suffer for the next two days until our cure is dispersed. Until that time stay strong and stay safe."

The President remained fixated on the camera in front of him for a few more seconds until the overhead light dimmed.

"And we're out. Thank you, Mr. President."

POTUS stood up from behind the Oval Office desk, a mere production façade to fool anyone watching that he had sent his message from within White House.

"Phone calls are already coming in from heads of state," a staff member announced. "They want the cure."

"Of course they do," the President replied. "Send it to all of them, whether they've requested it or not."

"Yes, sir."

One of his aides walked up to him and whispered in his ear. "We have a situation."

The President walked with his aide to a secluded corner of the room. "What is it?"

"Early this morning Robert Duncan, along with three others identified as Emma Duncan, Hobbes and Gabbi, escaped from the confines of Building Forty-Two and fled Area Fifty-One in a helicopter under the cover of darkness."

Shit. "What? How could this have happened?"

"Sir, a diversion was used, a fire alarm to be precise. During that evacuation the DCI countermanded your orders and boarded a helicopter."

"So you're telling me that all four of them escaped?"

"No, sir. There was one casualty."

"Who?"

"Emma Duncan, sir. She was shot and killed."

Fuck. If Robert didn't want to hang me out to dry before then he sure as hell does now. "Have there been any reports on their current whereabouts?"

"The helicopter was picked up briefly entering Las Vegas airspace, but it was only for a moment. Nothing since, sir."

Dammit. "I want them found."

"Yes, sir."

14

"And I want assurances that Thomas, or any of the others, never step foot out of Building Forty-Two."

* * *

The entire family gathered together in a single room, as a precaution, once rumors began to circulate that Emma had been shot during the escape.

"Do you think Hobbes, Gabbi and Robert got out?" Julie asked.

"I hope so," Thomas stated. "I just can't believe that Emma's dead."

Sam spoke up. "I hate to say it, but now we know for certain that they're going to detain us."

"That's just a fancy word for keeping us prisoners," Bill said. "Why are we still sitting here and not fighting for our own freedom?"

"And go where?" Kim told her husband. "We have nothing. No money; no vehicles; and no place where we'd ever be safe. Presidential pardons or not, we're currently holding the short end of the stick."

"Maybe," Bill conceded, "but the longer we stay here willingly the more time the President will realize he's made a mistake."

"Bill's right," Sam said. "They have their cure and we're responsible for taking Dr. Matsushita out of play for them." He turned to Thomas. "There's nothing standing in their way from putting you back on that table and letting Dr. Glover continue to work on you."

Laura visibly shuddered and Sam caught it.

"Sorry Laura," Sam told her. "I'm just trying to make a point."

15

"You definitely made it," she replied, "and I know we're all on the same page. And that means we all need to get out of here."

"And how do we do that?" Julie asked. "There are guards and cameras everywhere, not to mention the only way to the surface is in that damn elevator."

"We can try brute force," Sam offered, "but we wouldn't get far."

Bill nodded. "Yeah, not with the entire complex rigged with gas. We'd be out before we made any significant progress, not to mention having to contend with an unknown amount of guards on the surface; gunships; satellites…"

"Okay, okay," Thomas said, "we get it. So we need to create a list of what we need and where it's located."

Sam nodded. "For example, the Armory contains gas masks and small arms."

"Exactly," Thomas said. "But we're going to need much more than that to make it in the real world. We need money, a place to hide, supplies and a method of transportation to get us wherever that is. And we have to definitely figure out some of those answers while we're still guests here at Groom Lake. And there's more. I need to tell everyone that the DCI and I orchestrated the escape. I was the one that set off the fire alarm."

"What the hell?" Sam stated. "I thought you despised him for his role in everything that's happened to us?"

Everyone else stared at Thomas as he tried to explain the situation.

"I did. But the safety of all of you takes priority. Robert told me two things. The first was that he was going to expose the truth, to the world, about the President's intimate knowledge and involvement regarding Dr. Matsushita's virus. Robert knew that POTUS would never let him live to disseminate that information.

16

Second, and more importantly, Robert told me that the President won't recognize the pardons he's issued to us and will rescind our freedom."

Laura spoke up. "But I know he wasn't lying when he made the deal with us."

Thomas nodded. "I know, but look at our current circumstances. The President has the cure and is coming off as a hero. Dr. Matsushita is in custody and has been neutralized, thanks to Emily. But the world still knows who we are and what we're capable of. The President can't afford to just let us walk away."

"I don't like where this is headed," Kim said.

"Me either. But Sam was right when he commented that 'they're going to detain us now'. I mean, why wouldn't they after murdering Emma, which in turn means Robert, Gabbi and Hobbes were also targeted during their escape. We can't just sit here and hope that everything's going to work out in our favor. History has proven that course of action has never worked for us."

"Okay," Bill said, "I believe we all follow your logic. Go back to the part where we're somehow supposed to rendezvous with them in Palm Springs."

Thomas took the time and caught each pair of eyes before he continued.

"We're in serious danger and we can no longer stay here. Dr. Glover has tortured me and it's taken every ounce of will I have not to go over to his lab and kill him where he stands. But if I did that our current level of freedom would immediately come to an end."

Laura took Thomas' hand in hers and squeezed it gently as he continued.

"We all know that Building Forty-Two is going to remain on lockdown for the next few days until the rockets disperse the cure into the atmosphere."

"You know they're going to scrutinize our every move," Bill told them.

"Exactly, which is why we need to appear passive but stay vigilant at the same time."

Sam took the lead. "Bill and I will map out the security team's schedules and routines, and locate their Armory."

"I figured you'd want to do that," Thomas told him, "but I have a different idea about that."

"I don't understand," Bill said. "This is what Sam and I do for a living."

"True, and if I were them I'd never take my eyes off either of you."

Sam recognized the truth of Thomas' statement. "Alright. So what are you proposing?"

Thomas paused. "This may be a delicate subject at the moment...but..."

"We're family brother," said Bill. "Spit it out already."

"Okay. I propose Sarah, with her power of invisibility, help us."

"Absolutely not," Kim declared. "I will not allow my daughter to participate in any of this. She's been through enough already."

"Mommmm," Sarah rebutted, "I want to help."

"Don't talk back to me young lady."

"I'm thirteen and not a child. You can't tell what I can and cannot do."

Sarah stood up and promptly vanished from sight. Emily, Gavin, Edward, Craig and Amanda giggled. Edward then levitated off the floor and began to float around the room, a huge smile on his face. Craig started to phase in and out as they all watched Edward fly. Sarah reappeared across the room, beneath her airborne brother, and repeatedly jumped to catch him. The kids loved every second of their antics.

"I don't get it," Kim said. "Why is this so funny?"

Julie finally spoke up. "Because, sis, I now realize how much of an asshole I've been."

Everyone in the room stopped and turned towards Julie, stunned looks on their faces, especially Sam's.

"What does that mean?" Kim asked her sister.

"It means," Julie continued, "that I've been living in denial for far too long, unable to accept the truth that's been in front of me this entire time."

"Which is?" Sam cautiously tested.

Julie smiled at her husband. "That all of you are my family and that whatever circumstances led us to this point all we have are each other." She took a few seconds as Sam pulled her close. "I've been selfish, I know that now, constantly complaining and bitching. But the truth is I've been scared to death and all I wanted was for my family to be safe. What I didn't want to truly accept was that I need all of you in my life regardless of the circumstances, truly bizarre and out of this world as they happen to be."

Smiles formed on everyone's faces.

"I guess what I'm really trying to say is that I don't care if my children have special abilities. In fact, I'm glad they do, and so should you sis."

"Why?" Kim asked.

"Look at them, they're happy. And then look at where we are. We're trapped underground in a secret government facility and yet our children are still smiling. How amazing is that? But that's our current reality; we're trapped and we need to work together to find a way out so we can get back to actually being what we are, a family."

Silence permeated the room.

Julie spoke again. "Isn't anyone going to say something?"

Sam opened his mouth. "Honestly sweetie, I think we're all in shock."

Julie jokingly punched him. "You bastard."

"I'll pile on," Bill said with a smile. "Hey Laura, was Julie telling the truth?"

"In fact she was."

"Seriously?" Julie kidded. "You just had to go there, didn't you, Bill?"

Bill and the others chuckled. Julie turned to Kim.

"Sis, I'm sick and tired of being scared and so can you."

"I'm not scared," Kim replied as she defended her actions.

"We all are, but life isn't going to go back to normal, and at this point continuing to deny that is a waste of time and energy. I'm guilty and I've been selfish, and I freely admit it. But we need to move on and come to terms that our children now have unique abilities and only by banding together will we be able to survive any of this."

Sam hugged Julie. "I'm proud of you."

"Don't get me wrong, Sam," Julie replied, "I'm still glad that you're out of a job at SANDBOX."

Sam faltered. "Wait, what?"

"You heard me. You and Bill put yourselves ahead of your family time and time again. You know how I feel about that, which is why we moved to Hawaii four years ago. But we're not taking this moment to rehash that." She turned back to Kim.

"What I really want to know, sis, is how you plan to handle this situation."

All eyes were trained on Kim. Edward and Sarah walked over and sat down by their mother's side.

"It's going to be okay," Edward assured her.

"I can do what Uncle Thomas is asking," Sarah said.

Kim dipped her head and a single tear rolled down her face. "This isn't a game and I don't think you understand that."

"I get it," Sarah said.

"No, no you don't. Everything becomes real when you're hovering over your husband, in a hospital bed, who's been shot. The game, or at least the thought that everything was a game, immediately fades away when you realize your soulmate could have been taken away from you." She looked back at Thomas. "And now you want my children to step into harm's way? How am I supposed to deal with that?"

"Honey..., I...," Bill said and then faltered.

"Because," Laura offered, "haven't we already been dealing with it?"

Laura's words struck Kim right in the chest and sunk in. She faltered.

"Wow Laura, you're right. Until now you and Thomas have been the ones bearing the brunt. And now, with my kids given abilities, well, now it hit closer to home. I'm sorry. I didn't mean any disrespect. This is all completely new to me."

Julie put her arm around her sister. "It's new to both of us, but we're going to get through it together because we have to. Now, we need to plan on how we're going to get the fuck out of here."

3
Monday November 19, 2001

Two days later, after a whirlwind of mass production and engineering, the United States was ready to disperse the cure. Five hundred nuclear tipped missiles had their atomic payloads switched out and were all now in the final phase of prelaunch. Deep within NORAD a multitude of operators worked the consoles as the President looked on.

"Three-three-five through three-four-nine just came online in Nebraska. I'm showing green across the board. Please confirm."

"Roger that. Confirmed."

"I now show that all birds are green and prepared to fly."

"Green confirmed. Stand by." The operator turned to the President. "Sir, awaiting your launch authorization."

The President watched the enormous main screen and absorbed the incredible amount of work that had been accomplished in so little time. Missile trajectories crisscrossed the United States and were overlaid with cure disbursement projections.

We've lost so much in such a short amount of time, but we've also come a long way. I will be the world's savior and I will lead us into the next era of mankind.

The President swiveled his head and looked at a smaller screen to the right that constantly monitored the status of the Russian fleet and frowned.

If Demian Anatolievich thinks he can continue to threaten the United States then he's sorely mistaken. I'll give him just one more day before I blow his ships out of the water.

"Sir?"

The President refocused on the task at hand and addressed the servicemen and women in the room.

"Each of us here has been tainted by this deadly plague as it indiscriminately decimated one populated area after another across our great country. Its reign of terror ends now and we will take back this land. My authorization is omega-five-niner-sierra-charlie-xray."

The operator punched in the President's code. "Authorization identified and accepted. On your mark, sir."

"Mark."

Across the country silos spewed missiles into the sky and left white trails in their wakes.

"What's the countdown?"

"Two minutes until synchronized detonation, Mr. President."

"Very good. Carry on."

All eyes watched and never wavered from the monitors as the computers tracked each missile's progress and displayed it in real-time. The first minute ticked by at an agonizing slow pace for everyone in the command center.

"Sixty seconds."

I will rebuild this nation and make it stronger than ever before. And to accomplish that I'll need to utilize Thomas Clark and his family of freaks. Their powers, if properly harnessed, will elevate our country to a position of dominance; a position that can never be rivaled. But sacrifices will have to be made along the way, and those responsible for our current dilemma will pay the ultimate price; isn't that right, Dr. Matsushita?

"Twenty seconds."

The President stared silently at the screen as the final seconds ticked down.

"Five seconds."

24

"Four"

"Three."

"Two."

"One."

"We have detonation."

Satellites, who had been visually tracking hundreds of missiles, captured the exact moment as all five hundred rockets exploded in unison, at the edge of space. The air, above the United States, became chock-full of the cure as it filled the empty space and began its gradual descent back towards the Earth. Cheers instantly saturated the command center as a multitude of congratulatory hugs and handshakes were exchanged.

An operator took that moment to change the clock to display two hours. He then punched a button and it started to count down.

"Two hours until ground saturation is fully attained, Mr. President."

* * *

Throughout the country the effects of the cure, as it was breathed into lungs, were immediate. Nodules, on hundreds of thousands of infected people, shriveled and fell off their bodies within minutes, their smallpox symptoms annihilated. Still, chaos continued to grip the infected zones as buildings burned and bodies littered the streets. But for the moment a new sense of hope washed over the country.

The President, having seen the cure's results from a variety of surveillance cameras across the country, took to the air waves to make a new announcement.

"My fellow Americans, we have prevailed. The cure has been spread and all you need to do is breathe the air. Look outside and you'll know this to be true. It's time to celebrate!

"But this is just the first step. Now that this plague has been eradicated we need to come together to rebuild this grand nation of ours. Your government, along with your help, is committed to our survival and long-term prosperity. With that being said, I have ordered FEMA into the most heavily affected zones with the assurance that they will have medical and relief teams in place within twelve hours.

"Stay strong and keep your chins up because the worst is now behind us."

The President ended his speech and continued to look at the camera until the lights dimmed.

"And we're out."

He got up from the desk and made a beeline to his underground office where he immediately dialed a well-known number.

"That was a very moving speech, Mr. President. Congratulations on saving humanity. What are your plans now? Going to Disneyland?"

The President wasn't amused and his tone reciprocated his mood. "Move your fleet away from my coastline, President Anatolievich, or I will destroy it."

"Temper, temper, Mr. President. Consider it done. Now, with that bit of unpleasant business behind us, perhaps we should talk about your upcoming plans for Mr. Clark and his family."

"Plans? What plans? Mr. Clark is dead and so is Dr. Matsushita. Whatever future we were going to extract from them is no longer viable."

"Oh come now. You really don't expect me to buy that explanation, do you?"

"I don't care either way."

"Exactly my point, Mr. President. We both know you still have them and just like we both know you're going to keep experimenting on them."

"I can't stop you from thinking that."

"No, of course not. But know this. We'll be watching and waiting. Now, I will commend you on this cure. My people inform me that we'll be ready to spread it ourselves within the next twenty-four hours. Course, can you imagine what the public would think of you if they ever learned that you were the one responsible for the outbreak? It boggles my mind."

The President gripped the phone tightly as Demian Anatolievich continued.

"But that doesn't matter for the moment. I'll just hold that bit of information in my back pocket for a rainy day because right now we're both going to be extremely busy rebuilding our country's infrastructure. Take care, Mr. President, and good luck."

The line went dead. *That smug sonofabitch.* The President put down the phone. *It's time to move Thomas to a new location and deal with Dr. Matsushita once and for all.*

4
Tuesday November 20, 2001

The day after the rockets flew and FEMA began administering aid across the country, the President, back in the White House, made a video call to Groom Lake's Building 42. When Thomas, and the rest of the family, were brought to the large room they instantly discerned that Dr. Matsushita and Dr. Glover were already in attendance. But what they all noticed right away, and that was more disconcerting, were the excessive number of armed guards.

"Are you seeing this shit?" Bill whispered.

"Yeah," Sam replied. "I don't like it."

"Do you think they know about our plan?"

"I don't know. Anything's possible but we need to play along and see why they brought us here. You good, Thomas?"

Thomas hadn't taken his eyes off the two doctors since they'd entered the room and his mind was awash with murderous intent.

"Thomas?" Sam asked as he nudged his friend. "You good?"

"Yeah, I'm good."

Thomas stared at Dr. Matsushita. *What's stopping me from snapping your neck right here, right now? The world would be much better off without you in it. But there's a chance that these guards would then fire on my family so I can't take that risk. Not yet anyway. Count yourself lucky doctor, you sonofabitch. Your time is coming.*

The huge overhead monitor on the wall blinked on, the President's face appeared and everyone turned their attention towards it.

"Good morning everyone. I wanted to take this opportunity to thank you. The cure is a success and in time our country, and the

29

world, will be back to normal. However, I can't stress enough how many millions of lives were lost to this plague. But I'll address Dr. Matsushita and his role in that pandemic shortly."

The President locked eyes with Thomas. "Mr. Clark, what am I going to do with you now that the former DCI, Hobbes and Gabbi have vanished and are nowhere to be found?"

"I don't see why that is any of your concern," Thomas replied. "If I'm not mistaken, we all have our pardons and are free to leave."

"This is true."

"Good. Then we're leaving right now, Mr. President."

The family took a few steps towards the exit before the President stopped them.

"Don't let them leave."

The armed guards instantly raised their weapons. The family froze as Thomas turned back to readdress the President.

"You're a liar."

"I'm a politician, Mr. Clark. The truth is that when I issued you those pardons I actually meant it, at the time. But you need to look at this fluid situation from my point of view. Look at the impact the world has incurred as a direct result of your abilities."

"That's bullshit," Thomas spat out. "You and I both know that Dr. Matsushita was the one behind the genocidal attack on humanity."

"I don't disagree with you," the President said. "But the fact remains you have much to offer the world."

"You can twist your words anyway you'd like, sir, but we all know you're not one of the good guys, certainly not after sanctioning murder and then trying to justify it."

"I did what had to be done and I don't expect you to understand."

"The truth of the matter is that it was your desire, much like Dr. Matsushita's, to take from us. All you want is power, and you don't give a damn about who you have to step on to obtain it."

The President ignored Thomas' comment. "The world has drastically changed, Mr. Clark, and I'm going to need your assistance, whether you give it willingly or not, as we move forward."

"So you're saying our pardons are worthless?"

"No. What I'm saying is that you're new home is now Building Forty-Two. You can fight this change or you can embrace it. That's entirely up to you. In either case, welcome home."

Thomas gritted his teeth and clenched his hands as the President migrated his attention to Dr. Matsushita.

"Yamato Takuma Matsushita."

"That's Doctor Matsushita to you."

"Perhaps, doctor, you'd like to clarify why you decided to murder millions of innocent people. Make me understand."

"I don't have the time, Mr. President, nor do you have the intellectual capacity."

"Wrong answer, doctor. The fact is you tried to wipe out the human race, and for that I sentence you to death."

Dr. Matsushita smiled in defiance, a gesture the President wasn't prepared for. He took the bait.

"And what exactly do you find so humorous about your current situation?"

"I'm smiling because I have a two-part failsafe that I've been dying to use."

"What are yo…"

Yamato twisted around, stared straight at Emily, and spoke.

"Michelangelo."

31

Emily's eyes immediately glazed over. Before anyone realized what had happened Emily bolted away from Thomas and Laura towards Yamato.

"Em!" Thomas screamed.

Barely two seconds had passed before her hands found Yamato's arm, and when she did the command he had whispered to her, when they'd first arrived, activated. In less than a second she had unlocked his mind, giving him full access to his ability that she'd taken from him.

Sam and Bill rushed Yamato but he instantly took control of them, and then Thomas. Utilizing Sam and Bill as human shields he unleashed Thomas' full telekinetic power on the multitude of armed guards scattered throughout the room. Thomas, unable to control his actions, stripped the guard's weapons out of their hands before they could react and dropped them in front of Sam and Bill, who in turn armed themselves. Thomas then tossed the guards about the room like rag dolls; throwing them back and forth into one wall after another, their bones audibly splintering under the forceful impacts.

Sam and Bill, now armed and protecting Yamato, fired on the remaining guards that Thomas hadn't managed to neutralize yet. Blood sprayed the walls as their lifeless bodies hit the floor. The stench of blood, bile and gunpowder filled the room as the carnage concluded.

A mere ten seconds had passed since Yamato had spoken his failsafe word to Emily and Laura, Kim and Julie were left in utter shock. Their children, unfamiliar with such horror and bloodshed, especially at the hands of their own fathers, wouldn't let go of their mother's legs. Sam, Bill and Thomas stood there like statues, still under Yamato's control. Dr. Glover cowered on the floor next to Dr. Matsushita, his hands over his face.

The President had watched all of this in fascination, and in revulsion, as Dr. Matsushita used the three men to easily clear the room. When it was over he tried to appear confident and restarted the conversation.

"Impressive, Dr. Matsushita. I don't know how you managed to gain your power back but you realize you're not getting out of there."

Yamato smiled again. "Do you play chess, Mr. President?"

"Occassionally. What's that have anythi…"

"I mention it because I saw all the moves you were going to make long before you ever made them. I knew you would perceive me as a threat, abilities notwithstanding, and take me out of the picture. The fact is I allowed it all to happen so you'd think you had the upper hand. But your hubris got the better of you when you incorrectly decided to meet with me one-on-one."

"I don't understand."

"You don't have to."

"Enough then," the President announced. "What's to stop me from flooding that building with gas?"

"Nothing," Yamato replied. "But I'll be leaving before that will ever happen."

"You're not getting out of there."

"Oh, but I am. You see, I am the least of your worries."

The President grinned. "The world has the cure already. There's nothing else you can do."

"Mr. President, the world isn't prepared for what's coming."

The President's grinned faltered. "What are you talking about?"

"You thought my plague was something. Well, it wasn't. It was just the beginning. Now I'm going to make it Hell on Earth."

"Wha…"

"Remember when I told you I had a two-part failsafe? Well, I only used the first part. Here's the second part I whispered in your ear, Mr. President. Poseidon."

On the video monitor the President's face changed to one of pain. He clutched his chest as his heart gave out. His torso twisted and his face contorted as he slid out of his chair and out of view. Some Secret Service agents rushed from off-screen to his aid.

"Mr. President! Mr. President. Shit, he's having a heart attack. I need medical to the Oval Office right now! POTUS is down, I repeat POTUS is down!"

"Goodbye, Mr. President. The world will be better off without YOU in it."

Alarm bells started up throughout the facility as Dr. Matsushita, eyes wide, knew he was in full control.

"And NOW for the final act!"

Yamato slowly swiveled until he and Gavin's eyes met.

"Hello young one. I saved the best for you. I hope the booster I gave you works as I intended it to."

"No!" Laura yelled. "Stay away from my son!"

Yamato ignored her pleas as Stir appeared by Gavin's side, red yes blazing. Stir promptly bounded towards Yamato, throat in his sights. A moment before Stir would have landed the death blow he disappeared into thin air as Yamato took control of Gavin.

Yamato laughed loudly. "I'll give you props for trying, Gavin."

"Let him go!" Laura yelled.

"I don't think so. The world barely got a taste of what it's like to feel helpless and afraid, just as I did when the bombs dropped all those years ago. I only gave the world the cure so they could hold onto a glimmer of hope. But now, now I get to rip it all away!"

Gavin, under the control of Yamato, formed his portal in the middle of the room.

"Go ahead," Laura yelled. "Go on through!"

Yamato's smile was wicked. "Oh, I know what's on the other side, and now so will the rest of the world. It's time for everyone to die."

Out of the portal's depths a large hand, with talons for fingers, began to emerge. A shadowy head pushed through, its mouth ready to tear into whatever flesh it could get its hands on.

"OH SHIT! RUN!" Laura shrieked as she forced Kim, Julie and their children towards the room's exit, along with Tad.

Within moments the portal's exit overflowed as denizens of the Other Place rushed uncontested into the world. The shadowy creatures, that had already emerged, flew around the large room in a search of hosts. Some of them quickly fused themselves into the bodies of the dead soldiers while others caught the hectic movement of Laura, who had just pushed her gaggle of wives and children through the exit doors. Laura paused as she looked back at Emily, Gavin and Thomas, still under Yamato's control. The creatures surged towards Laura, talons and teeth extended, only to have Laura slam the door shut moments before they could get their hands on her.

The beings turned away from the closed door and targeted Dr. Matsushita, Thomas, Sam, Bill Gavin and Emily. They soared towards them and one of them took over Dr. Glover's body along the way. Yamato flinched and immediately commanded Gavin to disengage the portal. It winked out of existence and shrieks, from the remaining creatures, filled the room as they scrambled to inhabit the remaining soldier's bodies that littered the floor. Soon after, one by one, those bodies pushed themselves up off the ground. As each of them rose up Dr. Matsushita saw that their eyes now burned with a glowing red aura, something he hadn't expected.

That's strange. Nikolay or Rebecca's hosts never had red eyes. I'll have to figure that out later.

The broken and bullet ridden corpses lingered in place and just stared at them. It was then that Dr. Glover finally spoke up.

"Reopen the gateway."

Dr. Matsushita turned and looked at Dr. Glover, who was ten feet away, and fixated on the red eyes that gazed back at him.

"Reopen the gateway."

Intriguing. "Who are you?" Yamato asked.

"We are Ancient. Reopen the portal."

"If that's going to occur, and if I'm not mistaken, you'll need more hosts to inhabit."

"Yessssss," the voice out of Dr. Glover's mouth hissed as the twenty other corpses continued to remain statues throughout the room, their red eyes constantly watching.

"Very well then. Sam, Bill, Thomas. Go retrieve your wives and children from the hallway and bring them back here to me."

The three men, under the control of Yamato's mind-controlling ability, did as they were instructed and exited the room. Less than a minute later the doors reopened and everyone was reunited.

Julie, Kim, Laura and the five other children let out screams as the hoard of red eyed undead slowly swiveled to fixate on them. Sarah, Edward, Tad, Craig and Amanda quickly found solace as their mothers huddled to protect them.

"Reopen the portal," the being that inhabited Dr. Glover insisted.

"All in good time," Dr. Matsushita replied.

"Open it or we will tear you limb from limb."

"And that's exactly why I haven't reopened it."

Dr. Matsushita quickly took control of the five other children. They broke free of their mother's protective circle and ran over to the doctor's side.

"No!" Julie and Kim yelled simultaneously as the kids slipped out of their grasp.

Laura felt helpless and could do nothing as her husband, along with Sam and Bill, stood in front of Yamato, their minds no longer their own. Dr. Matsushita smiled as he grasped Craig and Edward's hands, who in turn continued the human chain until all seven children and the doctor were interconnected.

"Open the portal," Ancient commanded.

"I plan on reopening the portal, but not here."

Yamato released his control over Thomas, Sam and Bill. They each blinked a few times, as if coming out of a haze, and then took in their immediate surroundings. Sam and Thomas took a few steps towards their wives.

"What's going on?" Thomas asked.

"What happened?" Sam added.

"What the hell?" Bill stated as he looked back at the myriad of red eyes that were now focused on him.

Bill swiveled around, saw Yamato and raised the weapon he now realized he held in his hands. Yamato, along with the rest of the children, phased out just as Bill's finger depressed the trigger, Craig's power extending through all of them. The three-round burst passed harmlessly through Yamato and took chunks out of the wall behind him. Thomas and Sam snapped back into reality and faced Yamato.

"Nice try," Yamato said, "but as you can see I'm quite immune to anything and everything."

Thomas used his telekinetic ability to try and grab hold of Yamato, but it had no effect and Yamato smiled.

"The world wasn't prepared for my plague just like it won't be prepared for its dead to rise and overrun this planet. Perhaps we'll meet again, or maybe we won't. In either case, good luck."

Dr. Matsushita commanded Edward to fly straight up. The eight of them phased out and, collectively weightless, vanished through the ceiling. Ten seconds later, after having penetrated concrete, steel and earth, reemerged on the surface. Back in the large room the six adults had been effectively consigned to their death.

"Time to die," Dr. Glover moaned as the twenty pairs of red eyes sprang into action.

Sam and Bill instantly brought their rifles up to their shoulders, acquired targets and began to fire. Their bullets penetrated the dead flesh but didn't seem to slow them down. Thomas, on the other hand, had immediately moved to Laura, Julie and Kim's side and placed himself between them and the former Dr. Glover, whose red eyes glowed even brighter as he focused on Thomas.

"Die. Die. Die."

The doctor rushed Thomas, arms and hands extended, but was quickly tossed across the room as Thomas exerted his ability.

"They're not going down!" Bill yelled.

"No shit!" Sam bellowed.

The two continued to pump round after round into the rapidly advancing group of undead, backing away towards Thomas and the women as they continued to fire.

"Running low on ammo! Last mag!"

"Ditto!"

Dr. Glover extracted himself from the hole in the wall his body had made and stood back up. "We cannot die. We are immortal."

"We have to get out of here!" Laura shouted to everyone and moved towards the exit door.

"Shoot their legs!" Thomas directed at Sam and Bill. "Immobilize them!"

The two men began to hastily take out each undead's knees. The creature's advance slowed to a devastating halt as their only method of movement turned to dragging themselves across the blood soaked floor. Dr. Glover scowled and advanced towards Thomas once again but came to a stop ten feet away. Sam and Bill trained their weapons on him.

"Hold," Thomas said.

"But…"

"Get them to safety. I'll meet you there."

"Are you sure?" Sam asked Thomas.

"Go."

"Roger that."

Sam and Bill initiated the plan the group had come up with and headed towards the Armory, which had been successfully scouted out by the invisible Sarah two days prior. Thomas waited until he heard the door clicked closed, never taking his eyes off the doctor, or whoever he was, that stood ten feet from him.

"Who are you?" Thomas asked.

"We are Ancient."

The doctor's body was twisted, bones broken. But those injuries apparently didn't bother it whatsoever.

"What does that mean?"

"Your power is impressive, but it won't save you from us," the creature boasted. A cruel and evil smile slowly materialized on his face as the sounds of skittering dead on the floor pulled themselves closer.

Thomas was suddenly reminded of the doctor's heartless and sociopathic tactics and the torture he'd put Thomas through. Thomas was overcome by rage and brought his arms up, his hands formed in claws. Moments later the doctor's head imploded in a spray of blood and brain matter. However, the body remained upright and began to walk right at Thomas, much like the other twenty bodies that were pulling themselves along the floor.

Shit!

Thomas retreated out of the room and raced down the long hallway towards the Armory. Surprisingly he didn't run in to any opposition on the way. He turned the final corner and rejoined the others who had already donned Kevlar vests and rearmed themselves. The women held handguns as Sam and Bill stuffed magazines into their Kevlar vests. Gas masks hung from each their belts and Sam handed Thomas a loaded rifle as he approached.

"Anything new we should know about?" Sam asked.

Thomas took the rifle and then donned his own Kevlar vest. "Dr. Glover's dead."

"We know that," Bill said.

"I mean he's really dead," Thomas insinuated.

"Good," Laura expressed.

"But, he's not down. None of them are. They keep coming no matter what we do to them."

Thomas finished securing his vest, made sure his rifle was loaded and then they all moved out towards the elevator with Sam and Bill on point.

"What the hell was all that back there?" Julie inquired. "I thought Gavin's portal was only one way?"

"We all did," Laura replied. "But I heard Dr. Matsushita say he'd given my son a booster. It obviously worked."

"You can say that again," Bill said. "I'm just glad none of those creatures, or I, hurt any of you while we were under the doctor's control. I'm not sure I could have lived with myself if something had happened."

Thomas gritted his teeth. "We're going to get that bastard, one way or another."

"Damn right we are," Sam added. "But first thing's first."

The group fell silent as they approached the hallway that led to the surface elevator. Sam peered around the corner and saw that it was empty.

"It's clear. Move."

The six adults edged around the corner and filled the hallway. Thirty feet later they stopped in front of the large elevator doors.

"I don't get it. Why isn't this guarded?" Bill asked. "In fact, why haven't we seen a single individual since the portal incursion?"

"I don't know," Sam replied, "but my guess is that a silent alarm must have been activated during the initial firefight, which I don't' remember but obviously participated in."

"So they might be waiting for us on the surface as we step out of the elevator?" Kim asked.

"Potentially," Bill replied. "But what choice do we have. Dr. Matsushita has our children so we have to leave."

"Not to mention now stopping him from destroying the world using Gavin's portal," Laura added.

The six walked into the elevator and Sam pressed the button for the hanger. The doors closed and a moment later the steel box quickly rose towards the surface as each of them mentally prepared for the upcoming fight. Thomas, Sam and Bill stood in front, weapons ready as the elevator slowed and then stopped.

"Here we go," Sam whispered.

The large doors parted and the three men quickly advanced into the enormous hanger and into the crosshairs of ten soldiers, their own weapons aimed at the trio.

"DROP YOUR WEAPONS! DO IT NOW! DROP YOUR WEAPONS!"

In the distance, on the runway outside the hanger, Sam caught sight of Craig and Amanda obediently following Dr. Matsushita up the ramp of a large cargo plane.

"CRAIG! AMANDA!"

"DROP YOUR WEAPONS!"

Bill and Thomas turned their heads and witnessed the same thing Sam had seen, just as their children disappeared from sight inside the huge plane.

Thomas whispered under his breath. "Lower your weapons, I've got this."

Sam and Bill hesitated.

"You sure?"

"Trust me. There's no time to argue."

"DROP YOUR WEAPONS OR YOU WILL BE FIRED UPON!"

The trio slowly stooped and carefully laid their rifles on the hanger floor. As Thomas stood up he sprang into action and yanked all ten of the weapons out of the soldier's hands. Surprised and shocked looks flashed over their faces, but the fight was over before it began. Thomas wasn't in the mood, especially with his children at risk, and propelled each soldier fifty feet away in the blink of an eye. They landed hard on the concrete and were knocked unconscious.

Sam and Bill retrieved their weapons, and sprinted towards the cargo plane whose rear door had just retracted. Two seconds later the huge plane powered up and began to move down the runway. Sam and Bill stopped, took aim at the plane's multiple tires and opened fire. Sparks skipped off the runway and two tires blew out, but that didn't stop the cargo plane from accelerating out of range and lifted into the sky.

"FUCK!"

Thomas, Julie, Kim and Laura ran up to Sam and Bill and watched the plane that carried their children disappear into the distance.

5
The Other Place

The sun on Gavin's tiny desert island, situated in the vast Ocean of Time, was blotted out by the dark energy that swirled around it. Countless malevolent beings glided around the tiny speck of land in a constant, forbearing and endless circuit.

The Caretaker had positioned himself a good distance away from the island and observed the evil that continued to mass; its pulsating eagerness to escape the prison the Caretaker had trapped it in.

The Ancient is beyond anger and any type of reasoning. It is pure evil and will easily consume the world it desperately wants to escape to. I can't let it get away, but there's nothing I can do other than watch and hope.

A bright light appeared on the island, casting light and illuminating the blackness. The creatures surged towards it and began to disappear.

No!

But only a handful of the Ancient's mass vanished before the portal closed, denying the rest its freedom. The creatures buzzed around the lone palm tree, angry and distraught.

Gavin, don't open that portal again…I warned all of you what would happen if you did. The Ancient will kill all of you without a second thought.

As if the portal understood the Caretaker's thoughts, and scoffed, it opened once more. The jailed denizens of the Other Place streamed through it in hordes.

6

Tuesday November 20, 2001

"Mr. President, the world isn't prepared for what's coming."

The President's grinned faltered. "What are you talking about?"

"You thought my plague was something. Well, it wasn't. It was just the beginning. Now I'm going to make it Hell on Earth."

"Wha…"

"Remember when I told you I had a two-part failsafe? Well, I only used the first part. Here's the second part I whispered in your ear, Mr. President. Poseidon."

Poseidon?

The President's face suddenly contorted as his chest exploded in pain, as if a hand were squeezing his heart. He clutched his chest, twisted his torso and fell out of his chair out of view of the video monitor. Two Secret Service agents rushed to his side immediately.

"Mr. President! Mr. President. Shit, he's having a heart attack." He activated his wrist mike and called for help. "I need medical to the Oval Office right now! POTUS is down, I repeat POTUS is down!"

Dr. Matsushita gloated on the other end of the video conference. "Goodbye, Mr. President. The world will be better off without YOU in it."

One of the agents quickly stood up and disengaged the video feed to Building 42 and then knelt back down to assist the other agent. The President's right hand gripped his chest and his breathing was labored.

"Heart attack," one of the agents said. "He's having a heart attack."

"No shit. Medical will be here momentarily." The second agent locked eyes with the President. "Stay with us, sir. You're going to be just fine. But you need to breathe. Don't take your eyes off me, sir, and just breathe."

* * *

It hadn't taken long for the Medical team to determine that the President had indeed experienced a heart attack, but as they examined him further he had become more responsive, as he rebounded from the unpleasant and painful incident.

"Sir," one of the medical attendants said, "we need to get you to the hospital right away for further testing."

The President waved the professional away and ignored his recommendation outright. "I'm fine. I'm tired, but I'm fine."

"But, sir…"

"Get them out of here," the President instructed the Secret Service.

"Yes, sir."

The President sat back down in his Oval Office chair as the Medical team returned their instruments to their cases and left the room. His chest was still sore, and his left arm was slightly numb, but he was alive.

That sonofabitch tried to kill me.

He pressed a button on his desk and two minutes later one of his military liaisons; the same one who had been a part of hunting the Clark's down, entered the Oval Office and closed the door behind him.

"Sir?"

"Where are you with tracking down Robert Duncan, and the two others?"

"They've been trailed to Las Vegas where they went to ground. They've just been located and I have a team closing in on them as we speak."

"Good. Very good. I want them all taken out."

"Sir?"

"I said kill them. Kill them all. Is that clear enough for you?"

"Crystal clear, sir."

The man took his leave and left the President alone.

Oh Robert, you shouldn't have threatened me.

Before the President could continue his train of thought a sharp knock on the outer door interrupted him.

"Come," the President declared.

A high ranking General strode in with purpose and saluted. The President returned the salute.

"You don't look happy, General."

"No, sir, and neither will you."

"Spit it out."

"Yes, sir. The Russian fleet has turned back towards the American coastline."

Anger flared behind the President's eyes. *Dammit Demian!*

"Very well. Thank you, General. You're dismissed."

"Yes, sir."

The President steamed behind his desk. *You can't trust a Russian.* He pressed a very familiar button on his private line and the call was picked up three rings later over the speaker.

"Mr. President, what do I owe the pleasure of your call?" Demian Anatolievich, the Russian President, voiced with glaring disdain in his voice.

"What do you think you're doing, Anatolievich? The cure I gave the world works, so why have you redirected your ships back towards America?"

"Insurance, Mr. President. When I inform the world about the truth of the plague, and your intimate involvement with it, I worry you might overreact."

"Don't threaten me, Demian." A mild pain shot through his chest and he brought his right arm in an attempt to sooth it. "Dammit that hurts."

"Are you in pain? Is there a problem?"

The President, still somewhat out of it began to ramble. "Our mutual enemy, Dr. Matsushita, attempted to kill me earlier. And now I have you compounding the situation."

"Dr. Matsushita tried to kill you? Didn't you tell me he was neutralized?"

The President rolled his eyes. "Details, details. Apparently he programmed me with some code word while I visited Area Fifty-One that would entice me to have a heart attack."

Demian was unprepared for such a candid response from the President of the United States and took full advantage of it.

"While I'm sorry, naturally, to hear that you had a heart attack I must say I find it extremely alarming that you, the President of the United States, might not be in control."

The President finally realized what he'd said. "Wait, that's not what…"

"Furthermore, who's to say that you're in control of any, if not all, of your thought processes."

"Now look here dammit…"

"Thank you for the insight, Mr. President. I now feel even more justified about returning my fleet to your shores, with your new role as Dr. Matsushita's puppet. I wonder what he'll make you do next?"

The President gripped his desk tightly in absolute frustration over his lapse in judgment. "Let me make this as clear as I can for you, Anatolievich. Turn your ships around or I'll blow them out of the water."

"I'm tired of listening to you, and soon the rest of the world will be too. Take care, Mr. President, and I sincerely hope you feel better."

The Russian President ended the call which utterly infuriated POTUS.

"God dammit!"

The President collapsed back into his chair, tired, angry and incensed. His chest ached, and he was short on air, so he attempted to regulate his breathing. A few minutes later he was able to collect himself.

"How do I make this all go away? What the hell do I do now?"

7
Tuesday November 20, 2001

Thomas, Laura, Sam, Julie, Bill and Kim watched as the cargo plane that carried their children, and Dr. Matsushita, disappeared into the distance.

"Why didn't you stop them?" Julie declared.

"We took out a few tires," Sam answered, "in the hopes of grounding the aircraft, but Bill and I couldn't aim at any other part of the plane in fear of causing injury to our children."

"Don't worry, we'll find them and get them back," said Bill.

"How?" Kim asked.

Thomas spoke up. "The DCI and Hobbes will have access to satellites and other forms of intelligence we can utilize. So right now we need to stick to the plan and get the hell out of here before reinforcements arrive."

"Thomas is right," said Sam. "We're still in enemy territory so we can't dawdle. Julie and Kim, come with me."

"Where?" his wife asked.

"To acquire transportation."

Bill nodded. "Go with him honey. Thomas, Laura and I will scour the hanger for anything else we can use."

Two minutes later three SUVs drove into the hanger. Thomas and Bill raised their rifles, as a precaution, but quickly realized it was Sam, Julie and Kim. The SUVs stopped and backed up to where Thomas, Bill and Laura were waiting.

"What'ya find?" Sam asked as he exited his vehicle.

Bill started loading the three SUV with the new gear. "Radios, more weapons, ammo, some grenades and quite a bit of C-Four, along with remote detonators. We've been contemplating that maybe they were going to bury Building Forty-Two, with us inside of course."

"That's horrible," Kim said.

"Horrible, but definitely a surefire way for the President to cover this up. No wonder we didn't find anyone else inside."

They finished heaping the new equipment in the back of each SUV and closed the rear panels. Radios were then distributed to all three vehicles.

"Let's go," Sam ordered and hopped into one of the SUVs with Julie.

Bill and Kim took another one just as Thomas moved towards the driver's seat of the third.

"I'm driving," Laura told him.

Thomas hesitated. "Are you sure?"

"Yes. If you need to use your powers I can't have you distracted."

"Good idea."

They got in and in no time all three SUVs sped out of the hanger and hung a right down the large runway with Sam leading the pack.

"Stay close," Sam's voiced said over the radio to the other two SUVs behind him. "And call out if you see anything inbound."

"Roger that," Bill replied.

"Wilco," Thomas added. *Will comply.*

In the distance, as the runway came to an end, Sam eyeballed two jeeps blocking the dirt road that lead into the mountains.

"We've got company!" he squawked. "Two jeeps! Unknown hostiles! Peel off and fill the runway!" Without turning his head to look at Julie, Sam dropped the radio and readied his rifle, out his open driver side window. "Get your head down."

Julie removed her seat belt and managed to maneuver down to the floorboard. Behind him Bill veered right and Laura went left effectively making themselves three distinctive targets instead of one.

Four soldiers, two behind each jeep, opened fire on the incoming SUVs. Bullets impacted the grills, hoods and front windows as the three drew closer, but with three vectors to concentrate on at once the damage was minimal before Sam, Bill and Thomas were able to return fire. The four soldiers took cover as long automatic bursts stitched bullets across the jeeps, blowing out tires and exploding their windows. Before the soldiers could reacquire their targets Thomas used his ability and upheaved both jeeps end over end with a flick of his wrist while he hung out his window. The soldiers, now exposed, were tossed backwards a second later and landed with hard thuds on the rough earth. The three SUVs reconvened, rushed past the ambush site and drove up the dirt road.

"Nice driving," Thomas told Laura as he reloaded his rifle.

"Thanks, but I can't help but notice that either your powers are growing or you're just getting more proficient at using them."

"I actually think it's a bit of both."

Dust, from the three SUVs, kicked up and formed a cloud in their wake as they zipped up the skinny dirt road as the mountain pass came in to view.

The radio crackled with Sam's voice. "We're clear up front. Anything behind us?"

Thomas picked up their radio and keyed the talk button. "We can't see a thing with all this dust, but I've got us covered regardless."

"Yeah you do," Bill said as he chimed in. "We make one hell of a team. Did you see what Thomas did back there, Sam?"

55

"Yeah. Makes me glad he's on our side."

"No shit."

"Alright," Thomas said. "Enough with the 'thank the guy who has powers'. Let's make sure we get out of here and get to the rendezvous as planned."

"Roger that," Sam replied.

* * *

Ten minutes later the three SUVs breached the outer perimeter of Area-51, made their way to I-15 and headed south. What none of them had planned on, or were fully prepared for, was the multitude of bodies that littered the ground, sidewalks and freeway. Adding to that they needed to avoid vehicles of all sizes that clogged the interstate and surrounding roads. The stationary vehicles created a jumbled mess for the three SUVs to navigate, at a sustained rate of speed, and they had to avoid all the corpses at the same time.

"How do you want to proceed?" Sam asked over the radio.

"Keep going," Thomas replied, "but let us take point. I can push any abandoned vehicles out of our way as we drive down the freeway."

"Good idea."

Laura pulled ahead to the front and Thomas leaned out and started to use his ability to make room as necessary. As they progressed the reality of what had happened to the world, and what millions of people must have gone through, began to really sink in.

Kim was speechless. "We only heard about the plague while we were underground. But…but now that I see what it did with my own eyes…I…I…"

Bill lowered his tone to match the horrific situation they continued to drive through. "Yes, it's extremely unpleasant and evil what Dr. Matsushita did to the world. I'm sorry you have to see this."

"But you're used to this, right? It doesn't bother you?"

"Trust me, it bothers me. But Sam and I have been around this type of carnage for years. I hate to admit it but it becomes background noise."

"How do you train yourself to do that, to block all this out?"

He turned and looked her in the eyes. "By keeping your mind on the task or purpose at hand. Yes, the world is fucked right now and we could easily lose hope with the view that's just outside this vehicle. But there's a motivating force that's keeping me focused. Do you know what that is?"

"Our kids."

"That's right. We're going to get them back and hopefully enact some revenge in the process. Hell, we might even get lucky and end up saving the world."

Kim chewed on her bottom lip. "I want to see that bastard die for what he's done."

"So do I. So do I." He waited a few seconds and then spoke up again. "You still with me?"

Kim nodded. "More than ever."

"That's my girl."

8
Tuesday November 20, 2001

Dr. Matsushita cringed as he heard the gunfire emanate from Building 42's hanger. A moment later, as the large cargo plane shot down the runway, he felt the aircraft lurch ever so slightly as two of its huge rubber tires disintegrated. Two seconds passed before the behemoth rose into the air and left both the runway and the danger behind.

That couldn't have been the soldiers, not after I instructed them to guard the elevator. Dr. Matsushita smiled in the cockpit as he looked out the window. *Well played Thomas. You escaped sooner than I anticipated.* The plane banked to the south and then righted itself, the two pilots under his control.

"Land at your standard runway in Vegas," he voiced out loud.

Dr. Matsushita left the two pilots behind and rejoined his gaggle of seven children who sat in the rear of the plane. *Aren't I the popular one? A real pied piper.* He sat down and buckled himself in for the upcoming landing as Emily, Gavin, Sarah, Edward, Amanda, Craig and Tad remained motionless in their seats under the doctor's control. He turned his head and spoke to the seven of them, knowing full well that none of them could participate in the conversation.

"I've won children. Millions of people have been annihilated, exterminated by my virus. The world is on the brink of chaos as governments scramble to maintain order and a sense of security to their panicked and grief stricken citizens. But when we land I will take any hope the people of this world might be grasping on to and firmly tear it from their grasps."

The smile on his face grew bolder.

"Las Vegas will become the epicenter upon which I purge the Earth of what remains of humanity. And Las Vegas is fitting; an institution of gambling, whores and capitalism. What a fitting location for me to bring this planet to its rightful end."

The cargo plane touched down at JANET and taxied as close as it could to the security building which would house the exit. The rear door lowered, but before Dr. Matsushita exited he made the two pilots extract their service weapons, place them under their chins and pull the triggers. With those loose ends tied up he walked the seven children through the corpse ridden security checkpoint and out of the airport.

Strewn around them, as they walked towards the Vegas strip, was evidence that his plague had been wholeheartedly successful. He took it all in and reveled in his handiwork.

Bodies, and the crows that fed on them, were absolutely everywhere.

Burned out cars.

Smoke from smoldering buildings that had either caught or been set on fire.

Emptiness.

Quiet.

Nothing.

This is absolutely beautiful; breathtaking. What I've done to the world has surpassed my wildest dreams.

The seven children, oblivious to the rampant destruction and endless parade of corpses, trudged behind Dr. Matsushita like puppets, devoid of any emotion or individuality. They finally came to a stop at the intersection of Las Vegas Boulevard and Tropicana Avenue, smack dab in the middle of the large street junction. Around them on the four street corners, rising high into the air, were MGM, New York New York, the Excalibur and the

Tropicana hotels and casinos. A small twenty foot wide open section of road, surprisingly not taken up by the numerous vehicles that congested the road, was accessible. He took his puppets to the center of that area and began to prepare.

9

Tuesday November 20, 2001

Gabbi, refreshed from her shower in one of the MGM penthouses, and wearing a very comfortable robe, looked out a large window over Las Vegas as the morning sun illuminated the strip. She appeared lost in thought as Hobbes approached from behind, drying his hair with a towel and wearing his own robe.

"How're you doing?" Hobbes asked her.

Gabbi jumped, ever so slightly, and turned towards him as he joined her.

"Better I think. I'm just not used to all this death. It's all around me, like hands around my neck; choking me."

"I know how you feel. I was the one who threw up, remember?"

Gabbi allowed herself a small smile as she shifted her body back towards the expansive windows that surrounded the penthouse.

"Yeah you did. I have to say, in a way it was cute."

"Cute?" Hobbes countered with astonishment. "Blowing chunks into a potted plant hardly constitutes cute. Perhaps I should feel your head to make sure you're not sick."

She giggled. "Stop." Her smile faded. "All I mean is that you're still human and this obviously bothers you."

"How can't it? The city appears wiped out, and this is just a drop in the bucket of what that bastard did to the rest of the world. I can't...I just can't wrap my mind around it. It's too much..."

Gabbi reached out and took hold of his hand. "It's okay to be human, and I'm really glad that you are."

Gabbi stepped in close and tentatively kissed Hobbes. His brain immediately exploded in a multitude of sensations as his lips finally returned the affection Gabbi offered. He pulled her close as they began to devour each other. As their robes fell to the floor the world outside melted away, amidst all the chaos, uncertainty and death. Together they found a moment in time where none of that mattered anymore.

* * *

Five hours later a polite knock on the penthouse door startled them. Hobbes peered through the peephole and saw Robert's face. He opened the door and let the former DCI in.

"I'm glad you two are safe."

"We're fine," Gabbi told him. "Where have you been?"

"On a supply run, but I already told you that."

"For six hours?"

"What can I say? I had to remember where some of my CIA safe houses were located. After that it was a matter of successfully navigating to one of them, entering and stripping it of everything useful. I need your help with what I brought back."

"Where?" Hobbes asked.

"It's in the elevator. Gabbi, we'll be right back."

Hobbes and the DCI walked around the corner to the private elevator and pushed the call button. The doors slid open to reveal a number of stacked hard cases.

Hobbes pulled the first two off the pile and deposited them in the hallway. "Wow. It looks like you've been busy, sir."

"Very. Let's get everything back to the penthouse."

Five minutes later, after a number of trips back and forth, the supplies had found a new home.

"So what'd Santa bring us?" Gabbi inquired.

"A bit of everything," Robert replied. "Weapons, food, water, satellite phones, communication gear and more."

Hobbes eyes lit up. "I'll start setting things up."

"Good because I seriously need a shower." The DCI started to walk away and then turned back. "Is everything alright?"

"What do you mean?" Gabbi asked.

"I don't know. Something seems different."

Hobbes and Gabbi shared a quick glance.

Hobbes spoke up. "You're tired. A shower will make you feel like a new man."

"You're probably right. Anyway, I hope you two are rested because we're going to be here for the next three days before we head out to meet Thomas in Palm Springs."

* * *

Three days later, Tuesday morning, the trio repacked the hard cases and deposited them just outside the private elevator in the MGM lobby. Robert disappeared outside and thirty seconds later a large SUV pulled up outside. Together the three loaded the vehicle and then piled inside.

"We have a full tank and three five-gallon containers of gas in the back. That should be enough to get us there without having to pull off the freeway."

"How do we know that Thomas, and everyone else, made it out?"

Robert gave Hobbes and Gabbi a hard look. "We don't know, but we stick to the plan that Thomas and I came up with."

"But..."

"The rest it up to them."

Robert pulled out of the MGM. As their vehicle picked their way around obstacles, on the way to I-15, movement in the sky caught their attention. It was a cargo plane.

"That's odd," Hobbes stated.

"Very," the DCI added.

They watched as a large plane began its final approach to McCarran. Robert changed course and headed towards the airport.

"What are you doing?" Gabbi tested.

"That's an unmarked cargo plane."

"So."

"So, that plane definitely originated from Area Fifty-One and for all we know Thomas could be onboard. We're checking this out."

* * *

"Shit."

Robert lowered his binoculars and made his way off the roof of the SUV he'd been standing on to get a better look down the long road.

"What?"

"I can tell you this much, it's not Thomas."

"So who was on that plane?" Gabbi implored.

A grimace emerged on Robert's face. "It's Dr. Matsushita and he has all seven children with him. They're headed away from the airport towards the strip"

Gabbi didn't like his answer. "He has Gav and Em?"

"What the hell?" Hobbes said. "What's he doing here?"

"We have to save them!" she insisted, somewhat frantic.

"I don't know what he's doing here and it can't be good," Robert said, "but we're no match for the doctor."

"But we have to save them. All of them."

Robert spoke in a calm and collective tone. "Easy. Yes. But the three of us are not equipped to do that which is why you two are going to stick with the plan and go meet up with Thomas."

Hobbes was skeptical. "The plan was for all of us to go to Palm Springs."

"You're right, it was. But we have to stay flexible and that means I need to stay here and keep my eyes on Dr. Matsushita until you bring the cavalry back with you."

Robert walked to the back of the SUV and opened the hatch. Inside he extracted a satellite phone and handed it over to Hobbes. He placed another one, along with a handgun, food and water in a backpack and closed the rear door.

"We'll use these phones to keep in contact. If anything changes I'll call you. When you meet up with Thomas have him call me right away. Now get the heck out of here."

Gabbi gave the DCI a quick hug. "Be careful."

"I will. You too."

Suddenly, in the distance, they picked up distinctive sounds of helicopters rapidly approaching.

Robert pushed them to the ground. "Down. Get down and don't move."

Twenty seconds later two Blackhawk helicopters headed for the strip, filled with armed soldiers, flew overhead.

Robert stood up. "This isn't good."

"What do we do?" Gabbi asked.

"Get in the SUV and get out of here, right now. I need to keep my eyes on the children and see what these helicopters are here for, but my guess is that they've come here for the doctor."

Hobbes and Gabbi got in the SUV and closed their doors as Robert hefted his backpack over his shoulder.

"Are you going to be okay, sir?" Hobbes asked.

"I will be if you can find them. Now go and make sure to take care of each other."

Gabbi backed the SUV up and left the DCI behind them. As he grew smaller in the mirror Gabbi looked over at Hobbes.

"Do you think we just did the right thing?"

"He knows what he's doing," Hobbes told her.

"That's not the same thing."

"No, no it's not. But we're doing what we can to reunite our family and that's a good thing."

10
Tuesday November 20, 2001

"Echo-Base, Sierra-One and Two are inbound to target's location."

"Roger that Sierra-One. Proceed."

Beneath the White House the President, along the Secretary of Defense, a handful of military advisors and technicians, watched the footage from a bird's eye view as the two Blackhawk helicopters entered Las Vegas airspace.

"This is so surreal," the President said. "I knew the plague killed millions of people, but look at the city. Nothing's moving at all. There are just bodies everywhere. It's dead."

"Sir," one of the techs said to the President, "I've got movement outside the designated target's location."

The President leaned forward. "There are survivors? Show me. Put it on the main screen."

The large viewer switched from the two helicopters and fixated on a lone SUV in the middle of Las Vegas Boulevard, south of the Tropicana.

"Closer."

"Yes, sir."

The satellite zoomed in and captured three adults conversing by the rear of the vehicle.

"Closer. I want faces."

The tech maximized the zoom. As the auto-focus corrected itself three familiar faces filled the screen.

The President smiled. "I've got you now, Robert."

They watched the trio separate as Gabbi and Hobbes entered the SUV while Robert hefted a backpack. Moments later the vehicle drove south and the former DCI began to trek north.

"Mark both the vehicle and the DCI as secondary targets and continue to track them. In the meantime, take us back to the main event."

The large screen swapped back to the street junction situated between the MGM and the Excalibur. The satellite image clearly indicated that Dr. Matsushita had seven children which had formed a protective circle around him. It was then that the Blackhawks entered the surrounding airspace.

"Echo-Base, this is Sierra-one. We are on station. How should we proceed?"

"Tell the Special Ops team to neutralize the doctor from a distance," ordered the President.

The technician relayed the command. "Sierra-One. Eliminate target from the air."

"Echo-Base. Target is using children as human shields. Cannot confirm engagement without additional human casualties."

The President keyed the technician's microphone himself. "This is the President of the United States and your Commander in chief. I'm giving you a direct order to open fire. Do it!"

"Understood, Echo-Base, but these are children's lives we're talking about."

"Don't question my authority," the President roared. "Just do your damn job!"

"Negative, Echo-Base. Sierra-One cannot comply. Will engage target on the ground."

The President whipped around and addressed the Secretary of Defense. "I want that man court-martialed for disobeying my direct orders."

The SecDef begrudgingly nodded his head, disagreeing with the President's firmness to endanger the children, but quietly backing the team leader's decision, and upcoming attempt to remove them from danger.

On the screen Dr. Matsushita looked to the sky and extended his right hand, middle finger extended, and smiled.

"That smug sonofabitch. Those soldiers don't stand a chance."

* * *

Dr. Matsushita heard the familiar sound of helicopters and drew the seven children around him. As the two Blackhawks appeared further down the street he turned to face them.

Well, that didn't take long. I wonder who's watching me on satellite right now. He raised his right arm into the sky, gave it the bird and grinned. *Take that.*

The Blackhawks, a hundred feet away, kicked thick ropes out of both sides and, within a matter of seconds, twelve Special Ops soldiers fast-roped out of the helicopter, and immediately took up positions behind the numerous abandoned vehicles scattered throughout the street. The soldiers advanced, their weapons pointed at Dr. Matsushita, until they were only ten feet away. Red dots, from the soldier's lasers, dotted his chest.

"Let the children go!" Sierra-One demanded.

"I'm glad you're here," Dr. Matsushita said as he commanded the children to join hands. After they did exactly that they grasped his. "You're just in time."

"Take him down!"

Dr. Matsushita, along with the seven youngsters, phased out before the bullets could penetrate his body. Round after round cut through the air and passed through Yamato, punching holes in the vehicles behind him.

"What the hell?" Sierra-One breathed out, not believing what he'd just witnessed. "Reload and reengage! Echo-Base, are you seeing this!?"

"My turn," Dr. Matsushita told the twelve operators.

Gavin's portal opened in the middle of the street. A second later, creatures, both dark and horrifying, poured out of it. The twelve men shifted their attack to the new threats and let off bursts of automatic weapon fire, to no avail, as the darkness washed over them. In the creature's wake, all twelve operators having been tossed to the ground, slowly stood up and faced Dr. Matsushita once more; their red, glowing eyes staring at Yamato. Some of the creatures turned back and focused on the doctor and the children, to take them as hosts as well. But each time the creatures attacked the doctor they merely passed through him and the gaggle of children. The beings eventually became frustrated and rejoined the other apparitions that continued to swarm out of the portal and into the world.

Dr. Matsushita was not amused. "That's gratification for you."

All around the street junction dead bodies began to pick themselves off the ground, defiantly standing up. Dozens turned into hundreds, and then thousands as the denizens of the other realm began to inhabit the dead.

"Echo-Base! Echo-Base! This is Sierra-Two! Our team is down! What the fuck is happeni…"

The creatures, mouths wide open and teeth ready to kill, attacked both Blackhawks. The pilots, unable to defend themselves, were summarily populated. Seconds later both helicopters listed to their sides and tilted towards the ground, their controls yanked back and forth by sporadic hands. The helicopter blades struck the ground first, cutting up chunks of pavement and the cars it plunged into. The frames of the aircrafts hit next, crushing numerous undead underneath, leaving a huge trail of destruction in the road behind them. Fires broke out in the downed crafts until one of the fuel tanks exploded, scattering bodies and vehicles everywhere in an enormous fireball.

* * *

Robert Duncan observed everything, through his binoculars, after the two Blackhawks arrived on scene and failed to takedown Dr. Matsushita. When the portal opened up after that he could only watch as the darkness quickly spread in all directions, the dead rising up off the street in its wake. He zoomed in on one of the dead and saw red eyes staring back at him.

"Shiiiiiitttt," he uttered.

Robert dropped his binoculars and yanked the satellite phone out of his backpack. He punched the first saved number and the phone auto-dialed.

"Sir?" a familiar voice answered.

"It's me Hobbes. Don't come back here. Whatever you do, don't come back here."

"I don't understand. What's going on?"

"I…"

Robert looked up just as a creature, talons extended, flew right at him.

"Sir? Sir? Are you there?"

11
Tuesday November 20, 2001

The President, along with the SecDef and other personnel in the PEOC (Presidential Emergency Operations Center) beneath the White House, gasped collectively in horror as the wave of darkness rippled outwards from the portal's epicenter. The satellite's feed captured the dead, scattered throughout the large intersection, rise up off the ground. While the blackness continued to spread it struck the twin Blackhawks that hovered over the street. Seconds later both aircraft tilted forward and to their sides, apparently out of control, and swiftly collided with the ground. Their initial impact drove cars and bodies in all directions, spilling fuel all over the street. Fires quickly ignited and one of the downed helicopters exploded which sent an enormous fireball into the sky. Shambling corpses affected by the explosion, their red eyes ablaze, burned as the hungry flames consumed both clothes and flesh alike.

The portal winked out of existence and the vortex of beings invading the Earth came to an abrupt halt. The darkness had spread throughout Las Vegas and, as the satellite zoomed out, thousands upon thousands of people, previously dead, now ambled freely about.

"This isn't happening," the President mumbled. "This can't be happening. What has Dr. Matsushita done? Las Vegas…it…it was dead, but now…"

POTUS placed an anguished and distraught hand to his forehead as he continued to mutter.

"What do I do? I'm the President, but I don't know what to do. What do I do?"

The SecDef made his way over to the President's side. "Sir, I…"

POTUS cut him off as an idea took hold in his mind. "I know what to do."

"Your orders, sir?" one of the techs asked.

"Nuke Las Vegas," the President ordered.

The technician became uncomfortable. "Sir?"

"You heard me. I want Las Vegas obliterated right the fuck now!"

"But…but, sir, our nuclear launch system doesn't work that way. And even if it did we don't have any nuclear missiles pre-targeted to our own cities."

The SecDef took over. "He's right, Mr. President. I saw the same images you did but we can't just bomb one of our own cities. That's insane."

"Don't tell me what I can and cannot do. We have been invaded and we must strike now to contain it." He pointed at the live feed of Las Vegas. "Any further inaction will result in this world's ultimate demise."

The SecDef shook his head back and forth. "Do not continue down this course of action, sir, or I will have you relieved of duty."

"You're a fool, Mr. Secretary," the President shot back, "but I'm still the leader of this country and my people depend on me to act in times of crisis. And that's what I'm going to do."

POTUS strode to the closed outer doors of the PEOC, opened them and gave instructions to the Marines and Secret Service agents stationed there, who snapped to attention at his presence.

"Remove the Secretary of Defense from the PEOC immediately."

"Yes, sir."

The two Marines strode past the President, their new task in hand while one of the Secret Service agents became worried.

"Is there a problem we should be aware of, Mr. President?"

The President ignored the agent and turned to watch the Marines place their hands on the SecDef's shoulder. They marched him out of the PEOC and right past him.

"Don't do this," the SecDef pleaded. "Innocent lives are at stake."

"Thank you for making my point for me," the President replied. "That's exactly why this needs to be done." He addressed the Marines. "Hold him here for the time being."

"Yes, sir," they replied.

The President reentered the PEOC, closed the doors behind him and bee-lined back to the technician behind the large computer console.

"Now, where were we?"

The technician gulped as the President loomed over him.

"Our country is under attack and the lives of its citizen's rest solely in my hands. I need a nuclear missile launched. Make that happen."

"I...well...," the tech stammered, "I respectfully decline. I don't want to be responsible for this. Where's your man who carries the Football?"

"The briefcase which contains the Nuclear Football, as you well know, is available while I'm away from the White House. We're in the PEOC so stop dawdling. Make this happen before it's too late."

The tech looked at the other men in the room for support but received only blank stares in return. He turned back and resigned himself to the task at hand. He brought up the nuclear arsenal on the computer screen and a prompt immediately filled the screen.

"Yes, sir. I need your access code."

The President withdrew a laminated card from his coat pocket and handed it over. On it were a dozen codes separated by sequential line numbers.

"My authorization code is line five."

The tech keyed the code into the computer terminal and the prompt disappeared. In front of him appeared the United States of America's entire nuclear inventory; everything from land based silos to submarines.

"Sir, you are clear to proceed. The system will challenge your identity prior to launch."

"Understood. Show me the Arizona catalog."

The tech nodded and his hands flew over the keyboard. Seconds later the screen was replaced with a condensed list of Arizona's nuclear portfolio along with the top-secret locations those warheads were located in.

"There," the President pointed to. "Prep one missile from that location to target Las Vegas."

The tech gulped and keyed in the information. A five minute countdown appeared on the screen alongside a final authorization sequence.

"Sir, I need your final verbal code followed by a retinal scan."

"Very well," the President replied. "Enter Alpha-Two-Tango-Niner-Three-Oscar-Mike-Eight."

The computer accepted the code and waited for the scan. The President leaned in and placed his right eye close to the retinal scanner that protruded from the console. A green vertical laser line scanned his eye from top to bottom.

"It worked, sir, we're live."

The President leaned back as the five minute countdown on the screen began to tick down. Ten seconds later the PEOC's private line, reserved for the President during emergencies, began to ring. He made no movement towards it.

"Sir?"

"Let it ring. It's going to be NORAD wanting to confirm that I'm the one who actually initiated this launch. They'll try to convince me to abort and I don't have time to convince them otherwise."

The tech dug deep and found his courage. "Sir, are you sure this is the right thing to do? You're going to nuke an entire city that resides on US soil?"

"I don't want to but you've seen for yourself what Dr. Matsushita has brought into the world. The nuke will succeed in annihilating the creatures that have made the dead come back to life, and kill the doctor in the same strike. If I have to sacrifice one city in order to save the entire world, well, that's any easy choice…and one I've already made."

More phones started to echo from the console and the technician ignored them. Abruptly a scuffle emanated from the other side of the PEOC's doors.

"Let me go dammit!"

The door opened and four men, consisting of Marines and Secret Service, restrained the SecDef where he stood.

"What are you doing!?" he stammered. "I just took a call from NORAD and they told me there's a nuclear missile in countdown to launch."

"Let him go," the President ordered. "But if he takes a step towards me please feel free to shoot him."

The men released the SecDef who immediately straightened his crooked uniform.

"I need you to stand down, sir," he told the President. "Cancel the launch."

"Negative. The time to act is now before the epidemic spreads. I let Dr. Matsushita fool me once before, but not this time. This time I stop his plan before millions more end up dead."

"This is lunacy and you know it. You just threatened to have the Secret Service shoot me."

"No. Lunacy is doing nothing and I will not allow you to interfere while the world hangs in balance on the difficult decision I've made right here, right now. Mankind may judge me, but I know I'm taking the correct and only course of action. Millions are dead and entire communities have been wiped out from the plague. What do you think's going to happen when those millions rise up and slaughter the rest? I can't and won't let that happen."

* * *

China's early warning system blared, followed by the UK's, Russia's, Germany's, and the rest of the worlds, as the missile lifted off from its silo and into the clear Arizona sky.

"Compute that trajectory!" the Chinese officer on duty bellowed. "Now!"

"Working on it, sir. Initial readings indicate that they're firing...," he paused as he verified the data, "...on themselves."

"That doesn't make any sense."

"It's what the computer is telling me."

"Then you or the data is wrong. Run diagnostics immediately because I need to know why our sensors haven't picked up additional warheads."

Twenty long seconds passed as the system verified the data.

"Sir. The system is working fine. The United States has launched a nuclear missile on one of their own cities."

"Has the President of the United States lost his mind? Tell me where the missile will impact?"

"Verifying. No, this is correct. Detonation will occur within the city of Las Vegas."

* * *

The SecDef took a tentative step towards the President. "Sir, stop this before it's too late."

"Take another step and I'll have them shoot you."

The SecDef stopped in his tracks. "You don't have the authorization to blow up one of our cities. One man isn't supposed to have this much power at this disposal."

"If you haven't noticed it's quite a different world out there. We lost a great number of our government hierarchy to the plague and now we stand on the precipice of losing the rest of the world. Don't lecture me on the abuse of power when I'm doing everything I can to stem the flow of evil that has invaded our world."

"One minute, thirty seconds, sir," the tech stated.

"I implore you, stop this madness."

"Have you not seen what's happening in Las Vegas right now?" the President asked as he pointed to the live feed. "What part of 'genocide' don't you understand?" He paused. "Or maybe I appointed the wrong man to the position of Secretary of Defense? When it comes to responding to the World Trade Center attacks you're onboard sending troops to the Middle East. But now, as the dead rise, you have trepidations? Explain to me what am I missing?"

"One minute."

"Annihilating an entire city, not to mention killing any survivors that are in the area, isn't the right course of action. American citizens won't understand, and neither will the world. I'm giving you one more chance to stop this before it's too late."

The President pushed his chest out. "You're giving me one last chance, is that what I just heard you say?"

"Yes, sir, that's correct."

"My order stands, Mr. Secretary, and there's nothing you or anyone else can do about it. It's too late."

"Thirty seconds."

"No, sir, you're wrong about that."

The SecDef turned on his heels, pulled his phone out and speed-dialed NORAD. "Proceed with missile deactivation and nuclear lockdown, authorization Zulu-Charlie-Juliet-Four-Six-Zero."

"No!" the President bellowed behind him. "Stop him!"

The Marines knocked the phone out of the SecDef's hand and onto the floor who then turned around, a smug look in his eyes, and stared at the President.

"It's too late."

"Ten seconds."

The President, flush with anger, turned towards the live feed. The technician had already zoomed out to track the missile. As the seconds ticked down the rocket continued to bear down on Las Vegas from high above.

"Five seconds."

They all watched as the massive missile streaked downwards out of the sky and hurtled into the top of New York New York. The missile, inactive and now just a ballistic nightmare, penetrated multiple floors before it came to a halt somewhere inside the casino's interior. A large section of the building broke away from the impact and plummeted to the street below.

"You sonofabitch! What have you done!?"

"I…," the SecDef began to say before the President cut him off.

"Shut up!" He turned to the tech. "Queue up another missile for launch."

The tech typed away at the computer but a large warning popped up on the screen.

"I…I can't, sir. You've been locked out. There's nothing I can do."

The President pointed at the SecDef. "Get him out of my site. Come to think of it, that goes for everyone. Get out!"

The tech, and the other men in the room, seemed visibly relieved to be banished from the PEOC. As the door closed behind them, leaving the President alone, a new line began to ring.

What the hell does he want?

The President picked up the phone. "What is it, Demian?"

"Have you lost your mind, Mr. President? You launched a nuclear attack on your own soil."

"You have no rationalization to judge my actions, Anatolievich. You haven't seen what Dr. Matsushita has brought into our world."

"What are you talking about?"

"I'll show you. Do you have a satellite over Las Vegas right now?"

"No."

"Then let me send you what's going on so you can see for yourself." POTUS quickly compiled an email and shot it over to the Russian President, along with a link for him to click on. "There. Sent."

"Got it. I'm bringing up the video now." He watched the footage as the darkness swept through the streets, unabated. "What the…? You can't be serious. The dead are being inhabited by those creatures and coming back to life."

"That's what I was trying to stop," the President implored.

"This footage is disturbing, Mr. President, and will help me convince the world that you've lost your mind."

"What? I'm trying to save it."

"Why don't we let the people of the world be the judge of that, alright? In the meantime it appears I have no other choice than to release the facts that you caused the outbreak that caused the death of millions of innocents. I believe it's time for you to be replaced."

"How dare you. Don't threaten me, Anatolievich, you know you're just as culpable."

"I don't know what you're talking about. I clearly wasn't the one who just attempted to 'nuke' one of my own cities. I'm sure the American public will surely want to know about that reckless endeavor as well."

"Dammit! Dr. Matsushita is the one bringing death into this world, as we speak, and you're engaging in politics. These creatures won't care who they inhabit. They're death and they need to be stopped. Help me."

"I don't think so, Mr. President. But I do appreciate the footage you sent me. Thank you."

"You bastard."

"And, why I'm thinking about it, I'll task a satellite to watch over Las Vegas as well. I wouldn't want to miss anything."

"Go to hell."

"You first, but it looks like your version of hell is clearly underway already. I'm glad my fleet is headed back to America, I wouldn't want any of those 'things' to escape your borders."

"Anatolievich, this isn't over!"

"Goodbye, Mr. President, and good luck."

The line went dead. A split second later POTUS picked up a conference room chair and chucked it across the table. The chair nicked the table and came to a rest on the far floor.

Get a grip. What should I do? I have to do something.

The President picked up his private line and dialed.

"Send another Spec Ops team to Las Vegas. I want the DCI tracked down and eliminated, if he's not dead already. Then I want the team to converge on the SUV that contains Gabbi and Hobbes."

"What do you want the team to do with them?"

"Nothing as of yet. Let me know when they've been taken into custody."

"Yes, sir. However, there's something you need to be made aware of. I've gotten word that Building Forty-Two wasn't destroyed, as per your instructions."

"What? Why not? What happened?"

"The surviving soldiers said the family escaped."

"Shit."

"The C-Four explosives, that were going to be used, are missing as well."

"I don't care about that. I'm done playing around. Find Thomas and his family. Find them and have them wiped out."

"Yes, sir."

"The laws of nature must be brought back in to balance, and that means this has to end sooner than later. Thomas and Dr. Matsushita need to be wiped off the face of this planet."

12
Tuesday November 20, 2001

With Laura at the wheel, leading the convoy of three SUVs, Thomas continued to lean out the window and clear a path as they drove down I-15 into the heart of Las Vegas. Abandoned vehicles cluttered the freeway, in both directions, which severely inhibited their progress. Scattered about were bodies, ripe and bloated from the continued exposure to the elements, situated both in and out of the cars. None of it was pleasant to drive through; a constant reminder of what the world had undergone.

"Are you okay?" Laura asked her husband.

"What do you mean?" he replied as he used his ability to maneuver yet another automobile out of their way.

"I mean, are you getting tired? Do you need to rest?"

"Surprisingly, no, but even if I were tired I wouldn't stop. That sonofabitch has Emily and Gavin and I won't rest until they're safe."

Laura drove around another corpse as the radio on the seat next to her crackled to life.

"Umm, everyone," Bill's voice said, "stop your cars and take a gander out your left windows."

Laura slowed to a stop, along with Sam and Bill behind her. Everyone stepped out of the SUVs and formed a group as they tracked the large object barreling down out of the atmosphere. An enormous vapor trail followed behind it.

"Holy crap," Julie uttered. "What the hell is that?"

"That," Sam replied, "is a harbinger of doom."

"You can say that again," Bill said.

"I don't get it? What does that mean?"

Sam took hold of Julie's hand. "That's a missile."

87

Kim became alarmed. "Then what are we standing around for? We have to get out of here."

"There's no time," Bill tried to explain. "because by the look of it that thing's going to pack one hell of a wallop when it detonates."

"And why is no one panicking except my sister and me?" Julie stated.

"Because I think we're all tired of this constant fight," Thomas said. "But, truth be told, I'm more interested in why our government deemed it necessary to target Las Vegas."

Ten seconds later the enormous missile struck the top of New York New York and plowed deep into the building's interior. The six of them stood there and braced for the explosion, but none came.

"What just happened?" Laura asked as they watched a huge chunk of the building break off and tumble to the ground.

"There's no way that thing was a dud," Bill told them.

"Then apparently," Sam said, "it's our lucky day."

"It's time for you to die," a voice declared behind them.

The six of them quickly turned on their heels and were confronted with fifty or so red-eyed cadavers, in various states of decay, shambling towards them. Most of them were located on the north side of the freeway barrier, but a dozen were on the south side. More could be seen coming towards them from the streets of downtown Las Vegas.

One of the dead spoke up again. "It's time for you to die."

Sam and Bill simultaneously raised their rifles as Thomas propelled the closest ones away from them. Bullets ripped into some of the others which knocked them off balance and to the ground.

"Back to the SUVs!" Sam bellowed.

Laura, Julie and Kim didn't need any further convincing and retreated to the safety of their vehicles as the men continued to engage the advancing undead.

"Get in!" Laura yelled.

Thomas pushed another bloated and diseased covered carcass away, made his way to the passenger side and climbed in. Shortly thereafter Sam and Bill followed suit, shooting bursts from their weapons as they did.

"Moving!" Laura voiced into the radio and then slammed the shifter into drive.

The three SUVS took off down the interstate and left the walking dead behind them. Thomas hurriedly took position out the side window and unclogged the lane in front of them. A mile later Laura finally took her foot off the gas pedal and the SUV slowed to a stop. All around them, as they'd experienced north of Vegas, lay the bodies of the dead.

"What gives?" Bill queried over the radio.

Laura picked up the handheld and replied. "Look around, nothing's coming for us anymore."

"And?"

Thomas leaned over and Laura keyed the transmit button for him. "We just drove through the same creepy shit we had to deal with underground when Dr. Matsushita opened the portal the first time. And that means…"

Sam spoke up. "…Dr. Matsushita's in Vegas."

"And so are our kids," Bill added.

"Exactly," Thomas said.

Everyone got out of the SUVs, nervously eyeballing the dead, and reconvened.

Thomas voiced his observation. "If the dead are being taken over this far out then I can only imagine what the rest of Vegas is already full of."

"And that would also explain," Bill said, "why that missile was inbound. Someone's looking at Las Vegas right now."

"But who?" Sam asked. "The President's dead."

"That doesn't matter right now," Laura told them. "What matters is that our children are in the heart of sin city and surrounded by creatures from another realm, red eyes and all. We need to do something before this epidemic spreads across the world, and that means separating Gavin from Dr. Matsushita, whatever that means."

"I don't mean to sound disheartening," Bill said, "but we're grossly underequipped to deal with an opposition that must number in the thousands."

"You don't want to rescue our children?" Kim questioned.

Bill instantly put his hands up. "I never said that. All I'm saying is that we don't know what's in there and, more to the point, this could easily turn into a suicide run."

"But maybe we're left with no other choice," Sam said. "Maybe we have to sacrifice ourselves in order to stop the rest of the world from dying."

Julie made a face. "I don't like what I'm hearing."

"Neither do I," Kim included.

Thomas took control of the conversation again. "This isn't on any of you. This is on me so I'll be the one who goes in."

"Alone?" Bill scoffed. "Oh please. Even with your powers you wouldn't make it. There are too many variables in play. You need backup whether you like it or not."

"What he said," Sam added. "You're not going in alone Thomas, end of story. However, with that said," as he looked at Julie, "you're not coming with us."

"What?" Julie expressed. "Like hell I'm not."

"I'm going too," Kim said.

"It's too dangerous," Bill told them.

"I don't care," Kim replied. "We should stay together. We've all been trained at the range. We can defend ourselves."

"This is nothing like the range and you know it," Bill told her.

"This isn't up for debate," Julie stated. "Figure out a plan that includes all of us or none of us are going in there. We've come too far together to split the group up again."

"You can't be serious?" Bill tested.

Sam was dumbfounded. "This isn't a game, Jules. Those 'things' will tear you apart if they get their hands on you."

"You know all too well that you not coming back to me happens to be my worst nightmare," Julie argued. "If you think I'm going to let you out of my sight, when the shit is this bad, you're absolutely mistaken."

"That does double for me," Kim said.

Thomas shut them all up. "You're all coming."

"We are?"

"They are?"

"What'd you have in mind?" Laura asked him.

Thomas smiled. "I have a plan."

13

Tuesday November 20, 2001

Dr. Matsushita watched in fascination as the creatures rapidly expanded out from the boy's portal in all directions, after their attempts to take over the eight individuals were thwarted by Dr. Matsushita as he engaged Craig's phasing ability. The twelve Special Ops soldiers, their weapons useless against the oncoming horde, were the first to be inhabited by the dark beings, red eyes blazing. The dead, numbering in the hundreds that surrounded the portal's radius, followed suit.

Seconds later the surging wave of evil washed over the two Blackhawk helicopters and continued, unabated, down Tropicana Avenue. The hovering aircraft, their pilots anything but human began to deviate off course, tilting forward and out of control. Dr. Matsushita couldn't take his eyes off the seemingly slow advancement of the helicopters as they plummeted into the ground. Their hard impacts scattered vehicles and bodies in all directions and compounded the destruction when one of them exploded in a devastating fireball.

Dr. Matsushita's smile faded as his brain began to mull things over. *These creatures didn't hesitate, even for a second, to occupy my body. I won't be able to stay phased long enough for the world to become overrun because the children and I will need to rest to regain our strength. I seriously need to rethink my strategy before I continue.*

Gavin's portal snapped shut and the stem of creature's invading the Earth came to an abrupt halt. One of the soldiers, now merely a husk for the being inside him, came forward.

"Reopen the portal," it demanded.

"I don't think so," Yamato replied.

"Reopen it or we will tear you limb from limb."

"That's what one of you threatened to do to me before, and yet none of you have realized it's not a very compelling threat. Without me the portal doesn't open ever again. I wonder what it'll take for you to finally figure that out."

The creature paused and contemplated the issue it'd just been presented with. "Reopen the portal," it repeated.

"I actually plan to," an exasperated Yamato said, "but you have me at a disadvantage if you decide to occupy my body, and believe me that's not part of my plan."

The soldier's red eyes stared at Yamato, unwavering and unblinking for an agonizing minute before it opened its mouth to speak once more.

"We extend our gratitude to allow you and your children safe passage. You will not be inhabited, we give you our word."

"Our word? And why should I believe you?"

"Your words contain truth and we need to escape. You must trust us; you will not be targeted."

"I want to believe you. Who or what do you call yourselves again?"

"We are Ancient. We are many. We speak for all of us, and for those eager to arrive to this world. We have been trapped in another plane of existence, contained there by another."

"Trapped? By whom?"

"An entity we know only as the Caretaker."

"The Caretaker?"

"That is correct."

"So why did this entity contain you?"

"That is our business."

"Oh, come now," Yamato said, "you've peaked my interest…"

The creature's gaze shifted upwards. Dr. Matsushita followed and his eyes instantly fixated on the large object plunging down out of the sky.

A missile? They seriously launched a missile and thought it could stop me? Those idiots.

The object drew closer and Yamato, in the final seconds, was able to get a better view.

Oh no. That's a nuke. Please, not again.

Yamato verified he and the children were still phased out as the nuclear missile made contact with the top of the New York New York. He closed his eyes, remembering the intense and bright light that washed over him and his family when he was a boy in Japan, and braced for the explosion that would harmlessly pass through him. But instead of a devastating release of fire and destruction, the missile merely disappeared inside the building with a loud crunch; and a huge chunk of the building broke off and toppled to the street below.

"What was that…object?" the creature asked.

Yamato wasn't sure whether to be relieved or not. He did know, for certain now, that the US government had eyes on exactly what he was attempting to accomplish in Las Vegas and the desperate measures they intended to take to stop him.

"That was a nuclear missile, and if it had detonated it would have destroyed this entire city and everything in it. Perhaps even you."

"We are Ancient. We cannot be destroyed."

"Maybe. Maybe not. But trust me when I say that those weapons will definitely slow down any progress you intend to make."

The two turned towards a new source of interest as sporadic gunfire sounded off in the distance.

Yamato smiled. *Good luck to whoever's out there trying to survive. Soon you'll take your last breath as hell is unleashed upon this world.*

When the gunfire faded away the two resumed their standoff.

"So I have your word that none of us are to be taken over, correct?"

The solider nodded. "Yes. You and your offspring are exempt; safe."

Yamato chuckled. "They're not my offspring."

"That doesn't concern us," Ancient replied.

"Very well. I believe we have the same goal in mind, the end of the world."

"Yes. Your world will come to an end as we transform it into our new one."

"It sounds like we have a deal then."

Yamato silently commanded Craig to disengage his ability and the eight of them became solid once more. In that instant, and on a whim, Yamato tried to take control of the soldier's mind. It didn't work and the ensuing smile on the creature's face sent a chill up the doctor's spine.

"A feeble and obvious attempt, but one we understand. Reopen the portal before we rethink our arrangement."

Yamato countered. "We need to rest before we can continue."

"You are stalling. Do not defy us," the creature said as he took a menacing step towards the doctor.

Yamato stood his ground. "And don't threaten me, Ancient. We want the same things but we're still human, and humans require energy and rest to function efficiently. Your patience will be rewarded."

The soldier paused. "Our patience was once limitless, but that changed the moment we were given a glimmer of hope of escape.

96

And now some of us are here while others beg to join us. Open the portal."

Yamato shook his head. "Not until we eat and rest. I'm not against you. You will make this world your own, in time, but for now those are my demands. If you recall we want the same thing, so what choice do you have?"

The soldier stood fast but eventually relented. "We understand. You, and the children, will be honored appropriately. As we speak a location is being prepared to ensure both your comfort and dietary necessities. Will this be acceptable?"

Yamato smiled. "It's a start. Please, lead on."

Before the soldier could lead Dr. Matsushita anywhere a new disturbance was heard off in the distance.

"Now what?"

"Someone is coming," the creature stated. "We are under attack."

They twisted their heads but Dr. Matsushita was unprepared for what he saw next. Barreling down Tropicana Avenue, directly towards them, was a huge tanker truck. The front window was missing and the man behind the wheel had an arm out, readjusting any vehicles the tanker would have run into out of its way. In the tanker truck's wake, directly on its heels, were two SUVs.

"Unbelievable. Thomas, what the hell do you think you're going to accomplish? And you obviously brought Sam and Bill with you to join in this doomed endeavor. This is going to be hilarious."

"Leave this to us," Ancient stated.

"Alright, "Yamato said. "Have at it."

As if on cue, hundreds of undead swarmed out of neighboring casinos and buildings towards the moving tanker. Those hundreds quickly turned into thousands as they surged towards the incoming vehicle, choking the street. As the horde of bodies packed the intersection there was nowhere left to drive and SUV's forward motion quickly ground to a halt, surrounded by undead. Sam and Bill fired weapons out their windows, with little effect, as the inertia of Thomas's huge tanker continued to propel him forward through the tide of bodies and vehicles.

Panic set in in the back seats of both SUVs as Kim and Laura, in Bill's vehicle, and Julie in Sam's, could feel the immense pressure of the undead mass pressed against the outside of their SUVs, tearing at it to get at them. Even Sam and Bill instantaneously discerned they'd made a tactical mistake as they continued to shoot.

Thomas, unaware of the imminent plight his family now faced, continued to drive over and through the colossal throng of undead in his way. As the writhing corpses bounding off the truck's grill, and with the street clogged, Thomas was no longer able to properly clear a path. Powerless to change course the large tanker truck clipped a stationary vehicle and, with the help of so many undead working together, the truck tilted to one side and capsized. Thomas, not able to adjust the momentum, grabbed hold of the steering wheel and braced himself. The tanker finalized its death throes and landed on its right side, violently shoving bodies and cars out of its way until it came to a rest forty feet away from Dr. Matsushita and the children. The tanker's contents, which contained an ample supply of fuel, surprisingly didn't split open upon impact.

The undead rushed the toppled cab, scrambling up its sides towards Thomas who barely had time to recover from the crash before he could defend himself from the incoming boarders. The first few to reach him were instinctually thrust away. As more climbed to attack him Thomas finally regained his senses. He climbed out his open window, pulled himself up and stood on top the fallen tanker, the intersection completely packed with undead. Gunfire continued to erupt behind him in the street and Thomas looked back, in anguish, at the two swarmed SUVs.

"I'll take it from here!" Dr. Matsushita yelled at Ancient. "Leave them alone and give them some space!"

Sam and Bill stopped shooting as the undead mass moved away, perplexed and unaware of what was occurring by the toppled tanker further down the street. They shifted their gaze through the front window and saw Thomas standing on top of the overturned tanker clearly engaged in some sort of conversation.

Collectively the undead ceased their attacks as they backed away and formed an open perimeter around both the tanker and the two SUVs. Relief washed over Thomas when he saw this and he turned back to gaze down at Yamato.

"A valiant attempt, Thomas. But seriously, what did you really hope to accomplish? You must know by now that you're no match for me."

Thousands of undead stared at Thomas, packed together like sardines, and remained stationary. Thomas eyeballed them warily before he replied.

"We came for our children. Give them to us and we'll leave."

"You rushed into danger and caused all this havoc to retrieve your children?"

"Absolutely."

"Or maybe you think I got lucky and want to save them before the next nuclear missile the government launches actually works this time?"

Thomas clenched his teeth together. "They're only going to slow you down now that you've won, Yamato. Why not give them up so you can concentrate on annihilating the rest of the world?"

99

Yamato pondered what Thomas had said as he searched for the alternate reason Thomas had risked his life to reach him. Nothing immediate came to mind.

"Alright Thomas, perhaps this is your lucky day because I'm feeling generous and I truly understand how important family can be. Of course, my family was taken from me, burned right in front of my eyes. So with that in mind you must know I'm not going to give up all of my creations. You may have everyone but Craig and Gavin. The rest are useless to me now and will only slow down my process."

Amanda, Edward, Tad, Sarah and Emily all shook their heads side to side as if coming out of a long sleep. Gavin and Craig remained transfixed, still firmly under Dr. Matsushita's control. Thomas wasted no time, jumped down off the top of the cab and paused, suspicious of Yamato's intentions and nature.

"Come to me," Thomas called out to the children. "Come over here."

Slowly the five children, now under their own will, made their way to Thomas' side. Yamato smiled and continued.

"You see Thomas, I have a heart."

"You and I both know that's a stretch."

Yamato shrugged. "Regardless, you should take a few seconds and look around you. The world is already changing. In fact, it's coming to an end."

"Why? Why do this?"

Yamato sneered. "I suggest you leave Las Vegas and get far away while you can. My new friends are going to tear this world apart and it's only a matter of time before you're pulled into the abyss, just like everyone else."

"You're a monster, Yamato; a pathetic nobody."

"Careful, Thomas. I could easily take control of you right now and make you dance around in the street like a puppet until I decide to let these creatures rip you and your family to shreds. So make a choice. Leave and live, or stay and die. Either way I know you'll never make it. Your death is inevitable."

Thomas picked Emily up in his arms as the four others huddled close to his side.

"This isn't over."

Yamato's laughter echoed down the street. "You know where to find me, but when you return don't expect to find me in such a generous mood." Yamato turned towards the soldier. "Open a path and allow them to leave."

The undead moved backwards and swiftly created a drivable avenue for the SUVs. Sam and Bill, once Thomas motioned to them, slowly drove forward towards Thomas. Julie and Kim opened the doors as the children ran to the vehicles, and pulled them inside, tears of joy streaming down their faces. Laura pulled Emily to her chest, scooted over so Thomas could get in.

"Go," Thomas told Sam while he kept his eyes on Yamato.

"Where are Gavin and Craig?" Sam asked. "Where are our boys?"

Julie, with Amanda in her arms, wasn't having it. "Where's Craig? Where's my son!?"

"Turn around and go," Thomas replied sullenly. "He didn't release them. They're not coming."

Sam, as the undead allowed, made a sharp turn and headed back the way they'd come with Bill behind him.

"What's going on?" Bill asked over the radio. "We're missing two."

Thomas took the radio from Sam. "He's keeping them so he can pursue his agenda. There was nothing I could do. If we don't keep moving Yamato will kill us and then continue with his plan."

"Fuck," was the only response Bill could muster.

"No no no," Julie repeated. "I want my son. I want my son!"

A tear rolled down Sam's hardened face as he drove towards I-15, further away from the harsh epicenter they'd just left behind.

"We can't leave them," she pleaded. "Go back, Sam. Please, go back!"

"We don't have a choice, Jules," Sam told his wife. "We have to stick to the plan no matter what the sacrifice."

"No! We can't! That's our son we're talking about!"

Julie reached for the wheel but Sam blocked her hands before she could grab it.

"Stop it!"

As Julie wept Sam took a moment and glanced in the rear view mirror. There he caught Thomas' eye.

"Thank you for what you did and I'm sorry, to the both of you. I wish there was another option."

Laura's voice emanated from the back seat, a quiet certainty to her voice. "So are we."

The two SUV's reached the freeway and pulled to a stop next to the one they'd left behind. With the mob of undead in the distance, still bunched together around Dr. Matsushita's position, everyone dismounted and stood together on the overpass. Their mood was dour, having left two of their own behind in enemy hands, and no one wanted to talk about it. Bill pulled out the binoculars and zoomed in on Dr. Matsushita in the distance.

"He's still there."

"I know I agreed to this," Julie said, "but please don't do this. Please."

Sam pulled Julie and Amanda close to him. "It's going to be alright," he breathed. "There's no other choice."

Bill lowered the binoculars, looked over at Kim and their two children, and then turned to Thomas.

"Hey…uh…maybe I should be the one who…"

Thomas slowly shook his head. "I appreciate the thought, but we all know we're here because of me."

Laura wiped the tears from her face as Thomas extracted a detonator from his pocket. They saw a red light appear as he armed the device.

"Together?" Thomas asked Laura.

She could only nod and she placed her hand on top of his. Tears flooded Thomas' eyes as they pushed the detonator's button in unison. The overturned tanker truck, loaded with C-4 plastic explosives, disintegrated. The tremendous and massive blast disgorged undead and cars in every direction. The shockwave shattered windows for blocks as the tanker's fuel covered everything in a one block radius with fire.

"Holy fucking shit," Bill muttered.

Everyone cringed as Bill brought the binoculars back up to his eyes. Water spewed out of the ground from broken water pipes amongst the devastating and colossal hole the explosion had created. Heavy smoke and debris filled the air, fluttering down out of the sky and coming to rest on what remained of the street. The entire area, now in ruins, resembled a war torn battlefield.

Bill scanned the area as the smoke lingered finding pieces of the dead everywhere he looked.

"Anything?" Thomas asked. "Tell me it's finally over. Tell me Yamato's dead."

* * *

103

Dr. Matsushita watched Thomas, and the majority of his family, drive away.

Knowing Thomas, he gave up far too easily. Maybe I broke his will, or maybe there's something I'm not seeing. Would he leave without more of a fight or did he know he was clearly outmatched?

Yamato commanded Craig to phase out as he held both of the boy's hands. Without the other five children to constantly control he discovered he now had more energy to allocate to the task at hand.

"Why did you let them depart?" questioned Ancient.

"To break his spirit. If I killed him now I wouldn't have enjoyed it. But knowing that two of his family members are still under my control, well, that's an entirely different psychological conundrum for him to endure."

"Very well," Ancient replied. "When will you open the portal again?"

"Soon, very so…"

The tanker truck exploded before he could finish his sentence. An incalculable amount of destruction passed through Dr. Matsushita, Craig and Gavin before his brain registered what had happened. The soldier's body, which'd stood next to him, disintegrated in the blink of an eye. Cars, bodies, concrete and everything else caught in the enormous blast was either vaporized or destroyed. The mammoth crater left in the street, where the tanker had resided, was a clear indicator of the massive devastation. Fire consumed everything and burned all around him.

At first Yamato thought a nuclear missile had blown up. But, as he focused past the localized destruction and fires, he saw that buildings a block away were undamaged. He looked down at his body and made sure the three of them were intact. He smiled and was happily delighted. They were still very much alive.

"Nice try, Thomas. Although I can't believe you chose to sacrifice two of your own to kill me. My hat's off to you."

Yamato caught movement from his peripheral and turned towards it, the children's hands still clasped in his own. A female with red eyes, and recently deceased by the looks of her, worked her way around the fires towards him.

"Form the portal or we will take our deal off the table."

"Ancient, is that you?"

"We are Ancient."

"Yes, you apparently are." Yamato contemplated the request. "Very well. I'll open it for a bit and then we need to rest."

"Agreed."

Yamato concentrated and Gavin's portal popped into existence. From its depths the unending tide poured forth once again.

* * *

"It didn't work," Bill told them.

"What?" Julie and Laura expressed at the same time.

Thomas took the binoculars from Bill and looked through them himself. There, in the distance and through the fire and smoke, he saw Yamato and the two boys. A few seconds later the portal reopened and death began to stream through.

"We need to get out of here right now." Thomas told everyone. "The portal's back open."

"So what are we supposed to do now?" Kim asked the group.

Thomas paused before he got in his SUV with Laura. "He's not leaving Las Vegas; that much is certain. So we need a new plan, which in this case is the original plan. We have to reconnect with Robert, Gabbi and Hobbes and figure this shit out before this evil has a chance to spread."

14
Tuesday November 20, 2001

The President looked up from the desk in the PEOC when a knock came on the Command Center's doors. He still brooded over the conversation he's just had with the Russian President, Demian Anatolievich as the large monitor on the wall, behind him, continued to play current satellite footage of downtown Las Vegas.

"Come."

The door opened and the technician who'd previously helped him launch the nuke at Las Vegas entered the room.

"Sir, there's been some activity in Las Vegas you should be made aware of."

"What is it?"

The tech motioned towards the monitor on the wall. "Have you been watching, sir?"

The President shook his head. "No, I've been otherwise engaged."

"Not to worry. May I?"

The President nodded as the tech sat down at the console he'd previously occupied.

"Let me rewind the footage." After a few clicks of the mouse the tech was ready. "Okay, sir, it's coming up now."

The President turned to scrutinize the monitor and watched as the missile collided with the New York New York hotel.

"I've seen this already," POTUS said with noticeable contempt.

"Yes, sir. Keep watching. Let me zoom in."

The screen altered its view as the camera zoomed in above Dr. Matsushita and someone else.

"Wait a minute," the President said. "Who the hell is the doctor talking to? He's wearing a soldier's uniform. Did one of the SpecOps operators survive?"

The tech zoomed in closer and froze the footage as the soldier turned his head skywards. There, unmistakably, a pair of red eyes stared back at them on the monitor.

"Never mind, that man isn't human anymore. Is that all you wanted to show me?"

"No, sir. This isn't it."

"Well get to it then."

The camera zoomed out and the footage fast-forwarded until the satellite picked up a tanker truck and two SUVs barreling down the street towards Dr. Matsushita.

"Okay," the President said, "now this is getting interesting."

The video resumed normal playing speed as the President watched the scene play out.

"Thomas went to all that trouble, and danger, to rescue those children. But he still left Dr. Matsushita behind with two of them. Interesting."

"There's a bit more, sir," the tech countered.

"Really? Show me."

The satellite footage skipped ahead and continued again seconds before the tanker exploded.

"Whoa!" the President exclaimed, clearly not prepared for the remarkable blast of energy.

The raw devastation that the explosion caused to the area was exceptional, not to mention the carnage. Hotel windows blew out up and down the Vegas strip as fires plastered both the road and surrounding buildings. A colossal crater remained as the smoke began to clear, debris and bodies tossed everywhere.

The President smiled. "Are you trying to tell me that Dr. Matsushita is dead?"

The tech responded by zooming the satellite footage in and highlighting the doctor, very much alive. The President's face twitched and his smile faded.

"Sonofabitch. How? How could he have survived that?"

"It appears, sir, that he extended one of the children's abilities, namely the phasing skill, and extended that to shroud the three of them from harm. I'm afraid that even if the nuclear missile had detonated he wouldn't have been killed."

Shit! The President whipped around. "Where are Thomas and the others right now?"

The tech typed in a few keystrokes and recentered the satellite over three SUVs that traveled south on I-15.

So Thomas wants to stop Dr. Matsushita as desperately as I do, going to extreme lengths to kill him even if it meant sacrificing his own child. Very interesting. That means Thomas has acknowledged the overall stakes, and in doing so he realizes that actions must be undertaken, no matter what the cost.

"Have them picked up, non-lethally, and extend them my personal invitation. Inform them we need to chat about combining forces against our common enemy. Have them flown to Colorado. I'll meet them at NORAD."

15

Tuesday November 20, 2001

Gabbi glanced at Hobbes while she continued to avoid obstacles as they drove south on I-15.

"What do you mean the DCI told us not to come back?"

"That's what he said," Hobbes told her, "and then the phone went dead."

"Do you think we should go back?"

"I don't know. I'm going to call him back."

Hobbes hit speed dial on the satellite phone and waited for it to connect. A few seconds later he heard it ring. Seven rings later Robert still hadn't answered. After twelve Hobbes thumbed the 'end' button.

"Nothing," he said.

"Shit," Gabbi replied. "What do you think that means?"

Hobbes sighed. "I have no idea, but I could have sworn I heard panic in his voice."

"Seriously? From him? If that's true it can't be a good sign."

"No shit."

"So should we go back or not?"

Hobbes shook his head. "He gave us specific instructions to meet up with Thomas, so that's what we're going to do."

"And the DCI?" Gabbi asked. "What about him?"

Hobbes paused. "I really don't know but we'll figure that part out later, okay? Right now we have to concentrate on making it to Palm Springs."

* * *

BLAM!

The loud sound made both of them jump. Gabbi immediately had to fight to keep their SUV on the road as the steering wheel tried to rip free of her hands.

"What the hell was that?"

"It's yanking me to the right," Gabbi tried to explain.

Hobbes rolled down the window and heard the thumpthumpthump of their shredded tire.

"You've got to stop. The front right tire blew out."

"That's easier said than done."

Gabbi lifted her foot off the gas and gripped the wheel even harder. She managed to maintain control and pulled to a stop, in the middle of the interstate. She shut off the engine and together they got out to inspect the damage.

"Damn," Gabbi said. "I must have run over some glass or a chunk of metal. That tire is completely shredded."

"The road's littered with debris. I'm surprised our tires lasted this long."

"But we're only fifteen miles south of Las Vegas and we're not making good time, especially if the interstate continues to be this clogged with so many abandoned vehicles and rotting corpses. I had enough of the dead back in Vegas. Yuck."

Hobbes winked at her. "I hope that wasn't the only thing you had enough of…"

She managed a smile. "Very funny, but now's not the time to make a pass at me. We have to replace this tire and get back on the road. But that doesn't mean we won't be able to find some private time later. Now let's get the spare."

Hobbes wavered. "Umm, where is it is?"

"It's attached to the undercarriage. The tools to release it are in a side compartment in the back, including the jack."

"Oh."

"You've never replaced a tire, have you?"

"Is it that obvious?"

"I think it's cute. Would you like some help?" she teased.

"Maybe."

"We'll work on it together."

They opened the SUV's rear door and extracted the necessary tools from a side compartment. As Hobbes scooted under the vehicle to loosen the bolts on the spare Gabbi began to loosen the front destroyed tire's lug nuts.

After a minute of silence Gabbi broke opened her mouth. "I hate to bring this up…"

"What is it?" Hobbes asked.

"Well…I…I'm worried the world's never going to be the same; that it'll never return to the way it was before the plague killed all these people. What if there isn't a solution and society falls into some form of anarchy?"

Hobbes struggled with a rusted nut. "And here I thought that you sporting your purple hair and tats you'd easily embrace anarchy."

"You're right, in most forms, but not the 'end of the world' scenarios. How does the world bounce back from something as serious as this without screwing it up even more?"

"Honestly?"

"Yeah."

"I don't think we will," Hobbes told her.

"What do you mean? Why not?"

"Because this isn't Star Trek."

"You're referencing Star Trek right now?"

"I'm a nerd, like you are, so why not? Mankind hasn't united and has refused to move forward together. Instead we're focused on hate, power, greed and self-preservation. Each of those traits will come in to play as people's fears are used against them during this crisis. I'd go as far as to say that it's inevitable. Society is doomed."

Gabbi shrugged. "I feel the same way, I was just hoping you'd come up with something a little more positive than what's swimming around in my head."

"I hear ya. All of this is scary as hell. How are we supposed to process so much death and destruction? It's just not going to happen. The damage is done and the survivors will have to live with these horrific images for the rest of their lives. I just wish there was some way I could have stopped Dr. Matsushita from committing these atrocities in the first place."

Gabbi removed the last lug nut and locked the jack in to place under the side of the SUV. Hobbes extracted the spare and rolled it over to her.

"This is messier than I expected," he said when he noticed that both their hands were covered in grease and muck.

"Welcome to the world of 'getting your hands dirty'."

"I think I'll stick with sitting behind a computer, thankyouverymuch."

She chuckled and began to pump the jack. Hobbes noticed Gabbi has something else on her mind.

"What is it?"

"Nothing."

"Come on. Out with it."

"I feel bad for thinking it."

"You know you can tell me anything," he said.

She stopped working on the jack and stood up to face him. "Okay. Here's what's bugging me. What if Thomas is ultimately responsible for all of this?" she said as she swept her arm around to infer the state of the world. "Could he have stopped it from happening in the first place?"

"Are you saying that Thomas wanted this to happen?"

Gabbi shook her head. "No. You and I both know he and his family. There's no way they wanted this. No, all I'm asking is what do you think his role is when it comes to the deaths of millions of innocent people?"

"I know he blames himself, if that's what you're asking. I'm sure he's second guessing every decision he's ever made that allowed Dr. Matsushita to succeed with his plan. And that amount of anguish I wouldn't want to wish on anyone."

"You're right. I don't know what I was thinking. Of course I know he's one of the good guys, it's just that…"

Hobbes finished her sentence for her. "…just that I wish things could have turned out differently."

"Yeah."

He smiled at her. "It's going to be alright."

"How could you possibly know that?"

"That's easy, because you're here with me."

She blushed a little. "You smooth talking sonofabitch. Come here."

She placed her left hand on his cheek and pulled his lips to hers. Before they could savor the moment they heard noises off in the distance, in the direction they'd come from. Hobbes wasted no time to extract his handgun as they ducked down beside their SUV. Ten seconds later they watched as vehicles advanced on their location.

"What should we do?" she asked.

"I say we stay hidden until we discern whether they're friendly or not."

"And if they're not?"

He lifted his handgun. "Then we're not. Anarchy rules."

Through the window of their SUV they could see that three other SUVs were almost upon them. But something odd caught Gabbi's eye so before Hobbes could stop her she stepped out from behind the car and into the path of the oncoming vehicles.

16
Tuesday November 20, 2001

"I can't believe we left Craig behind," Julie repeated again. "I can't believe we left our son back there."

"Jules, your daughter and I heard you the first hundred times," Sam told her. "Please, just try and relax."

"Fuck you!" she snarled. "This is too much. How could you just leave like that?"

"Because we'd all be dead if we stayed," he shot back. "Look at the bright side. The plan was thwarted which means Craig and Gavin are still alive, alright. But we had to leave and you damn well know it. I promise you we're going to get our son back."

"How?" she pleaded.

"We're going to figure that out when we regroup. Now, our daughter needs you so get your shit together goddammit."

Julie turned towards Amanda, who sat in the seat next to her, and saw a frightened thirteen-year-old girl who desperately needed her mother. She reached for her daughter and they clung to each other. Sam breathed a sigh of relief as he continued to drive down I-15, the rearmost vehicle of the three, as the sun began to slip behind the mountains.

* * *

Bill, in the center SUV, along with Kim and their two recovered children, Edward and Sarah, continued to drive in silence. Kim sat in the back seat, her arms around their two children, thankful that they were alive and out of Dr. Matsushita's clutches.

117

Edward broke the silence. "Do you think Gavin and Craig will be alright?"

"That evil sonofabitch," Bill said, "needs them which means he'll keep them alive."

"But," Sarah asked, "didn't you try to kill them?"

Her question made her parents very uncomfortable.

"It's complicated," Bill told his daughter.

"But it's true, right?" she persisted.

"We didn't want to but there wasn't any other option. We had an opportunity to end this blight that's pouring into our world, so we took it. The good news is that they're still alive because our plan failed."

Sarah contemplated her father's answer. "Would you have sacrificed me to save the world?"

Bill glanced in the rearview mirror and caught Kim's eyes. They implored him not to continue down this train of thought. But Bill knew his daughter deserved an honest answer.

"Yes sweetie, I would have, and you should know that I would sacrifice myself if it meant saving you or the world."

Sarah absorbed her father's statement and seemed to find solace in it, much to Kim's surprise. Edward, on the other hand, challenged it.

"You'd really would have let us die?"

"If there wasn't another option, yes I would."

"Why?"

"You might be too young to fully comprehend this concept yet son, but I'll tell you anyway. I'm a soldier and your Uncle Sam and I have fought alongside each other for the past two decades. Together we've been in situations, more than once, where the outcome appeared bleak. Our survival relied on every man in our squad fighting to stay alive. However, sometimes the only way to

118

ensure that survival is to sacrifice one of your own, so that the rest go home to their families. Does their sacrifice cause me pain? Absolutely, but the point I'm trying to make is that sometimes there isn't a choice. Sometimes someone you care about has to die. Do you understand?"

"Kind of," Edward replied.

"Okay, how about this. What's better, everyone in the world dying, or just a few?"

"How about no one?" his son countered.

"That would be ideal, but we're not in control of this situation, are we?"

"No, not at all."

"That's right, we're not and that means we have to do whatever it takes to regain that control; to stop the bad guy from winning."

"And that means sacrificing one of our own?"

"I hope not, but if it came down to saving you, your sister and your mother's lives I would take that bullet in a second."

"Bill," Kim said, "this isn't a suitable conversation."

"Maybe not before, but look around us, the world is under attack. I won't coddle my children and neither should you. If you haven't noticed we're in the fight for our lives, and right now we're losing."

*   *   *

"We have to go back for them," Emily insisted.

"We will," Laura told her as Thomas continued to hang out the passenger side window to clear a path for their convoy.

"When? He's my brother."

Laura wasn't happy with the current situation either.

"Dammit, I don't know. When we come up with a new plan, okay? Do you think your father and I were elated when he decided to martyr your brother? We weren't but we didn't have a choice. Now that we know he's still alive you'd better believe we want to save him, just like we rescued you and the others."

Emily crossed her arms as Thomas pulled himself back inside.

"What's going on in here? All I'm hearing is arguing."

"Our daughter is unhappy with our decision to leave her brother behind, amongst other things."

Thomas picked up on the nuance immediately and turned his body towards Emily.

"How're you doing?"

"Me?" she replied. "How am I doing? Are you kidding me right now?"

"Okay, okay. Take it easy. We're all on edge but the last thing we need to do is tear each other's throats out. We have to remain united if we're going to get through this."

"Like blowing Gavin up?"

Thomas flinched and took a few moments before he responded. "You don't get the luxury of second guessing our decisions young lady. We risked everything to save you and, whether you like it or not, we'd do it all over again because that's how important you and your brother are to us. So don't think for one second that your mother and I came to that decision lightly because we didn't."

"Stop!" Emily yelled.

Laura and Thomas jumped in their seats. "What?"

"Stop!" Emily lifted her arm up and pointed out the front window with excitement. "It's Gabbi!"

120

Sure enough, a woman with purple hair stood in the middle of the road, her hand up in greeting in the fading day's light. As Laura slowed Thomas grabbed the radio.

"We're pulling over. It appears we've just run into Gabbi."

The three SUVs rolled to a stop. Emily bolted out the side door and ran to Gabbi who plucked the ten-year-old off the ground and gave her a monstrous hug.

"It's sooo good to see you again," Emily said.

"You don't know the half of it. You're a sight for sore eyes."

Thomas, along with the others, exited their vehicles and walked over just as Hobbes emerged and joined the group. Handshakes and hugs, along with numerous smiles, were exchanged between everyone.

"Where's the DCI?" Thomas finally asked.

Hobbes spoke up. "He stayed behind in Las Vegas to observe Dr. Matsushita and then we lost contact with him."

"The last thing he said," Gabbi added, "was for us not to come back."

"Walk us through what happened," Sam told them.

For the next few minutes Gabbi and Hobbes recreated their harrowing escape that included Emma's death, their helicopter ride, camping out at the MGM and culminating in spotting Dr. Matsushita's plane landing in Las Vegas.

"Try calling his satellite phone again," Bill said.

Hobbes went back to their SUV, retrieved the phone and returned. He redialed but it was never answered.

"Shit," Sam said. "We really needed his CIA contacts and equipment to mount any type of rescue."

"So what the hell do we do now?" Laura solicited.

Hobbes tentatively raised his hand. "They have drones I could fly at Nellis Air Force Base just north east of Vegas."

Bill shook his head. "Have you seen what's happened to Vegas?"

Hobbes and Gabbi were confused. "No," they said in tandem.

"Dr. Matsushita," Thomas told them, "made Gavin open the portal. Las Vegas is now overrun with walking dead."

"Shit," Gabbi whispered.

"And that means going back there is incredibly dangerous," Bill said.

"But," Hobbes continued, "if I could gain access to a drone station we'd have some serious firepower at our disposal."

"They don't get it," Julie stated. "They didn't see what we saw."

"What are you talking about?" Gabbi asked as she looked around at everyone's sad faces. She fixated on Thomas. "What the hell is going on?"

"Dr. Matsushita escaped Building Forty-Two by mixing Craig's phasing ability with Edward's flying power."

"I don't get it."

"He was able to extend their powers by holding their hands. All eight of them flew into the ceiling, through four stories of concrete right in front of our eyes."

"Okay…so what am I missing? Why don't we want to get our hands on a drone?" asked Hobbes.

Thomas continued. "We tried to kill him by blowing up a fuel tanker. He, along with Craig and Gavin, were phased out. At this point I think he'd just laugh at a hellfire missile being fired at him."

"I hate to state the obvious again," Kim said, "but we have to assume that Gavin and Craig are going to be standing next to him the entire time, so targeting the doctor also means targeting those two boys, and I'm pretty sure no one wants to make that decision again."

"No," Julie said, "no we don't."

"Shit," Gabbi said. "Okay, what else did we miss?"

Bill answered her question. "Oh, how about the nuclear missile the government launched at the city."

"A nuclear missile?" Hobbes said with an open mouth. "Seriously?"

"It didn't explode, obviously," Bill added, "but it sure as hell left a gaping hole in the New York New York."

"Holy shit."

Thomas put his hands up to quiet everyone down. "The world is imploding around us and every second we don't do something more darkness floods into this world. Without the resources Robert could have made available to us I don't know what course of action we should take. We could continue to run, but in doing so we leave two of our own behind, and who knows how long we'd last before that cloud of evil overtakes us. We could go back and try to stop Dr. Matsushita with the weapons and gear we have on hand."

"We'd never make it through the darkness," Laura stated. "We all know that shit would inhabit our bodies and there'd be nothing we can do to stop it."

"So we don't do anything?" Kim asked. "We're giving up?"

Sam and Bill cocked their heads to the side and then, as if on que, brought their rifles up.

"Everybody get to cover!" Sam ordered as he and Bill searched the early evening sky.

As the family scrambled to the sides of their vehicles Thomas, and the others, finally heard what Sam and Bill had picked up on prior.

"What's that sound?" Julie inquired.

"Multiple helicopters," Sam told her, "and they're coming right at us."

"I got'em," Bill said. "Coming in from the west."

Sam shifted position and quickly scanned the area to make sure everyone was behind something.

"How do you want to handle this?" Bill asked.

"If they start anything I'm pulling them right out of the sky," Thomas replied with a growl. "I'm tired of this shit."

"What Thomas said," Sam answered. "Follow his lead."

"Roger that."

Two black helicopters vectored straight at them, slowed down and began to hover fifty feet away.

"Hold," Sam told everyone.

The loudspeaker, on one of them, came to life. "Stand down. I repeat, stand down. We've been sent here by the President. We are going to land. Do not engage."

Sam and Bill shared a quick glance and sighted in their rifles as the two helicopters descended to the ground. A single soldier exited, unarmed and with his hands up, and walked towards them.

"I've got him, Thomas," Sam stated. "If he starts any shit he's the first to drop."

"Understood."

Thomas stood up and made his way towards the advancing soldier. The two stopped a few feet from each other on the berm of the interstate.

"Mr. Clark?" the solider asked.

"Who's asking?" Thomas replied.

"May I put my hands down?"

Thomas nodded.

"My team and I were sent here by POTUS to…"

Thomas interrupted. "The President is dead."

"Negative, sir. He's alive and he saw what you attempted to do in Las Vegas. I'm here, on his behalf, to offer safe passage to NORAD in Colorado. POTUS is well aware of the unstoppable force that's invading the world and has requested your help to put an end to it."

17
Wednesday November 21, 2001

The entire family, aside from Gavin and Craig, boarded the military plane, wearily located a seat and sat down. Just an hour prior they had believed, once again, that they were going to have to fight for their lives as the two black helicopters bore down on their position. But, with the fate of the world hanging in the balance, a semblance of luck appeared to be on their side for once. Still, it had taken a good deal of convincing from Thomas to get them all on the plane and headed to Colorado.

As the aircraft took off into the evening sky the children, absolutely exhausted, curled up beside their mothers and immediately fell asleep. Soon afterward Laura, Julie and Kim, along with Gabbi and Hobbes, followed suit as they reached cruising altitude. With everyone settled in, and no soldiers onboard, it didn't take long for Thomas, Sam and Bill to gather together.

"What the hell have you got us in to?" Bill stated with a particular hardness to his voice. "We're right back in the President's crosshairs again. What's stopping him from blowing this plane out of the sky and being done with us once and for all?"

"I'm afraid I'm with Bill on this one," Sam added. "This is an incredible risk we're taking."

"I'll admit," Thomas told them, "that there's a possibility that this might be a trap. But realistically, it doesn't matter."

"What?" Bill uttered with some astonishment. "You're not throwing in the towel on us, are you?"

Thomas shook his head. "No. But let's consider our circumstances. Evil is flowing into this world, unimpeded, and spreading out across the land at an astonishing rate. How long,

127

without the DCI's help, do you think we could have driven before it eventually overtook us? An hour? A day? A week? I don't know and neither do either of you. Taking the President's offer is threefold. One, he's alive and realizes he needs our help. Two, it removes our families from immediate danger. And three, we'll have the same equipment and support, if not better, than what the DCI could have offered us. So, if this is a trap we're walking in to, well, the joke's going to be on him because right now we need each other to combat these creatures and take the Earth back. End of story."

The two chewed on Thomas' thoughts for a bit before Sam opened his mouth.

"The President betrayed us before."

"I'm well aware of that, but if there's a chance he can help us get Craig and Gavin back, and stop this sweeping epidemic in the process, than it's worth the risk. We've been through too much together already to stop now, but I'll completely understand if I have to go forward on this by myself."

"Sam and I," Bill instantly said, "aren't going anywhere."

"No, we're not," Sam concurred. "But I don't think our wives, or our children, fully comprehend how bloody this is going to get, whether we're successful or not." Sam took his time and looked at Bill and then at Thomas before he continued. "We're brothers and we'll do whatever we have to do to end this, together."

18
Wednesday November 21, 2001

Just after midnight, in Las Vegas, Dr. Matsushita kept a watchful eye on Craig and Gavin as they slept.

They're so tiny and innocent, yet so deadly and necessary for my plan.

He shifted his gaze towards the dead woman who sat across from him and stared at the red eyes that never wavered from his.

"How's your advancement coming along?" he asked the creature as he ate.

"More consistently if the portal remained open," the being inside the woman replied. "But to answer your question, we are gradually beginning to inhabit this world, mile by mile. Based on current estimates we'll have conquered this land mass within four days. After that the rest of your world will be swept aside."

"So what's your real story, Ancient?"

It chuckled, the corpses' sagging flesh rising and falling. "You do not possess the capacity to understand our plight."

Yamato frowned at the obvious dismissal, unaccustomed to such blatant disrespect. "And yet here you are, free, because of me," he shot back.

The woman's hands clenched in anger knowing full well it was necessary for Dr. Matsushita to remain alive, but craving to kill him nevertheless.

"Very well, I'll dumb it down for you."

"Thanks," Yamato answered sarcastically.

"We are Ancient."

"I've got that part down already."

The creature continued unabated. "And we once controlled the fate of every sentient being in the universe."

Yamato stopped eating. "The entire universe?"

"Correct."

"But that, as I know it, contains an endless amount of space."

"More than your pathetic human race will know or ever hope to discover, especially now on the verge of your extinction."

"Good for you. So what happened to you? Something obviously toppled you off your throne."

"We grow tired of your incessant prattling."

"How cute," Yamato teased, "I got under your skin, so to speak. What's the matter, too painful and humiliating to talk about?"

The creature clenched its hands again, the nails digging deep into its bloodless palms.

"We were blindsided; tricked by a coalition of our opposition. And while the details of this event are unimportant, our resulting imprisonment is."

"How long?"

"Time is but one unit of measurement that binds this universe, and sadly it's the only one you're aware of. We've been trapped since the beginning of time."

"The beginning of time? What does that mean?"

The creature sighed. "It's irrelevant that you don't comprehend. Suffice it to say it's been an eternity."

"I see. And you mentioned that this Caretaker, you referred to, was the one that imprisoned you?"

"Partially. The Caretaker has always been our jailer."

"So let me get this straight. You're not the souls of individuals who have died here on Earth?"

The creature scoffed. "Hardly."

"And yet this Caretaker oversees the Earth's denizens in the afterlife. Interesting."

"I don't see why that would be interesting. Your race is weak and poses no threat to anyone but yourselves."

"And yet 'we're' your salvation you're running to."

"Correction. Escaping to. When the boy's portal formed the first time we began to observe his interactions from a distance. Over 'time' we devised a plan that coincided with six others that had crossed over, unbeknownst to them."

"You're referring to Nikolay Dmitriev, aren't you?"

The creature nodded. "We are. We knew their plan was to attack your people…"

"They're not my people," Yamato assured him.

"Semantics. Their plan was to attack and turn your people into puppets as they crossed from the Caretaker's realm in to this world. Our plan was to utilize their distraction to perpetuate our own escape. But we arrived too late and our plan was foiled. Since then we have taken up residence around the boy's island while we endlessly wait."

Yamato raised his glass. "Well, you're welcome then. Glad I could help."

"Thank you," the creature reluctantly replied. "We had no choice but to come through to this world. We would have eventually escaped some other way."

"Of course you would have, I completely understand. So what's next after you take over Earth? Won't you be trapped here instead?"

"Perhaps," it replied, "but it'll be on our terms while we came up with a new course of action to reinstate our entity as the dominate force."

"That sounds like revenge."

"Indeed it does, because it most certainly is. Our anger is unified, and immeasurable, and the universe will suffer because of it."

19
Wednesday November 21, 2001

Russian President, Demian Anatolievich, kept his eyes leveled on the camera in front of him.

"Ten seconds, Mr. President."

"And this will be broadcast throughout the globe?"

"Yes, sir. It will be able to be viewed on the internet as well."

Demian nodded ever so slightly in acknowledgement as the seconds ticked down. He was finally given the signal to start his speech.

"My name is Demian Anatolievich and I am the President of Russia. For those of you, in the world, currently unaware of the dire situation unraveling in America, I present you with the following footage."

The monitor changed from the President's face to an overhead view of Las Vegas. Demian's voice continued to narrate as events unfolded.

"What you are looking at is a satellite view of Las Vegas. There, in the center of your screen, Dr. Matsushita is using Thomas Clark's son, Gavin, to open a portal to another realm. Once open, hordes of creatures begin to stream in to invade the Earth. But it's worse than that, much, much worse. The dead, that litter Las Vegas, start to rise up off the street as these beings from another realm of existence take over the bodies. Watch as this darkness spreads outwards from Las Vegas. America is under siege and once their creatures gain a foothold it's only a matter of time before the rest of the world will fall."

The footage was replaced with the Russian President once more.

"Ladies and gentlemen, and people of the world, the Apocalypse is here and the President of the United States is the one that needs to be held responsible for it. He is the man that sponsored Dr. Matsushita's research, the same doctor that created the virus that killed more than a hundred million people throughout the world. This President hasn't answered for those deaths…or should I say, those murders.

"On the website, scrolling below, you will find the evidence that corroborates what I've been telling you along with our raw, unedited satellite footage. Why am I, Demian Anatolievich, the first to bring you this news? Because the President of the United States wants to keep this information from you. But the question you need to ask yourselves is why would he do that, and more importantly, why hasn't he taken any action?"

Demian paused for maximum effect.

"Citizens of the world, if this invasion continues I will be left with no other choice than to launch a nuclear strike on the United States. And let me be clear about what I just said. In order to protect and preserve the world, before more lives are senselessly lost, I will nuke Las Vegas and any surrounding territories that have fallen to our common enemy.

"I urge the leaders of every great nation to rise up and demand answers before it's too late. But make no qualms about it, we are at war and you should all be afraid for your very lives."

20
Wednesday November 20, 2001

An assistant knocked on the President's door onboard Air Force One.

"Sir?"

"What is it?" he responded sleepily from his bed as the plane flew through the night sky.

"Sir, I apologize for waking you but you need to be made aware of a statement that Demian Anatolievich just broadcast."

The President lifted his head off his pillow, swung his legs over the side of the bed, sat up and rubbed his eyes.

I can tell it's going to be another long day. What has that sonofabitch done now?

* * *

Shit. Shit. Shit.

"I need to fire back and clarify this situation immediately before we're inundated with additional phone calls."

"I agree, sir," the President's Chief of Staff replied. "I have a few ideas but what do you have in mind?"

"For starters, I need to respond to the Russian President with the same level of threat. After that I need to assure our people that we're on top of the Las Vegas situation and that we're doing our best to contain the spread."

* * *

"My fellow Americans, and citizens of the world, my administration is well aware of the catastrophic events that are

135

occurring in Las Vegas. I attempted to squash these unprecedented, and unforeseen, happenings by launching a single nuclear missile at Las Vegas the moment the portal opened and the invasion began. However, my Secretary of Defense overrode my authority, at the last possible moment, and the missile was disarmed prior to its detonation. This entire predicament might have been avoided if that device was allowed to discharge. However, with that said, I'm taking steps to end this siege as we speak before it endangers further lives, both American and abroad."

The President shifted in his seat.

"That brings me to the Russian President's comments about striking American soil with his own nuclear arsenal. Mr. President, your words have consequences. Let me give you fair warning that any overt actions, by your country, will be met with a swift response. I, nor the American people, will be threatened because in doing so you will have to answer both to me and the might of my military.

"Now, as to the point of Dr. Matsushita and his responsibility of the millions HE murdered, I admit I was culpable. Dr. Matsushita duped both me, and Demian Anatolievich, with a serum derived from Thomas Clark's powers, created on American soil. The serum, in question, was administered to both American and Russian soldiers and led to disastrous consequences, namely the death of millions as the deadly virus, created by Dr. Matsushita, swept across the globe. I take responsibility for my part in this but I have yet to hear Demian Anatolievich admit to any wrongdoing on his part whatsoever knowing full well the European epidemic erupted in Moscow.

"Citizens of the world, and my fellow Americans, know that I am doing everything that I can to thwart Dr. Matsushita's plan. I will close that portal, and end this invasion, you have my word."

The President held his gaze until the lights dimmed and the red bulb on the camera turned off. *The cat's out of the bag now.*

"I want thirty minute updates on the Russian fleet's movements, and I want immediate notification if any airborne planes or missiles are detected."

"Yes, sir."

The President decided on another course of action and went with it.

"Move us to DEFCON three."

"Yes, sir. Changing the Defense Readiness Condition from five to three across the board."

21
Wednesday November 21, 2001

Demian Anatolievich slumped back in his chair as he watched POTUS' bold rebuttal for the second time.

"He dares to throw me under the bus in hopes of diluting his own actions in this matter? That smug bastard."

Demian leaned forward and pressed a button on his intercom.

"I want continual live satellite coverage of Las Vegas and I want it broadcast live throughout the world on the website."

"That's going to take a few hours to setup, sir."

"Then stop talking to me and get it done."

He ended the conversation and continued to talk to himself.

"If the President of the United States won't show the consequences of his actions to the rest of the world then I will do it for him. Let the people's fear grow by the minute while he sits on his hands and does nothing to nullify the impending extinction of the human race."

His intercom buzzed.

"What is it now?"

"Sir," the military voice said on the other end of the line, "the United States has raised their defense level from DEFCON five to three."

Demian wasted no time. "Very well. Raise our level to match theirs and inform our fleet of a potential attack. After that's been handled I want to talk to the leaders of China, Germany, the United Kingdom, Canada and Mexico as soon as possible."

"Yes, sir."

With the call terminated he leaned back in his chair once more.

Two can play this game Mr. President, but it's not my country that's currently circling down the drain, is it? In a matter of hours

I will have the countries that border yours shouting for your head. And don't think for a minute I won't act on my threat. If it comes down to it, and the world needs a hero to save it, I will gladly step in to be that hero.

22
Wednesday November 21, 2001

The jet that carried the family members, minus Gavin and Craig, landed in Colorado just as the sun peeked over the horizon. The flight should have arrived hours earlier but the pilots were instructed to keep the aircraft aloft until the President arrived at NORAD. Once Air Force One arrived the family's plane was finally cleared to land. After a relatively smooth touchdown their plane taxied off the runway as Air Force One filled the windows. They came to a stop just two-hundred feet away from the behemoth aircraft as the pilots powered down the plane.

"Okay," Bill admitted as he took it all in, "that's kind of impressive."

"His method of transportation aside," Sam said as he placed a reassuring hand on his holstered sidearm, "we all know the President can't be trusted."

"Oh, obviously," Bill stated and took the moment to readjust his own holster. "So what do you think he brought us here for then?" He lowered his voice to a whisper. "To kill us?"

Thomas spoke up. "That's not going to happen."

Sam gave his friend an odd look. "You seem so certain of that. Why?"

"For the same reasons the two of you have already come to a conclusion about," Thomas replied. "Everything's changed and has spiraled out of his control. He's smart enough to realize that. True, he wanted us dead before in an effort to cover up his involvement. But now Dr. Matsushita is continuing to wreak havoc, on American soil, and the President has become desperate. Why else would he one, allow us to keep our weapons, and two, have us brought directly to him?"

Sam and Bill exchanged glances before they turned back to Thomas.

"Maybe to give us a false sense of security," Bill suggested.

Thomas nodded. "The thought did cross my mind but we all know the fate of the world's at stake and that in itself has already changed the rules of the game."

Sam's face turned serious. "This isn't a game."

"No, no it's not. But our sons are still out there and we both know, Sam, that we're going to need some help to get them back. Robert is MIA and he was our 'in' when it came to equipment and a plan of action. The way I see it we don't have any other choice than to deal with the President."

"It doesn't mean I have to like it," Sam said.

Thomas gave him a half smile. "You and me both brother."

"Don't forget to add me in there," Bill said. "Everything about this stinks."

One of the pilots emerged from the cockpit, pulled the handle and the door to the jet swung inwards. Sam, Thomas and Bill stood up and headed to the back to rouse their wives and children who had taken over the rear of the aircraft during the flight. Their children had sprawled out haphazardly in an effort to become comfortable, their legs and heads somehow keeping in contact with their mothers in one way or another. Gabbi and Hobbes, on the other hand, had positioned themselves in the middle of the plane, her head on his shoulder with his arms wrapped around her. A few bouts of whining ensued as their eyes opened and the reality of their situation flooded back to the front of everyone's mind.

"Where are we?" Julie asked as she peered out her window into the darkened morning.

"Colorado," Sam reminded her.

She took a moment before she replied. "Oh, right."

Two minutes later all thirteen of them exited the plane. As they stepped onto the tarmac a contingent of armed soldiers approached their position.

"I knew it," Bill hissed with hatred under his breath. "It's a trap." His hand slowly moved to his weapon.

"Easy," Thomas whispered back as he tried to soothe his friend. "Go easy."

At twenty feet the soldiers came to a halt. A lone officer, with two silver bars on his shoulders, broke away and walked up to them.

"I'm Captain Kirk."

"Seriously?" Thomas blurted out.

"What's your first name," Bill kidded, "James?"

The Captain, based on his stoic demeanor, was used to the ribbing he consistently received. He knew he shared a similarity between William Shatner's Star Trek character, Captain James T. Kirk, and his own for the time being. It was just another reason he couldn't wait for the day when he'd be promoted to Major.

The officer extended his hand. "Captain *David* Kirk, Mr. Clark. Would you and your family please follow me?"

"Follow you where?" Thomas inquired as he shook and released the Captain' hand. "And what's with the armed escort?"

The Captain glanced over his shoulder. "Protocol. But in this case, not to mention putting your minds at ease, they are an unnecessary distraction. Sergeant!"

"Yes, sir?"

"Dismissed."

"Yes, sir."

The armed men immediately withdrew back towards Air Force One.

"Better?" the Captain asked.

143

"It's a start," Thomas told him. "You mentioned us needing to follow you somewhere?"

"Yes. The President is awaiting your arrival within NORAD itself. I have a van to drive you to the facility."

"Just you?" Sam asked. "Nobody else?"

The Captain turned towards Sam. "I've been briefed on each of you, Mr. Paige, and I'm fully aware of your cautious nature, especially throughout these circumstances we find ourselves in. With that being said, I am unarmed and have been ordered to take you to the President without any undue harassment."

"He's telling the truth," Laura announced to everyone, "as much as he knows it to be."

"Fine," Thomas articulated. "We'll play along. Lead on, Captain."

* * *

The van, driven by the Captain, left the airfield and made its way to the outer gates of NORAD. Along the way they'd passed through three separate checkpoints and had ben quickly waved through by the sentries stationed at each one. The van approached the large mountain as it headed towards a two-lane tunnel bored out of the rock itself.

"Last chance to change our minds," Bill mentioned.

Thomas stared out the windows as the van entered the tunnel. "We might have a choice but we all know the world doesn't."

Bill remained silent as the sun's morning light faded away behind them. A humungous door eventually came into view, open and slightly ajar, that when closed would ensure the mountain fortress remained impregnable. The van pulled to a stop and the

Captain cut the engine. Outside armed soldiers waited patiently for the van's occupants to disembark.

"What the hell is this?" Sam demanded.

"This is the final security checkpoint before you enter NORAD's interior," the Captain explained.

"Is this going to turn ugly?"

"Not if you do as they say." The Captain opened his door, got out and closed the door behind him.

"Shit," Bill said. "Now what?"

Thomas opened the van's sliding door. "Let's find out," he said and stepped out.

"Sir, please relinquish any firearms on your person immediately," instructed one of the security personnel.

"No, I don't think so," Thomas shot back, his arms down by his side.

Two security men brought their rifles to shoulder height, their muzzles targeting Thomas' chest. Sam and Bill stepped out of the van and flanked Thomas, hands on the butts of their own weapons.

"Gentlemen," the same man demanded again, "I must insist."

Thomas smiled. "We're here by invitation of the President. If you have a problem with that then I suggest you take it up with your Commander in Chief. Otherwise, as I'm sure you're quite aware, I wouldn't want this situation to spiral out of hand." Thomas stared down all three men, along with the remaining security force behind them. "You know what I can do to you."

The soldiers shifted their feet nervously until a new voice spoke up behind them.

"Stand down, Sergeant."

The two men, visibly relieved, lowered their rifles as POTUS emerged around the thick bunker door. He made his way through the soldiers and walked right up to Thomas.

"Mr. Clark, and his family, have every right to be suspicious of my intentions because I betrayed their trust and tried to kill them."

"You're admitting it?" Bill asked.

"Why hide it?" the President countered. "It's true. And yet regardless of that truth you're all still here."

"We're here because you need our help," Thomas told him.

"That's correct, Thomas, I do. And in the same breath, you need mine."

Sam spoke. "And who's to say that after we've helped you take down Dr. Matsushita you won't betray us once again?"

"You mean kill you, don't you, Mr. Paige?"

Sam nodded.

The President continued. "It's a possibility, of course, but as you've seen with your own eyes the world has a more pressing issue at hand, don't you think? Besides, and forgive my bluntness, but you're missing two children and you're going to need my help to retrieve them."

Sam and Thomas flinched ever so slightly, but the President caught it nonetheless.

"So, Mr. Clark, it appears we need each other more than ever. Why don't we head inside so the two of us can discuss this like gentlemen while the rest of your family freshens up? I assure you the accommodations inside are top notch."

Sam shook his head. "No, sir, we're all staying together."

Thomas turned his head and gave his friends a look they'd rarely seen before. "Go ahead. Get your wives and children clean, fed and rested. I've got this."

"You sure?" Bill asked, knowing full well that Thomas meant business.

"Absolutely."

* * *

The President led Thomas to a private conference room while the others were led to a private suite. The President closed the door as the two of them entered the room.

"I'm not going to apologize for what I did to you and your family."

Thomas' right hand twitched as he held back the urge to strangle POTUS from across the room.

"I was protecting the country, and now look at what your abilities have led us to."

Thomas swallowed hard before he responded. "No, you were protecting yourself and you know it. The fact that it blew up in your face is on you, sir, but I'm not willing to stand here and debate that with you. Right now Dr. Matsushita is controlling my son, who in turn controls the portal. Craig, Sam's son, is keeping both of them phased out and untouchable. We have to come up with a plan to cut that portal off before the entire world gets overrun."

"That's why I brought you here. I figured if anyone could stop this madness it would be you."

Thomas paced a bit. "I'm working on it. I've been out of touch since we failed to shut Dr. Matsushita down in Las Vegas. Bring me up to speed."

"I witnessed your attempt. It was brave, yet ultimately pointless. The tanker's explosion didn't harm the doctor. But, on a side note, I have to give you points for saving the other children while deciding to sacrifice your own son."

"Points?" Thomas snapped. "This isn't a game we're discussing goddammit."

"You know what I mean."

147

Thomas calmed down and paced some more. "We tried but it wasn't enough. About the only thing we did gleam from our attempt, and the explosion, was that the creature's hosts can be slowed down..., perhaps even killed."

"That was my thought as well."

Thomas took the time to turn and stare at the President. "When exactly was that?"

"You don't know, do you?"

"Know what?" Thomas countered.

"I tried to nuke Las Vegas, to end this before it spread even further."

Thomas became uncertain. "When in the hell did this happen? And why, if you launched a missile, didn't it go off?"

"It was before you arrived in Vegas. The missile was in the air and my Secretary of Defense countermanded my order. The missile was disarmed in flight moments before it impacted."

"But...but our children were in there..."

"Oh give me a break, Thomas. You can't possibly hold that against me when you of all people made the exact same decision to sacrifice your own son for the greater good."

"Fine," Thomas conceded. "What's the SecDef's stance now?"

The President averted his eyes. "I don't think anyone wants to comprehend what they're seeing. Nor do they want to believe the darkness, that is spreading across America, continues to transform the living and the dead alike into...whatever these creatures are."

"Add me to that group," Thomas quietly stated. "This is insanity."

"On top of all this," POTUS added, "I have the Russian President threatening me."

"How?"

"He says he won't allow the rest of the world to become infected and will launch his own nukes to eradicate the problem."

"He publically said he'd nuke America?"

The President nodded. "To save the rest of the world. His words."

"Shit. We really need to come up with something fast to end this."

"Do me, and the rest of the world a favor Thomas, and do that. Whatever you need I'll provide, just fix this. Until then the Apocalypse is here and we're desperately short on time."

23
Wednesday November 21, 2001

Sam and Bill scrutinized the President as he and Thomas walked away together. Neither of them were happy that their friend wanted to confront the President alone, but at the same time they knew their family, after being on the run, needed to rest. Along the same lines they had no idea how Dr. Matsushita had treated their children while they were under his control and that naturally didn't sit well with them either.

Led by a NORAD staffer, the two caught up with their family as Thomas disappeared from view around a corner. A couple of minutes later the remaining twelve, including Tad, were shown to a private suite, with multiple bedrooms, deep within the NORAD bunker located in the mountains of Colorado.

"Where are we?" asked Amanda, Sam and Julie's thirteen-year-old daughter.

"Someplace safe," Julie answered, "I hope." Julie flashed Sam a look and he immediately caught her meaning.

"We're all going to be fine," Sam told everyone. "We're safe and out of harm's way. We've all seen and been through more than we can process, and trust me when I tell you that the mental fallout from these events will manifest themselves in one way or another in due time. With that said it's important that you all get as much rest as you can because our fight is far from over."

Nine-year-old Edward looked up at his uncle. "Why did that doctor do this to us? Why?"

"Because he could," Laura jumped in to explain, "and because he has something he wants to prove to the world he loathes." She looked around at all the children, including Emily, and continued. "There are bad people in this world and they do terrible things to

151

others. The one thing I need all of you to truly understand is that none of this is your fault. We're going to get through this, and we're going to do it together."

"What are you going to do with me?" Tad asked.

Sam fielded the question. "We'll put a call out to your parents so they know you're alright."

"But I'm not alright, am I? I have super-human strength now. My parents aren't going to want me now that I'm a freak."

"You're not a freak," Emily explained.

"Then what am I?" Tad insisted.

"You're special."

"What about Gavin and Craig?" Sarah interjected. "What are we going to do about saving them?"

"Uncle Thomas, Sam, Hobbes and I are working on that," Bill told his daughter. "But we need to focus on one thing at a time and collect our strength." He nodded at his wife.

Kim took the queue. "Alright. I need some of you to take showers while the rest of us get some food in our bellies. Who's hungry?"

* * *

Sam and Bill toweled off, changed and rejoined their family off to one side of the large room, away from the table the others were eating at. Hobbes sauntered over to them just as Thomas walked through the door. Thomas caught Laura's eye and motioned with his hand that he'd join them in a few. She nodded and turned back to the others.

"How'd it go with the President?" Sam asked.

"Aside from the significant gap of trust between us it appears we've been greenlighted to come up with and execute any plan we collectively brainstorm."

"No pressure," Bill said flippantly. "It's only the fate of humanity that hangs in the balance."

"No shit," Hobbes added. "What could possibly go wrong that hasn't already?"

Thomas raised his hand slightly to focus the other three's attentions. "I can't speak for any of you but I plan on going back to Vegas to stop Dr. Matsushita one way or another. My son is in there and he needs me."

"My son's in there too," Sam said. "There's no way in hell I'm sitting this one out."

"Make that three," Bill said as he displayed three fingers on his right hand. "We've been doing shit like this together since we were kids so I'm in."

"You'll need me."

Together they turned towards Hobbes.

"I feel like I'm partially responsible for this debacle, not to mention I technically still work for SANDBOX. Besides, you're my family now and I'm not going to let you down."

Thomas, Sam and Bill let rare smiles appear on their faces.

Sam answered. "We'd feel a hell of a lot more comfortable if you were watching over us with whatever we decide to do."

"Speaking of," said Bill, "what ARE we planning to do?"

"That's the question of the hour," Thomas replied. "I told the President we'd come up with a actionable plan by tomorrow and present it to him then. Whatever resources we need he'll take care of so the sky's the limit."

Sam looked at his watch. "That gives us twenty-four hours to come up with a plan to save our kids and nullify Dr. Matsushita, effectively saving the world in the process."

Bill piped up again. "Like I said before, no pressure. However, on a side and more personal note, I wanted to convey to both of you how sorry I am that we had to leave Gavin and Craig behind."

Sam made a face. "That's one way of saying we decided to sacrifice our boys for the greater good."

Bill lowered his head. "I know, I know. It was a shitty choice."

"The good news," Thomas offered, "is that they're still alive."

Sam nodded. "That they are. So don't feel sorry for us brother, feel sorry for Dr. Matsushita. When I get my hands around his neck he'll pay for the chaos and death he's brought on this world."

"More to the point," Thomas added, "we should feel sorry for Gavin and Craig. They have to suffer in silence while they watch creature after creature enter our world through that portal. I can't imagine what they're going through, unable to stop it from happening."

The four men were silent for a good ten seconds as they contemplated what Thomas had just said. Finally Hobbes broke the silence.

"So what are we planning to do?"

Sam took the time and looked at each one of them before he answered. "Whatever it takes."

24
Wednesday November 21, 2001

Within the invasion's epicenter, in Las Vegas, thousands of creatures continued to spiral out of Gavin's portal, unabated and starved for freedom. They soared desperately through the streets, down highways, over deserts and vast forests in one single-minded effort; to find hosts. The Ancient's area of control had dramatically increased and within its diameter a massive amount of territory had already been subjugated.

To the north the majority of Nevada had been swallowed up along with most of Utah, all the way up to Provo, leaving Salt Lake City the next to fall.

Arizona, to the south-east, had primarily been seized, which left Tucson as the next major city in the creature's crosshairs. Once that fell New Mexico's border would be in peril.

To the south the survivors of the plague, that remained in Los Angeles, San Diego and Tijuana, had already fallen, helpless and ill-equipped to fight against the never-ending onslaught that befelled their cities.

And the citizens who lived in the west faired just as well. The creatures rampaged through Bakersfield, Fresno, Merced, Mariposa, Yosemite, San Jose, San Francisco and up to Sacramento and Reno on their way towards the Oregon border.

People tried to run and hide as the wave of darkness washed through their neighborhoods, attempting to fight off the talon-wielding horrors with anything they could get their hands on. But nothing slowed down the evil surge as it relentlessly and tirelessly overtook mile after mile of American soil, transforming its people into unwilling hosts, their lives snuffed out as the shadows soaked into their bodies.

Satellites, miles above the Earth, from numerous countries, tracked and recorded the chaos that now heavily infected the sovereignty of the United States, along with the two Russian satellites. Around the globe people were glued to their televisions as they watched the live Russian broadcast. Occasionally the satellite would zoom in close to the ground, seemingly at the right moment every time, to show the flying creatures taking over a panicked crowd of people. In the ensuing seconds that always followed, as the beings invaded their new hosts, the humans would fall to the ground as they clawed at their heads and bodies. However, that activity would quickly dissipate as each of them peacefully stood up and looked skyward, their eye sockets now filled with a red and menacing glow.

Every time the world would collectively recoil, their minds failing to entirely grasp onto the impending reality that this was the new normal, and it was coming for each of them.

25
The Other Place

The Caretaker hovered overhead and watched helplessly as The Ancient continued to escape through the island's portal. His part in keeping this powerful being imprisoned was quickly coming to an end.

The impossible has come to pass and there's nothing I can about it other than watch it unfold.

The area around the small island pulsated with activity, the likes that this realm had never experienced before.

If The Ancient succeeds in fleeing, and is able to recombine in his natural form, there's no telling what will happen to the universe.

The Caretaker's demeanor changed to one of defeat as he continued to survey the mass exodus.

I've failed.

The portal snapped shut and the enormous grouping of creatures, made up of the Ancient, howled in agony as they whipped around the island in a new frenzy, desperate to leave as they waited for the portal to reopen.

A new thought crept into the Caretaker's mind. He dwelt on it for a bit, exploring the possibility that now presented itself.

It's a longshot, but I still have a card I could play.

26
Thursday November 22, 2001

In the center of Las Vegas, Dr. Matsushita, with both Craig and Gavin's hands firmly grasped in his own, smiled as the endless mass of creatures continued to discharge out of the portal.

The world has been brought to its knees and I'm the one who made it happen. The destruction that's ensued...it's...it's delightful. Sure, the history books will villainize me, but what do I care.

The doctor's mile faltered for a moment.

Wait. I must be seriously worn out because even I have to realize that no one's going to be left alive to write this particular chapter into any history book. Get it together.

It'd been nearly twelve hours since the three of them had started up the portal again, and Yamato was exhausted. And close by, seemingly never farther than ten feet away at all times, stood a red-eyed corpse. The Ancient never blinked as it incessantly supervised its escape via Dr. Matsushita. Yamato caught it's stare in his peripheral vision and twisted his head.

"Are you enjoying this?" Yamato inquired.

"Yes, we are, and more than your insignificant mind could ever comprehend."

Asshole. "Bold talk from a sentient creature that'd still be trapped if it wasn't for 'my' help."

The Ancient's red-eyes glowed stronger for a brief moment and then returned to normal. However, before their banter could continue the portal abruptly snapped shut as Gavin collapsed to the ground, unconscious. The Ancient became enraged as Yamato bent down to check the boy out.

"Re-open the portal! We're not done leaving that realm yet! Open it!"

Yamato snapped. "Back the fuck off! Gavin, Craig and I need to eat and rest. We can't keep up with your expectant pace."

"We don't care. Make the boy open the portal."

Dr. Matsushita released the boy's hands and stood up, effectively unphasing the three of them.

"And I don't care whether you care. You're not the one calling the shots around here. The fact is you need me infinitely more than I need you, and yet you continue to forget that little factoid. I'm starting to realize that you're not as smart as you think you are. Hell, if you had any brains at all then you wouldn't have been trapped in the first place, would you?"

The Ancient's eyes immediately intensified as its human host squared off against Yamato in the middle of the street.

"You're a pathetic race that needs to be wiped out."

Yamato grinned. "Those are some tough words from something that requires our bodies to subsist here on Earth."

"We should end your life right now," the Ancient threatened.

"Oh no, more empty threats," Yamato mocked. "But since you're a little slow on the current state of events, let me bring you up to speed. Without the boy's portal your remaining portion will remain imprisoned. And without my power to command the boy to open that portal, well, perhaps you can figure out the rest on your own."

"We could take over the boy ourselves."

Yamato stepped aside. "By all means, do it. He's right there, lying on the street." The seconds ticked by and the Ancient remained exactly where he was. Yamato stepped back to his original position. "I'll give you points for bluffing but not too many. You would have already done that if you had the ability to both inhabit and retain our powers. But we both know it doesn't work that way. The host dies and all that's left is a walking puppet." Yamato stepped back and bent down over Gavin again while Craig stood idly by, still under the doctor's control while the Ancient seethed. "So this is what's going to happen. We're taking a long break to eat and sleep."

"That is unacceptable."

Yamato continued unabated. "Or, if I'm not treated with respect, I can assure you the portal will never reopen. How's that work into your overall plans?"

The Ancient clenched and unclenched the host's fists as it tried to come up with an alternative plan, but it knew it had been bested, at least for now.

"Very well."

"That's better. That's much better."

27
Thursday November 22, 2001

A knock sounded on the outside of Demian Anatolievich's office door deep within the Kremlin.

"Come," responded the Russian president.

One of his assistants quickly opened the door and poked his head in. "They're waiting for you, sir."

"Very well," Demian replied.

As the assistant departed Demian slowly pushed himself out of his chair, his fatigued body protesting from the prolonged hours and lack of sleep he'd maintained since Dr. Matsushita's plague swept through Moscow and Europe more than a week before. He knew he was tired, and prone to snap judgments in his current state, but his country was looking to him for a way out of this horrific chapter, and he would not let them down.

I'll sleep when I'm dead.

Demian pushed his chair back, exited his office and made a beeline towards his main conference room. As he entered he immediately noticed that five pairs of eyes followed him from monitors attached to the conference room wall; and those eyes belonged to the leaders of China, Germany, the UK, Canada and Mexico.

Demian took a seat and said, "I want to thank each of you for agreeing to this meeting. I know it's both early and late in some of your countries, but the hard truth is that the world has arrived at a crossroads and sleep has eluded me for quite some time."

"I hate to break protocol, Mr. President," the Mexican President said, "but I have to assume you want to discuss the events that are occurring in America?"

"That's correct."

"Then forgive me when I tell you to get to the point. My country is already under attack."

Demian ignored the comment and maintained his composure. "The President of Mexico is absolutely right. We, and the people of the world, have run out of time. Earth is being invaded and people are being slaughtered. Granted, the majority of these have been American so far, but my people have calculated the growth projections of this 'darkness' and, quite frankly, we can't allow this invasion to proceed."

"Make your point," instructed the Canadian President.

"This incursion, as you can clearly see from my satellite footage, is spreading faster than anyone anticipated. I propose we act before our borders are encroached and our citizens within them annihilated. If we continue to sit back and watch, continue to do nothing, then what you've seen in America will soon arrive at your doorsteps.

"I propose," Demian stated, "that our only course of action is to launch a nuclear strike on the infected areas of the United States."

"You can't be serious?" the Prime Minister from the UK said. "This is America you're talking about."

"What other choice do we have? America hasn't acted in the best interests of the world as the invading creatures continue to expand their borders."

"The President of the United States," the Prime Minister countered, "launched a nuclear missile at his own territory."

"And it never detonated, which indicates to me that his own people countermanded his orders. If that missile had detonated this meeting may never have become a necessity. But that's not the position we currently find ourselves in."

"Once again," the Mexican President said, "what are you proposing, firing on the United States?"

Demian took a breath and let it out. "Not as a first resort. I need a consensus, from this group, that if left with no other choice you will all back Russia when I order nuclear missiles to be launched at the infected American zones."

China spoke up. "Why would you volunteer, or more specifically, why would you present Russia as a potential target to the U.S.?"

"For two reasons. First, I'm partially responsible for spreading the plague that ravaged our world. But more importantly, my fleet is stationed off the coast of America and can strike now. None of you have anything to lose unless you sit idly by and 'hope' this invasion will end on its own. Our lives depend on this war, that we never asked for, to come to a quick and decisive end. With that said, I will act if the American President refuses to." Demian took his time and looked at each and every one of them before he continued. "I need to know if you're with me or not?"

* * *

Demian Anatolievich returned to his office and initiated the connection. A minute later POTUS answered.

"I don't have a lot of time, President Anatolievich."

"That's something we both have in common then, Mr. President, so I'll get to the point."

For the next few minutes he laid out the ultimatum that unless POTUS nuked the infected areas himself Russia would be forced to do it for him, with the backing of five major countries.

"This is outrageous," POTUS exclaimed. "You have no idea what we're going through over here but suffice it to say I'm devising a plan, as we speak, to counter this incursion."

"Planning with whom? Thomas Clark?"

"That's correct."

"Interesting. Remind me, if I'm wrong of course, but didn't you tell me he was dead? Another lie, Mr. President?"

"Squabble if you want over the details, Demian, but you and I are actually in agreement for once. We both want that portal closed and these creatures off our planet. I don't appreciate being threatened and I will react accordingly. And aside from our personal beef with each other, the truth is that I need more time."

"Time is a luxury the people of the world no longer possess, especially you. The darkness is spreading across your country at an alarming rate, killing everything in its path. There is no cure for this other than a nuclear strike."

"You're treading on dangerous ground, Demian. Back off."

"You have three hours to act, Mr. President. I hope you decide to do the right thing."

"You son of a…"

But the line was dead already. The President hung up, cursed, and quickly made his way to Thomas Clark.

166

28

Thursday November 22, 2001

Thomas and his family, in the secure confines of NORAD, woke early Thursday morning to a light rap on their suite door. Sam and Bill, instantly on guard with hands on their weapons, cautiously opened the door to a female lieutenant who had been waiting patiently. She addressed Sam as soon as his head appeared.

"Good morning, sir. The President requests that you meet with him thirty minutes from now."

"Just myself, lieutenant," Sam clarified, "or everyone?"

"My apologies, sir. The President would like to meet with everyone."

"In thirty minutes?"

"Yes, sir."

"Alright. Thank you."

"You're welcome. I'll be back for you then."

"Very well, lieutenant."

Sam eased the door closed and looked over at Bill. "Here we go."

Bill nodded. "No kidding."

* * *

Thirty minutes later Thomas, Laura, Emily, Sam, Julie, Amanda, Bill, Kim, Edward, Sarah, Gabbi, Hobbes and Tad were led to a private conference room. Less than a minute later POTUS joined them.

"Mr. Clark, you and your family all slept well I take it?" he asked as he entered and took a seat.

"Yes, thank you," Thomas replied.

"Don't mention it. But let's dispense with the pleasantries. What have you come up with so we can move ahead with Dr. Matsushita's elimination?"

Before Thomas could reply the conference room door opened and someone poked their head.

"Mr. President, I'm sorry to interrupt but the Russian President is on the line for you."

POTUS sighed and stood up. "I'll be back."

The President closed the door behind him as he departed. Julie, Laura and Kim looked over at their husbands.

"What's he talking about?" Julie probed, a bit of alarm in her voice. "What's the President asking you to do?"

Thomas answered her question. "I'm going back to Las Vegas to end this. Sam and Bill have agreed to join me."

Julie slowly nodded knowing full well her son was still being held captive. "Will...will you be able to rescue Craig and Gavin?"

"We're going to do everything in our power to make sure we bring those boys back," Sam told her.

"But the reality," Laura interjected, "is that saving the world is our priority and that's something we all must come to terms with."

"You'd sacrifice your own son?" Kim questioned.

"No, not willingly," Laura answered. "But if it came down to a choice between saving him or saving the world, well, I'm afraid there's no real choice, is there?"

Kim lowered her eyes and clutched her two children on her lap a bit tighter. "I suppose not."

"I'm sorry," Sam told his wife, "but you know I have to do this."

"Just bring our son back to us, safe and sound, that's all I ask."

"That's the plan."

"I'm sorry to interrupt," Gabbi said, "but what IS the plan?"

All eyes turned to Thomas at the head of the conference table. He cleared his throat before he began. "Sam, Bill, Hobbes and I came up with an actionable strategy early this morning while you all slept. But, I don't think everyone's going to like it."

"Knowing Bill, probably not," Kim said, "but tell us anyway."

"The plan calls for six of us to parachute into Vegas."

"Six?" Gabbi inquired. "I don't understand."

"Neither do I," Julie added.

Kim persisted. "Who are the other three?"

Thomas finally answered. "Sarah, Emily and Tad."

Surprise washed over the three kids and their mothers.

"Over my dead body," Kim declared. "My daughter isn't going anywhere."

Emily looked over at Kim. "I'm going because we're a family. My brother and Craig need my help. Who are you to sit there and pretend that what Dr. Matsushita is doing doesn't affect you? Do you think I want to ever see that sonofabitch again? I don't, but my father has a plan and needs my help."

Laura gave Emily a hug as Sarah pulled free of her mother's arm and walked over to stand by her father. "I'm thirteen-years-old and Emily's right. I'm special now and I'll do whatever it takes."

Kim's mouth hung open as Tad joined in. "I'm in too. My parents didn't want me around so they sent me away to boarding school. I hated it there and part of me is glad that it was burned to the ground. But what I miss most, and what I've seen throughout all this chaos, is that you're all a family. I want that more than anything. If Mr. Clark needs my help then I'll lend my new found strength to the equation."

Julie, of all people, refocused the question at hand. "So you're saying the six of you are going to parachute into Vegas, is that what I'm hearing?"

Thomas nodded. "The plan is to utilize Sarah's invisibility, Tad's strength, and Emily's power of control against Dr. Matsushita while Sam, Bill and I, along with Hobbes in a support role, cause as much havoc and distraction as possible."

Before Thomas could continue the door abruptly opened and the President re-entered. He sat down, but he was clearly agitated. He quickly realized that everyone was looking at him.

"I'm not going to bullshit you. I just got off the phone with Demian Anatolievich, the Russian president. Five other countries are backing Russia and have ordered me to nuke the infected areas, starting with Las Vegas."

"Are you going to comply?" Sam asked him.

"It may come down to that," the President replied, "but not before I give you a chance to end this on your terms. I know your son is at risk, both of yours."

"Thank you, sir," Sam replied.

"Yes, thank you," Thomas added.

"Don't thank me yet. What you don't know is that he gave me three hours before he'd launch."

Sam tersely stood up. "What the hell? That's not enough time."

"I know," the President replied. "But that's my problem to deal with. Now, since time is of the essence, tell me what your plan is so I can immediately allocate equipment and personnel to this endeavor."

Gabbi butt in. "I have a question." She waited a few seconds before she continued. "I know I'm one of the odd ones out, which quite frankly is a new feeling for me due to my purple hair and tattoos, but I digress. My question is why should any of us trust you, Mr. President? You tried to kill us all before. If this plan is successful, why would you leave us alone after all this? And to further complicate matters, why would anyone is this world leave us alone? We'll be hunted till the end of our lives, always looking over our shoulders."

"We don't have time for this," the President stated.

"Answer her question," Laura articulated concisely, her eyes locked on POTUS, "because I know it's been bouncing around in many of our minds as well."

"You're being paranoid," the President said.

Sam walked slowly around the table and stopped an arm's length away from POTUS. "Your track record is shit, sir, so you're really going to have to convince us that you have our best interests at heart. Do I make myself clear?"

The President yielded. "I'll buy you an island in the Bahamas. You can live out your lives in peace."

"And use our money you took from us when you shut down SANDBOX to buy it is what it really sounds like," Bill uttered.

"Fine," the President said. "An island, your privacy and your money back. Deal?"

"I like what I'm hearing, but first thing's first," Thomas reminded everyone.

Sam leaned over and whispered in the President's ear. "I want this deal in writing, or trust me, we'll be back for you." He then walked back around the table.

POTUS regained his composure. "We need to move quickly so tell me exactly what you need."

* * *

An hour later, with preliminary operations for the insertion into Las Vegas underway, the President was informed of an impending threat.

"What is it now?"

"Sir, the Russian fleet has just launched a large sortie of aircraft. They're headed directly for the west coast and will enter U.S. airspace in one minute."

Sonfoabitch. Shit. Anatolievich, you'll pay for this. "Move us to DEFCON One and send those Russian ships to the bottom of the ocean."

"Yes, sir."

29
Thursday November 22, 2001

Three hundred miles off the coast of California, the Russian aircraft carrier *Kozlov*, flanked by numerous cruisers, destroyers and submarines, received a flash traffic transmission. The transcript was printed out, authenticated by two separate communications officers and then delivered to the Admiral who resided on the bridge. He unfolded the orders and read its contents.

> YOU ARE HEREBY ORDERED TO INITIATE
> OPERATION BOOGEYMAN
> ENEMY RESISTANCE: HIGH
> GOOD LUCK AND GOD SPEED

The Admiral, along with his entire fleet, had been expecting these orders from their President for the past twenty-four hours and, because of that, had maintained an elevated state of readiness. The Admiral, along with the Captains commanding the other vessels that surrounded his aircraft carrier, had been briefed on the details of Operation Boogeyman the moment Las Vegas had become the breeding ground to an unknown race of invaders. The Operation had one task, and one task only, to cauterize the infection by any and all means necessary.

The Admiral picked up the handheld phone next to him, flipped a few switches and his voice was instantly broadcast to the other ships in his fleet.

"Now here this. Now here this. This is Admiral Korovin. I'm sure each of you has kept their eyes glued to the news stations and is aware that the United States has been invaded. That attacking force has overrun Las Vegas and has already extended their area of control. That territory, no longer held by the United States, continues to expand and has encroached into Mexico. This threat will continue to magnify, multiplying throughout the world unchecked.

"For the past two weeks we have maintained our distance from the United States. That changes today. Our orders are to eradicate this threat at all costs. The Americans will fight to protect what's theirs and treat us as the enemy. Fight them as if your life depended on it, because it does.

"Man your battle stations. We are at war."

The Admiral cradled the phone and gave the first of many orders to come to the various officers on the bridge. "Helm. Turn the fleet into the wind."

"Aye, sir."

"Flight Control. Inform the flight deck that as soon as we're in position I want our planes up ten minutes ago."

"Aye, sir."

"Weapons Control. Ready cruise and ballistic missiles for launch."

"Aye, sir. What about our submarines?"

The Admiral held up his hand. "I want them held in reserve for the time being."

"Understood, sir."

"How close is the American fleet?"

"Four hundred miles south of us and closing, sir."

* * *

Twenty-four Russian planes launched in succession off the deck of the *Kozlov*. The airspace surrounding the Russian fleet

174

was filled with a mixture of SU-25 fighters, armed with both anti-ship and air-to-air missiles, while the MIG-31 fighters were loaded with air-to-air missiles.

Thirty minutes later satellite tracking picked up a large mass of American planes, made up of F-16 Falcon's and F-15 Eagles on an intercept course, both from the southern fleet and a military base out of Oregon to the north-east. The Eagles were armed for air-to-air combat while the Falcon's were also equipped with anti-ship missiles.

"Admiral, the American's are coming in fast from the south."

"How many aircraft?"

"I count thirty, sir. One minute until optimal long range radar-missile launch."

Shit. "Launch our remaining fighters immediately and instruct our current fighters to engage."

"Yes, sir."

"Weps. I need firing solutions for both Las Vegas and the American fleet locked into the computer."

"Already done, sir. Both ballistic and cruise missiles are ready to launch on your command."

For Mother Russia. "Fire."

*   *   *

The *U.S.S. Constellation* formed the center of the American battle group that had been sent by POTUS to keep the Russian navy, operating off the coast of California, in check. They had been keeping close tabs on the Russians for many days, but Admiral Murdoch, in the past hour, had received an update that an imminent conflict could instigate shortly.

"Admiral, I've got new satellite contacts appearing on the scope. It's a possible sortie launch from the Russian carrier."

"How many?" Admiral Murdoch inquired as he leaned forward.

"Contacts are growing, sir." He studied his console for a few more seconds. "Confirmed. They're launching multiple birds."

"Understood. Inform the flight deck to prioritize launching. I want our Eagles up first to shoot down those bastards, followed by our Falcons to blow holes in the sides of their ships."

"Aye, sir."

* * *

Alarm bells began to ring throughout the NORAD command center. One of the operators scrutinized his console and began to holler.

"I've got a ballistic missile launch! I repeat a ballistic missile launch, originating from the Russian fleet, has been detected!"

A senior officer quickly verified the data. "Give me the number of inbound and their trajectories."

"Four, sir. Calculating." A few seconds later he had the answer. "They're all headed towards Las Vegas."

"Are they nuclear?"

"There's no way to tell."

* * *

"Ballistic missile launches detected!" announced the naval officer aboard the U.S.S. Constellation.

Admiral Murdoch kept his eyes on the radar screen in front of him. He barked out new commands.

"Spin up our tomahawk missiles and target their fleet. Launch when ready."

"Aye, sir."

"Prepare all counter-defenses. More than likely we're about to have cruise missiles fired at us. And finally, give the go ahead to our boys; give them the sign for weapons clear."

* * *

"Mother Hen to Vampire. Weapon's hot. I repeat, you have permission to engage."

"Roger that, Mother Hen," Vampire replied.

The group leader keyed his communications and took another look at his radar. It was filled with enemy targets that were just about to enter the range of his air-to-air missiles.

"This is Vampire. Call your targets, lock and engage at will. Gator, we'll clear a path for you."

Gator, the leader of the Falcons flying thirty miles behind the Eagles, replied. "We'd appreciate that, Vampire."

"I've got a lock."

"Ditto," multiple pilots said at the same time.

"Splash them, gentlemen," Vampire instructed.

* * *

Punk, the codename for the Russian pilot who commanded his squadron of sixteen MIG-31's, attempted to regulate his breathing. He was a seasoned aviator but he knew the looming air battle would be the largest he'd ever participated in. He watched the radar countdown until his long-range missiles enveloped the incoming American fighters.

The Americans are a formidable enemy, but they are no match to our superior tactics.

Punk opened a channel. "Lock targets and fi..."

Punk's MIG-31 abruptly exploded in a tremendous ball of fire, along with seven other Russian MIG's. The remaining sixteen Russian jets immediately broke formation; the MIG's banking as they climbed higher, while the eight SU-25's plummeted towards the ocean below to drop their anti-ship missiles.

Spuds, Punk's second-in-command, frantically reissued his squadron leader's order while he hastily veered to avoid an incoming missile. "Fire at will! Fire at will!"

* * *

Vampire smiled as eight enemy planes vanished from his radar screen. But he knew now wasn't the time to gloat; there were still adversaries in the air.

"Golf and Foxtrot. Concentrate on those SU-25's hitting the deck. Protect our ships."

"Roger that, Vampire."

Eight American Eagles immediately changed vector while the remaining sixteen remained on course. Additional missiles launched off the Eagles rails and sped towards the incoming Russian planes at inexplicable speeds.

"Thirty seconds until visual contact," Vampire informed everyone. "Get your fucking game faces on."

"Radar indicates another sixteen Russian aircraft are inbound."

"I see them, but they can't stray too far out without leaving their own fleet vulnerable to our thirty planes bearing down on them from Oregon."

* * *

The remaining eight MIG-31's regrouped and fired off a volley of their own long range missiles at the American planes while the SU-25's dove towards the water in an effort to launch their anti-ship ordinance.

Four more planes around him disintegrated before Punk finally locked his eyes on the Eagles in the distance. He was rewarded as five American aircraft were hit and plummeted out of the sky.

"Incoming!"

Punk, and the other three MIG's, engaged the eleven remaining Eagles coming straight at them knowing they'd never survive.

* * *

Collision alarms sounded throughout the American fleet as Russian cruise missiles screamed across the surface of the ocean towards them. These large missiles would easily tear huge holes in any vessel they collided with, severely crippling or sinking their targets.

"I count six....seven....shit, there are eight of them, sir."

"Range?" Admiral Murdoch asked.

"Ten miles and closing fast, sir."

"Nine miles."

The Admiral pressed a button on his intercom. "All ships, engage Phalanx anti-missile defenses."

The Phalanx CIWS, or close-in-weapon-system, was a swivel mounted Gatling gun that spit out 20mm radar-guided rounds at 3000rds/min. Their purpose was to obliterate any incoming anti-ship missiles before they reached their targets, typically from one to five miles out.

"Eight miles."

"Seven."

"Six."

"Five."

Multiple Phalanx's, aboard the majority of the fleet's decks, opened fire in sustained fire as the 20mm shells streaked out in an effort to destroy the eight Russian cruise missiles.

"Four."

"Three miles."

The Admiral gripped his chair and held his face rigged as his fleet's defenses propelled thousands of rounds over the sea.

"One down, sir! Two miles!"

"Four more destroyed! Three left. One mile!"

"All hands, prepare for collision," the Admiral voiced on an open channel.

"Another one down!"

The remaining two cruise missiles found their targets. One struck the side of a destroyer, on the outskirts of the fleet, and penetrated deep into its hull where it detonated. That explosion sparked off the forward magazine munitions store which blew the front of the destroyer clean off.

The second missile, having been grazed by Phalanx fire, was forced off course and clipped the rear of a cruiser. It exploded one-hundred feet away, bombarding the cruiser's deck with hundreds of fragments, crippling the vessel's engines.

"Damage report," the Admiral commanded.

"Two vessels hit, one terminally. There are men in the water."

"Begin rescue operations immediately."

The Admiral sat back in his chair, angry but determined. *It's up to you to end this now, Vampire. Avenge our fallen brethren.*

* * *

The eight Russian SU-25's, anti-ship missiles hanging from their wings, dove towards the ocean floor as quickly as possible.

"Engage afterburners!" Spuds ordered.

His wingman instantly voiced his concern. "We won't have enough fuel to get back to the fleet if we do that."

"Our job is to cripple the American fleet. We're already outnumbered which means we're not going to make it back to the fleet. Make peace with that and hit your afterburner before the Americans fire on us."

* * *

"Sir, they're trying to speed by us."

"I caught that," the leader of Foxtrot replied. "Lock and fire."

Two seconds later eight missiles leapt off the Eagle's wings.

* * *

The six Falcon's, led by Gator, bypassed the dogfight Vampire was engaged in by ten miles and zeroed in on the Russian fleet more than a hundred and twenty miles away.

"Any of them break off and follow us?" Gator asked his squad.

"Negative. Those Russian MIGs aren't going to last very long against our boys. However, we do have a new problem."

Gator acknowledged the new issue. "I see them. We've got sixteen new contacts coming into range. Reduce speed."

"Reduce speed? "Sir, what the hell for?"

"We're stalling for time."

"Roger that sir."

* * *

Spuds kept his eyes on his fuel-gauge, the distance to the American fleet and the eight incoming Eagles at the same time as his SU-25 sprinted a mere fifty feet above the ocean alongside his comrades.

It's time to send these Americans to the bottom of the sea.

"Ten seconds to launch."

The SU-25's wing next to him broke off as a missile slammed into it. The shockwave nearly pushed Spuds into the ocean, but he was able to quickly correct his trajectory while three more of his squadron blew up and splashed to their watery graves.

"NOOOO! FIRE! FIRE! FIRE!"

Eight missiles rocketed out from the remaining four SU-25's towards the American fleet.

Spuds smiled. "Good job comrades, good job."

Moments later the four Russian aircraft fragmented as the Eagles from Golf and Foxtrot finished what they'd started.

* * *

The Russian pilot pickled off a short-range missile and banked to his right away from the incoming Eagle only to find himself in the crosshairs of another American.

"Sonofabitch!"

His missile shaved the tail off the American aircraft just as his computer began to warn him that his own fighter had been locked on to. He turned sharply to his left and angled downward, hoping to throw off his opponent on his six. In the meantime, as he continued to evade the persistent American on his tail, his other three comrades were blown out of the sky around him.

*   *   *

This guy is good.

Vampire concentrated as he swooped and jerked his craft in an effort to stay behind the remaining Russian MIG in front of him.

"Status?" he voiced into his comm unit.

"We lost two in the engagement, sir. You have the final MIG in your sights."

Fuck. "Roger that. RTB to rearm and refuel ASAP. Do you copy?"

"You want all of us to leave you, sir?"

"That's an affirmative. I've got this."

"That's against regulations, sir. Splash this bastard already."

"Leave," Vampire ordered. "Do I make myself clear?"

There were a few seconds of hesitation before his wingman answered. "Roger that, sir. Good hunting."

Eight Eagles turned in unison and left combat as they headed back towards the fleet. Vampire knew the MIG, making evasive maneuvers in front of him, noticed their departure as he opened all channels.

"This is the American Eagle on your six. I go by the call sign Vampire. Acknowledge this transmission or I will shoot you down."

The MIG dove and attempted to pull an S-turn maneuver, but Vampire followed in his wake.

"Acknowledge or be fired upon."

Vampire's headpiece squawked. "I read you. You're an adequate pilot, for an American."

"You're not so bad yourself. Why don't we call it a day and end this. There's been enough killing already. Disengage and head back to your fleet."

The Russian pulled another tricky move but still couldn't shake Vampire. "We both know I won't have a fleet to go back to. And even if there was I'd be branded a coward. No, we must end this in battle so I can maintain my honor."

Vampire had heard the rumors of Russian valor but had never had to experience it first hand before. "It doesn't have to be this way."

"We both know it does. Good luck American."

The transmission ended as the MIG pulled a sharp downward turn to the right. Vampire followed him in and reacquired missile lock.

"In your honor."

He pickled his release button, sent the missile flying and the Russian's plane disintegrated.

* * *

"Eight new inbound targets detected."

"More cruise missiles?" asked the Admiral.

"Negative sir. They're Russian anti-ship missiles launched from the SU-25's."

Here we go again. "Sound collision and engage when in range."

"Yes, sir."

This time only one missile made it through the heavy Phalanx barrage and unfortunately slammed into the side of the same cruiser that had been previously disabled. The ensuing explosion ripped into the heart of the ship, at sea level, and it immediately listed to one side as it took on seawater.

The Admiral sullenly took in the scene through high-powered binoculars.

"She's going to keel over, Admiral."

"Prioritize the rescue operation. I want as many of our sailors recovered as possible."

*   *   *

"What brings you out here, Echo-One?" Gator voiced into his headset at the swarm of thirty aircraft inbound from Oregon.

"Nothing much, you?" Echo-One replied.

"Shall we?"

"I thought you'd never ask. We're engaging the remaining sixteen Russian aircraft while Sierra-Two, and his boys, along with you, target those tin cans bobbing on the surface from both sides."

"We can do that," Gator replied. "Thanks for the assist."

*   *   *

Admiral Korovin knew his aircraft had taken a heavy beating and it was only a matter of time before his fleet would become vulnerable to the American aircraft above. In fact only seven of his sixteen MIG's were left after the American Eagle's, from the north-east, had engaged.

"Admiral. I'm tracking multiple missile launches."

"Their vector?"

"One-nine-zero and zero-two-five, sir."

"How many?" the Admiral asked.

The sailor's face turned ashen. "Thirty-two, sir."

The Admiral launched himself out of his chair. "What!?"

"Oh shit, sir, an additional thirty-two have come on screen. We have sixty-four inbound anti-ship missiles vectoring straight at us!"

* * *

The President continued to watch the battle unfold on the large NORAD screens.

"Sir, your orders?"

The President calmly took everything in, knowing full well that two of his ships, and the majority of its sailors, hadn't survived the missile attacks while the Russian fleet had remained untouched.

"Send them to the bottom."

"Sir?"

"Sink them. Sink them all."

"Relaying those orders now sir. However, you need to see this. The four ballistic missiles are about to hit Las Vegas."

"Show me."

The large screen changed to the overhead Vegas satellite. Below, four white trails streaked down from the sky and impacted four buildings. The ensuing explosions were absolutely massive and destroyed large sections of the city and their inhabitants. But, those explosions were not nuclear in nature. As the dust began to clear POTUS spoke up.

"Show me the designated target."

The satellite zoomed in on a tower that remained upright and relatively undamaged.

"Good."

POTUS turned away and went to meet with Thomas, to make sure the upcoming incursion into Las Vegas needed any last minute assistance.

* * *

Fifteen minutes later, as the Russian fleet sank or lay crippled in the Pacific Ocean, Demian Anatolievich called the President of the United States in a full blown frenzy.

"HOW DARE YOU!" the Russian President screamed.

"You attacked us by launching missiles at Las Vegas. You know I wouldn't let that stand. Crippling your fleet was the only logical choice."

"You will pay for this in blood, I swear it!"

"Too late." POTUS terminated the call.

30
Thursday November 22, 2001

Dr. Matsushita sat on the comfortable couch and continued to watch the live satellite coverage of Las Vegas on his suite's enormous television. He was tired, but not nearly as worn out as Craig and Gavin, who were currently passed out cold on one of the beds in an adjoining room. Outside the kitchen, across the large suite, a woman stood motionless and stared at the back of the doctor's head. Her beautiful body was entirely intact and wasn't damaged in any way. Dr. Matsushita had found her dead, locked in the hotel's walk-in freezer and immediately requested that she become his new liaison. The woman quickly became an indoctrinated host to the Ancient to converse with the doctor. Yamato looked over his right shoulder and was met with her cold gaze and the red eyes that belonged to a creature not of this world. He enjoyed looking at her even though he knew that she was anything but human.

"Why don't you come over here and enjoy the fruits of your labor? Your empire is growing."

Ancient made its way over to the couch and reluctantly sat down. "Not fast enough."

Yamato sighed. "We've already been through this. These twelve hour shifts are draining." He turned back to the television. "You're lucky I find the destruction I've brought to this world this amusing or I might be tempted to stop."

"And if you stop you will die," Ancient threatened.

"Perhaps," Yamato countered, "but you'll be trapped in two different planes of existence and the proverbial joke will be on you, now won't it?"

189

Ancient seethed. It was unaccustomed to such blatant disrespect and had grown weary of it millennia ago by the hands of the Caretaker.

Its eyes flared. "You should watch your tone."

"Why? I'm enjoying the hell out of this. And, more importantly, it's not every day that I have the opportunity to get one over on a being that could, as you would say, squash me like a bug. The fact is we're both getting what we want, but only one of us in this room is lacking patience."

The host stood, walked over to the large floor-to-ceiling windows and looked out over the city. "We must continue to grow…, to escape. For the first time since we can remember, we can finally taste freedom."

Yamato joined the female host and gazed out the windows as well. "You'll have it soon enough. And think about it, when you do you won't have to deal with me anymo…"

Yamato's train of thought derailed as the first of many Russian cruise missiles began to rain down out of the sky. Massive explosions erupted throughout the city as the warheads detonated. Yamato noticeably cowered as the unbearably loud booms echoed throughout the city in rapid succession, flashbacks to his youth racing to the front of his mind. Multiple buildings slowly toppled around Dr. Matsushita's hotel as their foundations weakened and crumpled. Bodies of the Ancient, that once clogged the streets, were obliterated and had been replaced with rubble and debris. The smoke from dozens of fires clogged the air as the full extent of the considerable devastation to Las Vegas became clear.

"They are desperate, wouldn't you agree, doctor?"

Yamato found himself on the floor and slowly picked himself up. "It would appear so."

Ancient took in the destruction from atop the hotel and reveled in it, as if gaining strength.

"The people of your world," the female host finally declared, "are a nuisance. BUT, their attempts come too little, too late. We've expanded far beyond this meager city." Ancient turned to Yamato and watched as the doctor finally regained his composure. "This world is ours for the taking, and your people will soon know true suffering."

31
Thursday November 22, 2001

"Gentlemen, is everything here that you requested?"

The President of the United States hovered nearby as Sam, Bill and Thomas methodically prepped their equipment. Laura, Julie, Kim, Amanda, Edward, Sarah, Emily, Tad, Hobbes and Gabbi stood nearby as the three men continued to get ready. In front of them, laid out on a large table, were M4 carbines and Glock pistols along with a seemingly endless supply of magazines for both. Next to those small arms were fragmentation grenades, plastic explosives, tactical vests, helmets, communication headsets and head mounted cameras. Behind this smorgasbord were three parachutes that had been modified for tandem use by Emily, Sarah and Tad.

"Yes, sir," Sam replied. "We'd like to take more but there's the obvious weight issue to consider."

Sam was referring to the upcoming jump that would require each of the men to have a child strapped to their chest as well as all the gear they'd need. Due to the nature and pace of the mission, once they landed an additional airdrop of supplies would be completely out of the question.

"Of course," POTUS replied. He strolled over and gently picked up one of the head-mounted cameras. "And these?"

"Those are cameras, sir," Bill explained. "They'll enable everyone here at NORAD, especially Hobbes, to see exactly what we're seeing in real time."

POTUS smiled. "Excellent."

Kim spoke with and edge of caution in her voice. "I'm not sure I like that idea."

"While I agree with your thought, Mrs. Nicholson," the President told her, "that what we observe could be unsuitable for young eyes; I assure you there is no need for your children to watch."

Kim countered. "You mean aside from Sarah and Emily who, from the last time I checked, will be accompanying our husbands into hell. No, I expect they won't be traumatized from this experience whatsoever."

Thomas, Sam and Bill paused and collectively turned towards their loved ones behind them. They'd already been down this road many times over and everyone knew that deciding to take the children on the mission hadn't been an easy choice. But that decision hadn't been made by any of the adults and Kim knew her daughter, just like Emily and Tad, had demanded to be included.

"Mom, we're going to be okay," Sarah insisted.

Kim bent down on one knee so she could look her daughter in the eyes. "I know you want to believe that but this isn't a game. You could be hurt, killed…or worse."

"I'm old enough to make my own decisions. I won't turn my back on Gavin or Craig."

Kim collected herself. "It's true, you're thirteen years old. But that's all the experience you have sweetheart; just a very short thirteen years. I'm proud of you for what you're going to do; you just have to understand that as your mother I'm absolutely terrified to let you go."

"The truth is," a new voice announced from the shadows, "you have every right to be terrified."

All eyes converged on five individuals, two men and three women that appeared seemingly out of nowhere. The President held his ground as his two Secret Service agents immediately moved in front of POTUS, drew their weapons and pointed them at the advancing threat.

"Identify yourselves!" one of them yelled.

Thomas stood there with an open mouth. "Mom? Dad? Grandpa? Grandma? How…how is this possible?"

"Hello, son," Michael said. "It's good to see you."

As Thomas recovered from his shock the third female moved to one side and revealed her identity.

"Becca!" Emily shrieked and ran into the open arms of Rebecca. "I knew I'd see you again."

"I missed you too, Em," Rebecca said.

"What the hell is going on?" the President demanded as the two agents hesitantly lowered their side arms.

Thomas made his way towards his parents and grandparents and gave them each an enormous hug.

Laura answered his question. "Mr. President, these are the Clark's. Ed and Claire, Thomas' grandparents. And his parents, Michael and Betsy."

"I see. And the other?"

"Rebecca Cross. She worked for SANDBOX and was our personal bodyguard until she was killed."

The President took a second to put the pieces together. "You're saying that they're all dead?"

"Yes, sir, that is correct."

"Okay, but this is incredibly peculiar. I thought I'd seen everything. What are they doing here?"

"Let's ask them." Laura called out to her husband. "Thomas?"

Thomas broke free from his family reunion and walked the newcomers over to the President.

"Sir, I'd like to introduce…"

Before Thomas could continue Michael interrupted. "My apologies, Mr. President, but there isn't time for any pleasantries. The five of us are here to reinforce the urgency of your impending mission."

Sam turned serious and stepped in. "Michael, what are you talking about?"

"The Caretaker sent us to warn you."

"Warn us about what?" Sam insisted.

"Who's the Caretaker?" the President asked.

Michael ignored the President. "He sent us here with both a message and a warning, and that message is…*you have to succeed or the fate of the entire universe is at risk*."

"Sure," Bill said under his breath. "No pressure."

"Why didn't he come and tell us this himself?" Thomas inquired.

Ed chimed in. "You know there are rules that even he can't break."

"And yet you're all here," Laura pointed out.

Claire smiled. "He said break, not bend, and we're the loophole the Caretaker's exploiting."

Rebecca, with Emily's hand in her own, came forward. The gravity of her tone gave everyone pause. "Gavin's portal has to remain shut so the Ancient remains trapped, and that means you have to stop Dr. Matsushita by any and all means possible."

"That's what we intend to do," Thomas assured her.

"Who is this Caretaker?" the President asked again.

Michael finally answered. "Someone you'll meet sooner than later if this mission fails."

Thomas pulled his father away from the group and lowered his voice. "Where have you been? Emily hasn't been able to summon you or mom for years."

"That was our punishment for interfering in your lives. We took that risk but helped you anyway."

Thomas nodded. "And now?"

"Now son, now the Caretaker sees the risk you're about to embark on and wants you to know that every world in the universe will change one way or another based on your mission's outcome."

Thomas shook his head. "Shit. So he sent you with this wonderful pep talk? That's fantastic. I feel one-hundred percent better now."

Michael put his hand on his son's shoulder. "You misunderstand. He's rooting for you because he knows you're the only one who can change the course of carnage that's encroached the Earth."

"That's encouraging, I suppose, but I don't suppose he's going to lend a hand to help me out, is he?"

Michael grinned. "That's not how this works."

Thomas returned the inside joke. "Tell me something I don't know."

*　*　*

Ten minutes later, after multiple hugs, Ed, Claire, Michael, Betsy and Rebecca waved goodbye, and in a blink of an eye they vanished. With one set of goodbyes taken care of Thomas, Sam, Bill, Emily, Sarah and Tad began a new round. When that was tearfully completed the men gathered their gear and, along with the three children, were driven out of NORAD to an adjacent airfield where they boarded their plane. Each knew what lay ahead of them was exceptionally daunting, and without a doubt the most important undertaking they'd ever faced in their entire lives.

32
The Other Place

The Caretaker, high above Gavin's small island, persistently observed the mass exodus from overhead. Each and every time the portal reopened more of the Ancient escaped, to intensify and collate its power on Earth.

This madness has to stop.

He circled the island again craving for a solution to present itself. He stopped suddenly as an new idea began to shape in the back of his mind.

Would that really work? Could it?

A small smile turned the corners of his mouth.

Thomas will need an incentive to succeed and I have just the right people for that job.

* * *

Ed, Claire, Michael, Betsy and Rebecca reappeared in front of the Caretaker, their visit concluded.

"Thank you," he told them.

"Thank you for allowing us to see our son one last time," Betsy replied.

"Perhaps you'd all like to join me and watch how things unfold?"

"Don't you know how thing's turn out already?" Michael asked.

"Not in this instance, I'm afraid."

"Why not?" Ed pressed. "Time has no meaning here."

"This is true," responded the Caretaker, "but in this unique situation there is no past or future, there is only the present. And, to be quite honest, it is an entirely new sensation for me."

The five of them followed the Caretaker who began to grind on an entirely new thought. *Is it too late to stop Ancient from escaping? What if it does?* He paused. *You know exactly what it means; it means the destruction of another universe will be on my hands.*

33
Thursday November 22, 2001

The plane pulled up into the air over Colorado and banked towards Las Vegas while it continued to gain altitude. Onboard Sam, Bill, Thomas, Emily, Sarah and Tad tried their best to relax but it didn't come easily. Each of them knew, albeit not as much as Sam and Bill did, that what they were about to subject themselves to was going to be nothing short of frightening and creepy. However, each of them wanted to save Gavin and Craig, and the world, but deep down they each had a significant axe to grind with Dr. Matsushita that needed to be sated.

The reality of bringing the three children on the mission now weighed heavily on the three men. They knew that not only did they have to do their job but now they had to also look out for the safety and wellbeing of non-combatants, who were taking just as much risk as the adults were, if not more. Sam, Bill and Thomas didn't have to share glances to know that this mission could easily turn into a one-way trip for all of them, and that was something they were having a hard time coming to terms with. Thankfully Hobbes' voice interrupted their collective thoughts.

"Testing. One. Two. Three."

"We read you, Hobbes," Sam voiced into his headset.

"Roger that, Sam. I'd like to verify the cameras work if you don't mind."

"Understood."

Sam motioned to Bill and Thomas to switch on their head-mounted cameras, which they did. Sam then thumbed his on as well.

"All three powered on."

"Thanks," Hobbes replied. "Give me a few seconds to configure their signals."

The loud hum of the plane continued to fill the void as they waited.

"Got them," Hobbes announced, "and they're clear too. We won't have a problem back here watching what unfolds."

"Until the shit hits the fan," Bill whispered so only Sam and Thomas could hear.

"I didn't catch that."

"Nothing," Bill told him.

"Okay. Anyway, the techs here have ascertained a particular pattern in Vegas."

"What pattern?" Thomas asked.

"The portal..., well Gavin to be more specific..., keeps his portal up for twelve hours and then off for the next twelve. Rinse and repeat."

Thomas winced and clenched his fists. *Poor Gavin.* "What window are we in now?"

"The portal is currently down, and should be for the next six hours. If anything changes on that front I'll let you know."

"Thanks."

"And just to let you know, you're about thirty minutes out from your drop. If you need anything just holler."

"Will do."

There was a pause before Hobbes spoke up again. "Thomas?"

"Yeah?"

"I wanted to thank you for bringing me into the fold years ago. I know you could have sent me to prison, like Calvin, for the role I played. A day doesn't go by that I don't think about that. I was weak and should have stood against Victor and Calvin. I guess what I'm trying to say is, well, I'm truly sorry."

"I know you are. We all do. We trust you with our lives just like you've placed yours in ours. You're family Hobbes, plain and simple. I hope you understand that."

Hobbes sniffled on the other end of the conversation but held it together. "I hear you loud and clear. We all do."

* * *

In Vegas Yamato, Craig and Gavin sat around the large table as the female host served them food. Ancient knew this role was beneath this but it had been left with little other choice than to play along until Dr. Matsushita, and the two children, were no longer needed. As Yamato commanded the children to eat the female sat down across from him.

"So let's assume," Yamato began, "that your entire essence, for lack of better words, makes it through the portal. What happens at that exact moment?"

Ancient's red eyes deepened, as if that moment had actually arrived. "My power would be restored and the lives of this world would be snuffed out instantly."

"So you're without power now?"

"No. I am but in a weakened and vulnerable state, but still more than capable of destroying this planet. What you fail to comprehend, nor will you ever be able to, doctor, is that our strength is absolute and unstoppable."

Yamato put down his fork. "And yet, and correct me if I'm wrong, but you're currently escaping from a prison. Someone or something must have placed you in it."

Its eyes glowed with anger. "You consistently play a dangerous game with us."

203

Yamato grinned. "And your recollection seems to be hampered by your narcissism. But I get it, you and I are used to getting our own way. It's just that your playground is a heck of a lot bigger than mine ever was."

Its eyes dimmed. "You have no idea. But let's not mince words. I will enjoy killing you when the time comes."

Yamato raised his glass to toast Ancient. "The pleasure, at the moment, is all mine."

34
Thursday November 22, 2001

The plane's rear cargo door slowly lowered fifteen thousand feet above what was left of Las Vegas. Tad, Emily and Sarah trembled, each of them harnessed in to Sam, Thomas and Bill respectively as the wind whipped into the now open compartment high above the city. This was the first time any of the children had skydived as the six of them inched forward together and prepared to exit the aircraft.

Emily's hair blew up and tickled Thomas' face. Without taking her eyes off the vast, open space below her Emily raised her arms, grasped her loose hair and quickly knotted it. Thomas patted her on the shoulder.

"Thanks, Em," he said to her over the headset, which all three children were also wearing. "This jump won't be that scary. It's going to be okay. I love you."

"I know," she replied wide-eyed but eager. "I love you too, but right now I'm just thinking of Gav. Everything else around me is background noise."

Shit. Those words just came out of my ten year old daughter. She's missed out on her own childhood because she's endured so much over the years. It's just not right.

Thomas shifted his rifle to the side of his body and secured it with a Velcro strap so it wouldn't come loose to smack him in the head when he pulled the parachute ripcord. Sam and Bill had already secured their gear and were waiting for the red light to switch to green, the indication it was time to jump. The two shifted their gaze over to Thomas and the three of them took a long look at each other.

"Looks like we're all headed back into the shit again," Bill quipped. "Just like old times."

"Except this time," Sam added, "it's for all the marbles." He paused and then said, "It's time to get our game faces on."

Hobbes broke into the discussion over their headsets. "So far so good. The timing on the portal gives you roughly five hours before it comes back online."

"That won't mean a thing as soon as we're detected," Sam reminded him. "But at least we're not dropping in on a party already in progress."

"I hear you," Hobbes replied. "If anything changes I'll let you know right away. Good luck out there. We'll be watching."

The red light on the interior wall of the plane began to blink rapidly. Sam, Bill, Thomas, Emily, Sarah and Tad mentally prepared themselves for the next step, realistically the easiest part of their entire plan, the plummet.

"Here we go," Bill told his daughter.

"I'm ready," Sarah told him.

Bill allowed a prideful smile to stretch out across his face, but it was cut short as soon as the red light switched to solid green.

"GO GO GO!" Sam ordered.

One by one, in quick unison, Sam, Bill and Thomas, with the children strapped to their chests, exited out the back of the moving aircraft and began their rapid descent. As the plane pulled away each of the men released their drogue chutes, which immediately stabilized their heavy loads, and maintained they'd descend no faster than one-hundred and twenty feet per second.

"Comms check," instructed Sam.

"Good to go," Bill replied.

"I read you," Thomas said.

"You're all coming in loud and clear," Hobbes informed them. "Cameras are clear and functioning."

"Roger that," Sam replied as he checked the altimeter strapped to his right wrist. It read 12, 500 feet. He glanced down at Tad and adjusted the boy's arms a bit to mirror his own. "How're you doing?"

"This is awesome!" Tad exclaimed. "Holy shit, this is amazing."

Sam had long forgotten his first time freefalling out of a perfectly good airplane during his Jump training at Fort Benning, but he recognized the true exhilaration in Tad's voice.

10,000 feet.

9,000 feet.

8,000 feet.

"I've got a visual on the casino roof," Bill told everyone.

Sam slightly adjusted his eyes and found it as well. "I see it."

"Me too," Thomas added.

7,000 feet.

Much of the city below, as the six dropped out of the sky, was on fire. Without emergency crews to fight them, those fires ignited by the Russian missiles, had begun to spread unchecked throughout the city. The streets were filled with the husks of bodies, once alive, but now just hosts of the Ancient.

6,000 feet.

Thick smoke wafted over Las Vegas and significantly added to the complex and difficult landing they were about to attempt. The casino's roof, the same building that contained Dr. Matsushita, Gavin and Craig, was large enough, but the issue they knew they had to contend with were the crosswinds, especially during the last few seconds before they touched down. A sudden burst could quickly pull them off course, and change their roof insertion to a ground one; and they all knew the streets were packed with thousands of unfriendlies.

5,000 feet.

"Prepare to pull," Sam directed, "and then follow me in."

At 4,000 feet, after telling Tad to cross his arms across his chest, Sam yanked his ripcord and looked up to make sure his chute opened cleanly.

"Good chute," Sam said.

He placed his hands around the steering belts, looked down and reacquired the roof through the haze. Bill and Thomas quickly confirmed their own chutes had deployed and working as intended.

Sam let out a sigh of relief and concentrated on the arduous task at hand. The airstream fought against him and Sam constantly had to adjust his position relative to the roof. It was exhausting because the crosswind never let up. Behind and above him Bill and Thomas were experiencing the same issues.

Bill let out his frustrations through clenched teeth. "This fucking wind is a nightmare."

"No shit," Thomas instantly said, the strain in his voice clearly coming across.

"Just a little bit more," Sam assured them. "We're almost there."

The roof rapidly approached and Sam flared his chute to slow his descent. Just as Sam's feet came in contact with the gravel roof his chute was filled with another blast of air. Sam and Tad were yanked off their feet and dragged to one side, the edge of the casino rapidly getting closer.

"Ohhhh shiiiiitttt," Tad barely managed to mutter.

Sam slammed his fist against the emergency release button and the chute peeled away, off his shoulders and over his head in one swift motion. The very next second, no longer held aloft, Sam and

Tad slammed into the hard gravel, rolled over a few times and came to a dramatic stop against the side of a ventilation unit just five feet away from the long drop to the sidewalk.

Bill, the next to land after Sam, had witnessed Sam's abrupt and dangerous landing, and immediately spoke to his daughter seconds before their insertion. "This is going to be problematic. Hold on sweetie."

Sarah gripped her harness even tighter as Bill fought against the shifting winds. As his right foot touched down he and Sarah were violently propelled away from Sam and Tad towards another perilous drop off. This time the gust of wind filled the chute so quickly it dug into Bill's chest and knocked the breath out of him.

"Oof!"

Bill, clearly aware of the plight of him and his daughter, attempted to disengage his own emergency release, but his fist glanced off it and didn't activate. Sam rolled to his knees, disconnected Tad's harness, which freed his movement considerably, and ran across the roof towards Bill. But his friend was swept upwards and out of his grasp in seconds, sailing over the edge of the building.

"Bill!" Sam cried out as he reached out for him, but knowing full well there was nothing he could do as Sarah finally let loose a terrible and panicked scream.

But then Bill and Sarah jerked to a stop in mid-air, the chute completely billowed out behind them, incessantly tugging at Bill's harness. It was as if Bill was trapped in some sort of tug-of-war.

Sam paused. *What the fuck?*

"Bill!" Thomas yelled at him behind Sam. "Get with the program and release your fucking chute!"

Sam looked over his shoulder and saw Thomas with one arm out pointed at Bill. He'd just landed and now held Bill and Sarah's lives in his hand. Bill, still gasping for air, heard Thomas' booming voice in his ear and slammed his fist down on the release again.

Nothing.

The wind wouldn't let up and the chute strained even harder against Bill's frame, causing his face to distort in pain. Sarah, unable to do anything but look down at the street hundreds of feet below her, continued to scream.

"Pull us in!" she bawled.

"I can't!" Thomas told them.

"Why not!?" she persisted.

"Because the strain will kill your father!" Sam yelled back.

He yanked his rifle free, brought it up and aimed at the two main straps that connected the parachute to Bill's harness. Bill's eyes began to roll, the pressure contracting his lungs and preventing him from taking a breath. Sam wasted no time and emptied a full thirty-round magazine, cutting the straps, as he stitched the bullets from left to right. The parachute whipped away as Thomas used his power to gently bring Bill and Sarah back over and onto the roof.

Sam wasted no time to unhook Sarah from her father and cut away the remaining straps as quickly as he could. At first Bill didn't respond, but a few seconds later he took in a deep breath, rolled over and had a coughing fit as his hand formed a thumbs up for them. Sam stood up, dropped the empty magazine out of his weapon and inserted a new one as Sarah bent over her father.

"Back in the shit again. Fucking hell, what a way to start this one off. Yamato has to know we're here now. Regardless, exceptional move Thomas."

Thomas sloughed off his remaining harness as Bill finally sat up on the gravel roof.

"Thanks brother," Bill said hoarsely. "I owe you one."

As Sam helped Bill to his feet Tad and Emily joined the group.

"You good to go?" Sam asked Bill.

Bill nodded. "Yeah, although I'm sure I just gave my wife a heart attack."

"You're not too far off the mark," Hobbes immediately voiced over everyone's headset. "Your combined video footage had us all on the edge of our seats back here."

"Tell her I'm okay; that we're okay."

"She knows, but she had some choice words for you that I'm not going to repeat."

Bill nodded. "I bet. But that'll have to wait till later. Right now we have a mission to accomplish."

Bill and Thomas pulled their rifles out and charged them. Thomas then addressed Emily, Sarah and Tad.

"You know your roles so I hope I don't have to remind you to stay behind me and out of sight, okay?"

The three kids nodded. Then Tad and Emily each took one of Sarah's hands and vanished from sight, utilizing the same trick Dr. Matsushita had taught them.

"Good." Thomas turned back and nodded at Sam and Bill. "Ready."

Sam brought his weapon up in unison with Bill.

"Hobbes?"

"Yeah, Sam?"

"We're heading for the stairwell to get us off this damn roof. Commence with your side of things."

"Roger that. The drones are already inbound."

* * *

211

The sound of sustained automatic gunfire instantly altered Dr. Matsushita's demeanor and his head tilted up towards the room's ceiling. The female host looked out the window just as the remnants of a parachute zipped by.

"We are not alone," Ancient stated.

"No shit," Yamato replied. "Go take care of whoever these uninvited guests are. I need to stay here with the boys, and ultimately the portal you so desperately require."

Ancient rolled its red eyes and then closed them as it whispered, "Pathetic." Moments later hordes of undead, from the streets, rushed the casino doors. Once inside they clogged the stairwells as they tirelessly climbed the tower to protect the human occupants in the suite. Ancient knew he needed Yamato and Gavin alive until it'd completely transferred over from the other realm; a nagging reminder it wanted to squash as soon as possible because it was tired of the doctor's company.

Ancient opened its eyes. "Reinforcements are on the way."

Dr. Matsushita stood up and grasped both Craig and Gavin's hands. A second later the three of them phased out, now unable to be harmed in any way.

* * *

Ten drones, piloted by Air Force personnel within NORAD, dropped altitude and commenced their attack. Multiple Hellfire missiles leapt off Reaper's wings, accelerated towards the ground and detonated, adding to the destruction in the streets surrounding the casino. Hundreds, if not thousands, of the Ancient's hosts were annihilated during the first pass. High above the ensuing carnage Yamato watched as the female host winced ever so slightly.

"Problem?" Yamato asked.

"Hardly," Ancient replied.

* * *

Laura, Julie and Kim couldn't tear their eyes off the large screen. On it, split into four boxes were Thomas, Sam and Bill's live helmet feeds. The fourth continued to run the live satellite footage of Las Vegas. The thundering explosions that rippled the streets, as they all watched the satellite footage, echoed from all three of their husbands cameras. Kim, who had nearly feinted from the bloodcurdling screams of her daughter, had somehow managed to compose herself just as Sam, Bill and Thomas began to engage the enemy.

On screen they, along with everyone else in the large control room, watched as the three men, and the invisible trio behind them, advanced down the roof stairs to the top floor and opened the door. They stepped through and, with weapons up, advanced down the hallway towards the closest residential stairwell that would give them access to the room Dr. Matsushita, Gavin and Craig resided in, four stories below.

When Sam pushed open that doorway the grunts, labored footsteps and noise that filled the shaft overwhelmed them. Sam and Bill peered over the railing together and back at NORAD their cameras fixated on the hundreds of red-eyes that stared back at them. The entire stairwell, from the ground up, was packed to the brim and the tip of the undead mob was only three floors below them, and ascending at an exceptional tempo.

Sam and Bill wasted no time and depressed their triggers simultaneously into the closest undead. Bodies toppled over and slowed down their progression, but even after two full magazine

213

changes the tide of monsters advancing towards them clearly hadn't diminished in number whatsoever. It was a losing battle and time clearly wasn't on their side.

The throng of creatures moved to within two levels of their position. At the top of the stairwell, Sam and Bill made a third ammo change, ejecting their spent magazines and inserting new ones. Their smoking barrels told a story of their own as the two looked at each other, nodded and pulled two frag grenades from their vest pouches at the same time. On the screen everyone heard Sam speak.

"You go high and I'll go low. Time to break up this party."

Thomas' point of view changed as he crouched down and motioned to the invisible three children behind him to do the same.

"Fire in the hole!" Sam yelled.

As the mob moved higher towards them four grenades, two at a time, appeared on Sam and Bill's screens as they tossed them. The four explosions were absolutely deafening and reverberated up and down the vertical enclosure.

"Are you guys okay?" they heard Thomas ask the unseen children. "Did you cover your ears in time?"

"I think we're all okay," Emily told her father.

"Yeah, I am," Sarah confirmed.

"Me too," Tad assured him.

"Good," Thomas replied. "Now stay behind us."

Thomas moved past Sam and Bill and took the stairs down towards the incoming mob, which had been fractured by the grenades, but was quickly reclaiming its foothold from the endless supply that steamed in from the lobby.

"Thomas," Hobbes called out over the headsets, "what are you doing?"

Body parts were scattered everywhere and the stench of blood, bile and decomposition rose to the top of the shaft, filling everyone's nostrils with the scent of death. Sam and Bill had heard Hobbes, turned and caught Thomas' movement.

"What the hell are you doing?"

Without looking back Thomas answered them. "Stay on my ass. We're running out of time and not making any significant headway. It's time to do this my way. Hobbes?"

"We read you Thomas," Hobbes replied.

"Direct all drone firepower to the base of this hotel. You have to stem the tide of undead getting in here."

"Roger that. On it."

Sam, Bill and the invisible children followed about ten feet behind Thomas as he slung his weapon over his back. All eyes at NORAD focused on Thomas' camera feed as the oncoming horde made its way through the grenade carnage and surged at him. Thomas used his power and flung bodies, one after another, over the side of the railing. Step after step he moved downward towards their destination, now only two levels below their current location. Suddenly the building shook violently as multiple missiles impacted the casino's entrance. As the shaking subsided Thomas immediately fell back into his rhythm and carved out another level as the six of them made headway. Sam and Bill, unable to contain themselves, used the opportunity to fire over the railing at undead three to four levels below. They were close to confronting Dr. Matsushita, and rescuing their boys, and that renewed feeling of success kept them moving forward.

* * *

Back at NORAD a heated argument broke out between the President and one of the NORAD personnel some twenty feet away from Hobbes. Everyone's attention shifted over to them.

"You have to let them know, sir."

"It's not relevant to their mission. Now stand down. That's an order."

"Like hell I will. Their wives and children are watching. You can't deny them a last goodbye."

Hobbes pushed away from the desk, tore off his headset and boldly walked over to the President with Gabbi by his side.

"What the hell is going on?" Hobbes demanded, knowing full well he was addressing the President of the United States.

"Nothing you should be concerned with," POTUS told him.

"It sure doesn't sound like it," Gabbi blurted out.

"He knows he's lying," Laura said. "In fact, my guess is that whatever it is has everything to do with what's happening in Las Vegas." Laura's eyes spelled trouble. "Spill it you sonofabitch."

"Very well. The Russians have launched a nuke from one of their submarines off the west coast. It's inbound to Las Vegas as we speak."

Laura, Kim and Julie's faces went ashen and Gabbi's jaw dropped open.

"Holy shit!" Hobbes exclaimed. "How long till it impacts!? How fucking long!?"

"Eight minutes," the man who had argued with POTUS in the first place informed them.

"Fuck!"

"No, no, no," Julie and Kim began to murmur together.

Laura plopped down in the closest chair, speechless and stunned. *I'm going to lose them all in a matter of minutes.*

Hobbes rushed back to his desk and threw the headset back on. "Shit."

"What was that, Hobbes?" Bill replied. "Say again."

Hobbes fumbled for the words but he knew there wasn't any time to beat around the bush. "Uhhh, fyi guys, I was just informed that there's a Russian nuke inbound to your location."

"Wait? What the fuck?"

"Did you say a nuke?" Sam demanded.

"The President was trying to keep it hush hush. It launched from a Russian sub so the travel time is severely truncated. There's no way to destroy it in time."

On the screen Sam and Bill looked at each other as their new reality suddenly washed over them. Thomas, on the other hand, doubled down on his determination to clear a path to his son.

"How long?" Sam inquired.

"You have seven and a half minutes," Hobbes replied bleakly. "I'm...I'm sorry...I..."

"Forget it. It's not your fault. We have a job to do and we're pressed for time. Hopefully we can make it to Craig and have him phase us all out before it strikes. It's our only option. If we miss that opportunity tell our wives we love them."

NORAD fell silent.

* * *

Ancient was well aware of Thomas' progress down the stairs as its hosts, one after another, were expelled over the sides of the stair's handrails. It recognized the raw determination in Thomas' eyes and knew they'd arrive in this very room, seeking vengeance, very shortly. It wasn't worried about itself, but the Ancient needed

Yamato and Gavin to finish their work so it could fully inhabit this world, once and for all, so it turned to Yamato.

"They're coming. Open the portal."

35
Thursday November 22, 2001

One minute after the Russian nuclear missile was detected POTUS was on the phone with the Russian President, Demian Anatolievich.

"Call it off Demian. Destroy it! NOW!"

"Go to hell. You killed thousands of Russian sailors, and for what, so the darkness infecting your country could continue to spread?"

"You attacked us first, you sonofabitch!"

"Your inaction, Mr. President, may have doomed this planet. I merely took the necessary steps to ensure this doesn't happen."

"Attacking our fleet was an act of war. Nuking American soil is an act of lunacy."

"Perhaps, Mr. President, but only if you retaliate."

"And why wouldn't I?"

"Because the world already knows how weak you are, standing idly by why your own people are swept up in the wave of darkness. I, on the other hand, will be looked upon as the world's savior; a man of action who knew what had to be done and acted. Sure, you could launch your own missiles, and then I'd counter with my own, but to what end? Even if America somehow survived such utter destruction both you and your country would never recover, and you know it."

POTUS recoiled as if he'd been slapped in the face. He quickly came to the realization that Anatolievich had baited him. The Russian attack on the American fleet was merely a political chess move, even though thousands of men and women had lost their lives in the process. The world would view Demian Anatolievich as a savior who fought back against the most powerful leader on Earth in an effort to save the human race. If he fired his own nukes at Russia he'd seal the fate of America for generations to come. It'd all been calculated. *Checkmate.*

The President finally found his voice. "This isn't over, Demian."

"Tell yourself whatever you need to, Mr. President, to make yourself feel better. When my missile strikes Las Vegas, and this crisis comes to an end, I'll expect a public apology both commending and exonerating my actions."

POTUS could practically hear Demian's smile on the other end of the line and didn't respond.

"I believe you have other pressing matters to attend to, Mr. President. Have a good day. I know I will."

The phone went dead in the POTUS' hand and he flung it as hard as he could towards the wall, shattering it.

Get it together. The mission could still be a success. It's possible they could take out Matsushita before the missile hits. He paced back and forth, alone, in his office. *But their families are here, and watching as everything unfolds in real-time. So what, I just don't tell them. Sam and Bill are professionals but I can't take the chance that their impending deaths will throw them off their game.*

POTUS, with his new game plan, left his office and headed back to the control room. As soon as he entered he was immediately confronted by one of NORAD's worried personnel who began to relentlessly barrage the President with updates about the inbound missile they were now tracking.

* * *

Thomas propelled additional undead over the railing, their bodies tumbling head over heel to land forty stories below. He turned the final corner of the stairwell and laid his eyes on the target doorway. There, Thomas knew just beyond that door and down the adjoining hallway, his son was waiting for him. More undead shambled up the steps below as Thomas advanced, but the space the creatures occupied Thomas quickly emptied. Behind him Sam and Bill methodically targeted the empty husks, having easily lost count of how many they'd slowed down.

"I'm running low on ammo!" Bill announced. "Down to two mags!"

"Same here!" Sam proclaimed. "Keep firing! When you're out engage with your sidearm!"

Ten feet later Thomas placed a free hand on the fortieth level's door and pushed it in. They'd finally reached their destination. The wide hallway was clear of any undead as Thomas and Bill filed through first as Sam provided rear guard.

"I can't see you kids," Sam indicated. "Are you through? Are you inside?"

"We're all here," an invisible Emily answered just a few feet behind Thomas.

Sam fired a few more rounds down the clogged stairwell and followed that up with another frag grenade for good measure.

"Fire in the hole!"

Sam moved back, slammed the door shut and looked for something to wedge it closed. Bill quickly pointed at some hefty but decorative cement pots that contained a beautiful arrangement of flowers, now half dead from their lack of watering. Thomas pivoted, used his ability to lift two pots and placed them against the stairwell door. Moments later a barrage of fists banged on the other side in an attempt to get to them, but the heavy pottery prevailed.

"WE ARE ANCIENT!"

The trio instantly turned towards the new threat at the end of the hall, weapons up. A young woman, red-eyes ablaze, stood outside the target room and effectively blocked its open doorway.

"WE ARE ANCIENT!" the woman shrieked defiantly, taunting them.

Sam and Bill wasted no time and depressed the triggers on their rifles simultaneously as they aggressively advanced down the hallway together. The bullets perforated the female host in quick succession, and with such ferocity that her body was pitched backwards. As it landed on the carpet Sam and Bill instinctively changed out their magazines with fresh ones.

The female abruptly sat up, hinged at the waist. Her body, no longer pristine, was now riddled with wounds. One red-eye and part of its jaw remained. Somehow it was still able to speak, and its words drifted down the hallway into everyone's ears.

"And now you will perish."

The open portal expelled hundreds of denizens of the Ancient who shot out of the open doorway and down the hall. In a blink of an eye the hallway unexpectedly filled with flying creatures, past the female host and towards the closest two targets, Sam and Bill, who emptied their weapons into the black horde that bore down on them. Sam and Bill dropped their rifles and tried to reach for their sidearms, but it was too late. The creatures, talons extended, swallowed up the two men. Before Thomas could react he lost sight of his best friends, but their ghastly screams lasted forever as the fevered frenzy shredded their bodies.

"DAAAADDDDD!" Sarah cried out as the three children became visible, her hands now clasped over her mouth.

"Oh shit no," Thomas barely managed to hear Hobbes express in his ear before Thomas opened his own mouth in disbelief.

The mass continued down the hallway towards the remaining four, their long sharp nails dripping with Sam and Bill's blood. Thomas fell to his knees and screamed.

"NOOOOOOOOOOOOOOOO!"

Thomas shook his head and tried to focus.

"WE ARE ANCIENT!"

Sam and Bill instantly turned towards the new threat at the end of the hall, weapons up. A young woman, red-eyes ablaze, stood outside the target room and effectively blocked its open doorway.

Not again. Thomas took off like a rocket towards the woman, blowing past Sam and Bill.

"Kids!" he cried out. "Stay with me!"

"WE ARE ANcient…" the woman started to shriek but faltered as Thomas barreled towards her.

"What the fuck?" Bill uttered as his friend rushed past he and Sam at full speed.

On the run, and without hesitating, Thomas gathered all his strength, raised his arms and blasted the female host with as much of his telekinetic power as he could muster. The colossal force Thomas expelled slammed into the creature and propelled it backwards. It slammed against the wall, just five feet behind it, and continued its trajectory through the wall, plummeting forty stories to the street below.

"Everyone move!" Thomas yelled. "NOW!"

Thomas turned the corner of the open doorway just as a half-a-dozen talon wielding monsters whizzed by and out the door towards Sam and Bill. In that exact moment a snapshot formed in Thomas' brain, as if time had offered to stand still so he could fully comprehend the dire situation.

The hotel room was aglow from the portal's shimmering light. It danced across every surface and would have been mesmerizing to stare at if it wasn't for the ghastly beings that flooded out of it. Dr. Matsushita, Gavin and Craig stood next to the portal, by the large floor-to-ceiling windows, phased out; protected from anything and everything.

As Thomas burst into the room he and Yamato locked eyes. Yamato smiled; an evil, cocky smirk that pissed Thomas off to his very core. The snapshot ended as the six creatures zipped by Thomas. In the hallway Thomas heard Sam and Bill open fire on the new threats while new ones continued to pour out of the portal and focused on the new target in the room.

"Stop!" Yamato bellowed. "They're mine!"

The Ancient immediately halted its simultaneous attacks on Thomas, Sam and Bill, its talons inches away from tearing flesh from bone. The portal snapped shut and the remaining creatures quickly scattered out of the room to locate their own hosts.

Yamato stared at Thomas as Sam and Bill appeared through the doorway, weapons up and trained on him. The two fired a few bursts but the rounds passed right through him. Yamato chuckled as Sam and Bill reluctantly lowered their weapons.

"What did you really think you'd accomplish by coming back here?"

Thomas moved to his left which opened up the right side of the room considerably. "You have our children."

"You want me to believe you went through all of this just for your children? I doubt that very much."

"That's because you don't have children or a family of your own," Thomas stated. "In fact the only family you ever had were burned alive in front of your eyes."

224

Yamato shrieked. "HOW DARE YOU! I'VE WAITED LONG ENOUGH! IT'S TIME FOR YOU TO DIE!"

"DO IT NOW!" Thomas ordered.

Tad appeared out of thin air behind Dr. Matsushita, Gavin and Craig. As Yamato turned to investigate Tad raised his arms up and brought them down hard. The floor under Yamato crumbled and buckled from Tad's augmented strength, and Yamato, along with the two boy's hands he held, fell through the floor. The unexpected plunge caught Yamato off-guard and his normal instincts kicked in which caused him to involuntarily release his grip on Gavin and Craig as he fell. In mid drop the three unphased and landed with a resounding thud in the room below, dazed.

Emily and Sarah became visible. As Sam, Bill and Tad scrambled down the newly formed hole, Thomas used his power to pick up the two girls and safely traverse them down a floor before he joined everyone. Emily, following her mission parameters, was able to briefly touch Dr. Matsushita's exposed arm, to take control of him, right before he regained his senses. But his eyes focused on her and she went rigid, now under his control while the others helplessly looked on. Sam and Bill, intent on taking the doctor down, pointed their rifles at Yamato.

"Stop," Yamato calmly spoke.

Sam and Bill froze, their fingers halfway depressed on their triggers. Tad and Sarah also halted, their free will nullified. Thomas was the only one who could still move. Sam and Bill swiveled, under Yamato's control, and readjusted the business ends of their weapons at Thomas.

"Shoot him," Yamato commanded.

Thomas was able to rip Bill's rifle out of his grasp in time, but not Sam's, who proceeded to stitch a burst of gunfire into Thomas's chest from ten feet away. The impacts tore into his chest and punched a hole through the meat of his upper right arm. Thomas toppled over onto the floor and began to wheeze, the bullets in his chest stopped by his Kevlar vest, but his ribs had taken the brunt of the kinetic damage and had cracked, if not broken outright.

"Stop," Yamato commanded.

Yamato walked over to Thomas and stood over him, his grin even more devilish than before as Thomas's face bore the intense pain. His right arm hung useless next to him and spouted blood onto the hardwood floor.

"It's over, Thomas. You've lost. The world has lost."

Thomas tried to focus through the penetrating pain that wracked his body as a new snapshot filled his field of vision. His two best friends were lost, along with the children. Their plan had been foiled. He adjusted his position on the floor slightly and, in doing so, his chest exploded in pain.

"Aww, does it hurt?" Yamato teased. "Can I get you an Advil or something?"

"Go…fuck…yourself…" Thomas barely managed to express.

"I'd call for an ambulance, but I don't think one would make it. I guess I'll just have to stand here and wait for you to bleed out."

Thomas grunted and began to raise his left arm towards Yamato.

"I wouldn't do that if I were you." Yamato stated.

Sam and Bill, in unison, each took a step back and trained their weapons on each other. Thomas saw it and lowered his arm.

"Good boy. Now, we both know this is the end so I had the foresight to keep an old friend close by just in case you and I ever saw each other again." Yamato looked up at the hole in the ceiling. "You can come out and join us now."

From the floor above a familiar face appeared and jumped down to join them from above. Thomas' eyes opened wide. There, in front of him, stood what remained of Robert Duncan, the DCI. His body was ragged and his clothes were torn in a variety of places. But what made Thomas gasp, much like everyone back at NORAD who saw the same thing through Thomas' camera, were the Director's eyes, now red. Those eyes stared at Thomas as the husk of the Director stood there.

Shit.

"It was a miracle that I found him really," Yamato continued. "I happened to run into him early on. Funny, right?"

The former DCI opened its mouth. "We are Ancient."

Yamato took that moment to walk over and pluck Thomas' helmet off his head. He looked into the lens.

"Who's watching us Thomas? The President? Maybe your wife?"

"Go…to…hell…"

"Or all of the above?" Yamato smiled, pleased with himself. "I'm going to go with all of the above."

"Yamato," Thomas forced himself to say.

"What?"

"If there's…nothing I can do…to change this outcome…then please let me…hold my daughter…one last time."

Yamato thought about it. "Very well. But if either of you try something be aware that Sam and Bill will be the first to go."

Yamato released Emily from his control and she immediately ran over to her father, tears were running down her cheeks.

"Daddy! Daddy!"

She crouched down by her father and didn't know what to do. In that moment Laura's emotionally charged voice filled Thomas' ear. "Thomas, I love you. I'm going to miss you all so very much. I wish things were different, much different."

"I…"

Yamato looked over at Thomas.

Laura cut him off. "Don't say anything. Just know that I love you, Emily and Gavin. You mean the world to me." Laura paused. "You have thirty seconds until that nuclear missile hits the city."

Yamato focused back on the camera and spoke into it. "Hello, Mr. President. I must say I was impressed you survived the heart attack I gave you. But not to worry, your mission is a bust, as you can clearly see."

Yamato turned back towards Thomas.

"What method do you use to communicate?" He looked over at Sam and Bill. "Never mind."

He took a few strides, knocked the helmet off Bill's head, took the headset and placed it on his own head.

"Better. Now where was I? Oh right, reveling in my victory."

"I love you too," Thomas said into his headset. "And I love you…Em and Gav. You're my entire…world."

"What the hell are you babbling about now, Thomas?" Yamato voiced with some annoyance.

"Em and Hobbes," Thomas said as he began to force himself to his feet, "do your thing."

Simultaneously, as Hobbes ordered a drone to fire at the building, Emily summoned Yamato's dead parents and sister directly in front of him. The utter shock on Yamato's face was briefly captured before the camera slipped from his hands. His family began to berate and accost him in rapid Japanese, visibly ashamed and disappointed with Yamato's actions and life choices.

In that instant Sam, Bill, Tad, Craig, Gavin and Sarah snapped out of his control.

Thomas, up on one knee now, used his power to pull Craig away from Dr. Matsushita as Sam and Bill turned to engage the doctor.

Yamato realized he'd been duped and instantaneously commanded Gavin to reopen the portal. In the blink of an eye the gateway to the other dimension appeared.

A wave of darkness burst forth and knocked Sam and Bill off their feet. Their shrieks of pain fill the enclosure as the monsters begin to tear their bodies apart like piñatas.

NO!

Thomas, somehow now on his feet, noticed the incoming hellfire missile bearing down on them.

Gav and Em. I have to save them but there's nothing I can do. We only have seconds left to live.

"Five seconds," Laura managed to say, the images from the video feeds forever etching profound scars in the wives lives.

With the remaining strength he had Thomas formed a protective bubble around himself and Emily just as the missile struck the top of the casino. The explosion decimated the four floors above and the force of the blast sent a blast of raw energy down through the open hole in the ceiling. The wave of momentum washed over them and yanked Emily from his grasp as it blew out the glass windows. The room's furniture tumbled through the open windows and pulled Yamato, Tad, Sarah, Gavin, Craig, Emily and the remains of Sam, Bill and the DCI out into the open air.

NO!NO!NO!NO!

As everyone began their plunge, thirty-nine floors to the street, the Russian nuke dropped out of the sky, seconds away from

229

detonation. Thomas hobbled for the portal, still operational as Gavin fell towards the street.

"I love you too," he said into his headset, blood trailing on the floor behind him.

With the creatures still coming through Thomas used every ounce of strength in him to dive through.

"GO TO HELL!" he screamed as he disappeared.

The nuclear missile detonated over Las Vegas. The brute force of the explosion tore through the city and the shockwave flattened buildings and decimated everything in its wake. The falling bodies were incinerated moments before they struck the pavement; their ash swiftly combining with the rest of the destruction.

Thomas landed hard in the sand just as the portal behind him snapped shut. A high pitched wail transcended the island as the remnants of the Ancient trapped here knew its exit had just been permanently cut off. To say it was enraged would have been a gross understatement.

Ancient turned all its attention to the man who lay on the beach, the sand red from his wounded arm. Multiple hands picked Thomas up and collectively flung him into the waters that surrounded the small island. Thomas, completely spent, helplessly flew through the air and splashed into the shallow waters twenty feet from the beach. The hard impact jarred his body and pushed his broken ribs further into his lungs, puncturing them.

Thomas gasped for breath as blood ejected out of his mouth and poured down his chin. But Ancient wasn't finished enacting its vengeance and surrounded Thomas again. Their dark hands reached out, grabbed both of Thomas' arms and pulled in opposite directions. Thomas cried out in insurmountable pain and anguish as his right arm tore clear from its socket and then held aloft by

230

one of the creatures as a prize. Thomas flopped over in the shallow water, his left hand covering the jagged hole his right arm used to occupy. Blood squirted between his fingers and pooled in the water around his battered body. His life force ebbed away and he knew he didn't have long to live.

"BEGONE!"

Ancient gave one last look at Thomas, dropped the arm and fled the area in mass. Within seconds the skies around the island were clear and the sun once again drenched Thomas' face. The Caretaker lowered himself out of the sky and hovered over Thomas, silent. Thomas was unsure of the Caretaker's intentions but he never spoke. The next words Thomas heard were from someone all too familiar to him.

"The world is still ravaged," Yamato said as he stood on the island. "You didn't win, Thomas, I did."

Thomas averted his gaze away from the Caretaker and towards the man who had made he and his family's life a living hell, Dr. Yamato Takuma Matsushita.

"Bas…tard…," Thomas spit out, along with a sizeable helping of red blood that merged with the considerable pool that had already formed around his body.

Behind Yamato others began to appear. His grandparents, Ed and Claire. Next to them were his parents, Michael and Betsy.

"He..lp…me…"

But none of them moved a muscle. Rebecca materialized next followed by Sam, Bill, Sarah and Craig.

My friends, and their children…dead because of me.

Thomas choked on the blood in his mouth and tried to take another painful breath of air, but his damaged body fought back against him.

But then Emily and Gavin emerged. His children stood there and stared at him while Gavin stroked Stickers in his arms.

Thomas wanted to let out a torrent of tears, but he had nothing left to give

Em. Gav. Even Stickers. All dead because of me.

All of them stood there and watched Thomas die.

Why won't any of them help me?

Dr. Matsushita grinned and spoke as Thomas' eyes closed on their own accord. "The world is on fire Thomas, and it's all because of you…"

The Caretaker watched Thomas carefully as he fell to one side, half submerged in the Ocean of Time, his blood discoloring the clear, blue waters. It was then the Caretaker finally opened his mouth and whispered three simple words.

"Thomas, it's time."

Deep with Thomas a burst of energy bubbled to the surface. He channeled everything his inner being had, and then some, to communicate his final thought. With the ocean pulling his body down, like invisible hands, Thomas' mouth broke the water's surface one last time so he could announce his death roar to his entire family.

"NOOOOOOOOOOOOOOOOOOOOOOOO!"

36

June, 1948

Late at night twenty-eight year old, Nikolay Dmitriev, began to tail a man who'd just exited a downtown Moscow bar. Nikolay's target, now fifty feet ahead of him, briefly looked both ways before he crossed the street. Not wanting to lose sight of his mark, Nikolay quickly and silently mirrored the man and then hastily closed his distance to thirty feet. The man, seemingly unaware of the potential danger looming behind him, continued to walk straight ahead and turned left into an alleyway.

Nikolay smiled and readied the gun hidden in his right jacket pocket. *Perfect. Just like clockwork. Now, it's time to end this.*

Nikolay also turned left into the alley and stopped short. It was empty. He withdrew his gun and held it out in front of him while he scanned the environment.

What the hell? Where did he go?

Nikolay barely had time to register the movement to his right as the lead pipe slammed down on his wrist with an audible snap.

"YeeOuucchh!"

The gun skittered across the uneven pavement and came to a rest ten feet away as Nikolay clutched his broken hand with his good one. A follow-up blow to Nikolay's kneecap knocked him deftly off his feet and onto the pungent ground, amidst the considerable trash and dog shit in the alley.

Nikolay, in tremendous pain and unable to move, watched in horror as the man walked over and picked up his gun.

What just happened? What did I do wrong?

The man slowly turned the gun on Nikolay and came closer, his face finally visible in the moonlight.

"Hello son," Mikhail Dmitriev said to Nikolay. "You have no idea what a strange coincidence this is."

"Go fuck yourself, father," Nikolay replied between clenched teeth.

Mikhail continued. "To be honest I'm having a hard time believing you wanted to kill me."

"And why's that? It should be obvious. You are a member of the esteemed Russian Central Committee, the Politburo. You have power and I wasn't going to wait decades for you to die before I could take your place."

Mikhail's face saddened. "Then I suppose the dream I had last night is something that will haunt me until the day I die."

Somehow, through all the pain, Nikolay's face clearly displayed shock. "Dream? What dream? What the hell are you talking about, old man?"

Mikhail swept his hand around the alley. "This. I saw all of this happen, right down to you shooting me in the back and using my assassination to take my place in the Politburo."

"Impossible," Nikolay spat out.

"And yet here we are, but this time it played out differently and I have the upper hand."

Nikolay smirked. "You're not going to shoot me, are you father? How's that going to play out when the Committee discovers you killed your own son?"

"I expect my base of power will become even more solidified when they hear my son was mugged and brutally murdered. A pity really. Your mother will be heartbroken."

Nikolay's eyes opened wide as his father pointed the gun at him. In a last ditch effort he raised his left hand.

"Father! Don't!"

BLAM!

* * *

October, 1952

Thirty-two year old, Frank Russell, knew he had just blundered his first CIA assignment as he hurried towards the closest underground downtown Moscow rail station. Frank knew it was only a matter of time before the KGB agents, hot on his heels, caught up to him. He'd been working for the CIA for a few years now but this had been his first overseas assignment, and he'd jumped at the opportunity when it was presented to him. But now, as he looked over his shoulder for the hundredth time, he wished he'd never been that eager to leave the United States.

Frank took the stairs down into the station two at a time, careful not to slip on the rain soaked concrete. Just as he reached the bottom four KGB men appeared at the top, spotted him, and advanced down them in pursuit.

Shit!

Frank hurried into the station as his failed mission replayed in his head, his right hand patting his coat pocked to make sure the film was still secure.

Access the government building. Charm the secretary and use a diversion to take pictures of classified documents.

He'd done everything right until the secretary's boss, the same man whose office and documents he'd accessed, came back from lunch early. Frank, in haste, made his excuses and left. However, the man followed protocol and immediately called the incident in. Within minutes the KGB spotted Frank and had initiated their pursuit.

Frank heard a train approaching from down the tunnel and started to jog hoping to board it before the KGB caught up to him. Behind him he distinctly heard the sounds of multiple shoes as they finished their descent and entered the station. Spurned on, and with panic rising, Frank broke into a full sprint towards the sound of the inbound train.

Twenty seconds before it stops, then add boarding time on top of that. I'll never make it.

Hearing his pursuers gaining ground Frank decided to make for the far exit in an effort to confuse the men behind him that he'd boarded the train instead. But those hopes were dashed when four more men, obviously KGB, appeared in the distant stairwell and pointed at him.

I'm trapped.

Frank's face turned ashen as the realization hit home.

Escape! Run! Go!

Frank, without changing stride, angled to the right and bore down towards the exposed train tracks. He knew his only chance lay on the other side of the inbound train tracks which would effectively put a momentary barrier between him and the KGB. As onlookers gasped Frank leapt off the side of the platform and propelled himself over the tracks. He landed hard on the opposite tracks, his hands full of gravel. He stood up just as the train entered the station and formed a barrier he desperately needed. He allowed himself a smug smile as the eight KGB agents scrambled to get to him.

Too slow, Ivan.

Some of the civilians on the other side of the station, the side he was closest too now, eyeballed Frank with distrust, while others began to yell and point. A sustained blast of warm air blew Frank's overcoat around his legs. He turned his head and looked at what everyone was ranting at him about. Behind him, on the tracks he'd jumped on to, a fast moving train slammed into him. Frank never felt the impact as his body collapsed in on itself and flew forward. As the train operator applied the emergency brakes the film, once safely secured in his coat pocket, was crushed underneath the train's wheels along with Frank Russell's corpse.

37
Saturday July 28, 1962

The Caretaker watched Thomas carefully as he fell to one side, half submerged in the Ocean of Time, his blood discoloring the clear, blue waters. It was then the Caretaker finally opened his mouth and whispered three simple words.

"Thomas, it's time."

Deep with Thomas a burst of energy bubbled to the surface. He channeled everything his inner being had, and then some, to communicate his final thought. With the ocean pulling his body down, like invisible hands, Thomas' mouth broke the water's surface one last time so he could announce his death roar to his entire family.

"NOOOOOOOOOOOOOOOOOOOOOOOO!"

Thomas felt something change within him, as if his soul had just left his corporeal body. The dreadful pain he'd been experiencing suddenly vanished; gone as he floated towards an unknown destination.

What's happening?

Millions of stars were all around him. But then those lights increased their tempo and within seconds turned into streaks that raced past him at unfathomable speeds.

Thomas was frightened; terrified and unsure.

What's happening!?

The stars blurred together in one seamless cone of white light, their energy pulsating all around him. The vortex pulled his body towards its center and everything turned pitch black.

"WHAT'S HAPPENING!?" he cried out in panic.

As Thomas opened his eyes the children in the living room, along with the few parents all stared at him. Thomas silently looked back at them as his brain attempted to figure out what had happened.

What the hell is going on?

The memory of the assault on the Vegas casino was forefront in his mind, as were the excruciating incidents that occurred during it. He instinctively reached out with his left hand and tenderly placed it where his right shoulder would have been. Thomas' hand found warm flesh. As the audience around him scrutinized Thomas he turned his head and realized his right arm was still attached to his body.

But it's smaller than I remember.

"Tommy?" a familiar voice called out. "Tommy, are you alright?"

Thomas looked up as Betsy, his mother, bent down in front of him.

"What's wrong, sweetie?"

Thomas didn't know what to do and his mouth remained open.

"Tommy?" she said with sincere concern in her voice, her brows furrowed.

Thomas finally took in the entire scene around him. There, in the living room he grew up in, were some of the kids from his kindergarten class. Amongst them a very familiar, if not practically unrecognizable face, stared back at him.

Sam? Holy shit, its Sam, but he's so young.

Thomas finally looked down at himself and realized what this was.

It's my fifth birthday party all over again, the day I lose my mother. I can't go through this again. I have to warn her.

"I...I'm okay," he told her and somehow produced a huge grin on his face. "I was just kidding around."

Nervous giggles from the other children sounded off as Betsy smiled back at her son.

"Well, okay then. It's your birthday so I guess you're entitled to at least one joke. In the meantime I'm headed to the kitchen to prep your cake." She stood up and addressed the other children. "Does anyone want some cake?"

Multiple small arms shot up around the room.

"Good," she said. "Why don't you all find a seat at the table so we can sing 'Happy Birthday' to Tommy, okay?"

Betsy practically had to fight her way back to the kitchen as a dozen children scrambled past her to the dining room table. Thomas slowly picked himself off the carpet and stood up.

I'm five years old and short. Sonofabitch. He looked around the room again, nostalgia filling his brain. *But seriously, what the hell is all this?*

In the kitchen Thomas heard his mother and father start the song up as they emerged from behind the kitchen swing door.

"Memememememeeeeeee…..Happy Birthday to you."

The children were mesmerized by the cake and the five candles that burned on top as they joined in.

"Happy Birthday to you. Happy Birthday to Tommmmmy. Happy Birthday to youuuuuu."

A few of them kept going.

"And many more on channel four. And Scooby Doo on channel two. And Frankenstein on channel nine."

Thomas had somehow meandered to the head of the table and watched as his mother placed his cake down in front of him. At the far end his father, Michael, watched his son with a silly grin on his face.

"Make a wish before you blow them out, sweetheart."

All eyes were on Thomas as he hovered over his cake, the flames taunting him. He took in a breath and blew.

Don't let my mother die today.

The candles winked out under his gust and the table erupted into applause; each one of them eagerly awaiting a slice of sugary goodness. Betsy handed Thomas the cake cutter.

"Go ahead and carve out a piece for yourself."

Thomas did as he was told as his mother reached for a paper plate to put it on.

"Hold on there, kiddo, I must have left the paper plates in the kitchen."

She quickly zipped past Michael and into the kitchen. The sounds of cupboards opening and closing were soon heard before his mother reappeared with her purse in hand.

"Apparently I forgot to pick them up from the store. Why doesn't everyone go back to the living room and open more presents? I'll be right back."

A collective groan emanated from the table as the children scooted their chairs back and moped back to the adjacent room. As Betsy headed towards the front door Thomas got out of his chair and went after her.

"I need to talk with you," he said with serious conviction in his voice.

As Betsy turned Michael picked up on what was happening and came over.

"What is it?" she asked.

"I'd rather talk about it outside."

Michael opened the front door, a perplexed look on his face. The three of them exited and stood on the front porch together. Michael bent down so he was face to face with his son.

"What's on your mind, birthday boy?"

"Mom can't go to the store. It's not safe."

"What are you talking about? She goes there all the time. You know that."

Thomas remained steadfast. "Not today."

Betsy finally spoke up. "I don't know what's going on but we're ignoring our guests. I'll be back before you know it."

They don't get it. They don't know what I know.

Betsy left her husband and son behind as she hurried towards her car.

"Nikolay Dmitriev is going to kill you," Thomas bluntly stated.

She stopped and shifted her head. "What?"

"I don't know what's come over you but that's enough of that, young man," Michael declared.

"But…"

Michael placed his hand against Thomas' back and led him back inside as he whispered in his ear.

"Son, you're going to finish up your birthday party and then we're going to have a serious talk."

"You have no idea."

* * *

Thomas breezed through the opening of his gifts as fast as he could while he waited for the ill-fated phone to ring in the kitchen from the sheriff that would inform his father of his mother's accident. Much to his surprise, and shock, the front door opened thirteen minutes later and his mother sauntered back inside, a package of paper plates in her hand. Thomas' world immediately ground to a halt.

She's alive? But how? I don't understand. This is the day.

243

Michael watched the confusion wash over his son's face and his demeanor completely changed.

Tommy, what's going on in that head of yours?

* * *

For Thomas the rest of the present opening, along with the inhaling of the cake, transpired in a complete haze. Thirty minutes later the party was over and the kids were picked up. Shortly after that Michael, Betsy and Thomas finally had their house to themselves.

"It's time we had that chat," Michael stated as they maneuvered to the family room couch and sat down. "You have some explaining to do. But first, I believe you owe your mother an apology."

"You don't understand. I was trying to warn her. She was supposed to die today."

"Enough!" Michael yelled.

Both Thomas and Betsy jumped. She opened her mouth.

"I don't know what's going on, but whatever this is we have to remember that Tommy is only five years old. Yelling isn't going to solve anything."

That realization hit Thomas square in the face. *Holy shit, of course. They think I'm just a kid. Why would they take me seriously? I know I wouldn't.*

"Mom, I'm sorry," Thomas offered.

"That's better," Michael said.

Thomas turned to his father. "And as for you, I believe it's time you came completely clean, don't you think?"

Michael exchanged glances between Betsy and his son, but ultimately remained quiet.

"Tommy," his mother finally dared to ask. "What are you talking about?"

Thomas waited for his father to say something, but when it was apparent he was going to remain silent Thomas continued.

"Dad works for the CIA."

Michael laughed. "That's preposterous. What's gotten into you son?"

"The CIA?" Betsy whispered as if men wearing suits would hear her and kick the front door in. "Your father works for a company called Westen." She turned to Michael. "I don't understand. What's going on with our son?"

"I have no idea," Michael replied. "But whatever game he's playing it ends right now."

Michael stood up and reached for his son so Thomas dived in headfirst.

"Dad was a political science major and recruited out of college by Richard Moore. In October of fifty-two he began his training at Camp Perry with Instructor Green and Instructor Jones."

Michael froze and his face contorted. There, sitting in front of him, was his five year old son spouting the truth, and he had no idea how his son knew what he knew. He slowly sat back down as Thomas continued.

"In March, of fifty-four, you made a drop..."

"What's a drop?" his mother interjected.

"You want to field this one, pop?" His father didn't respond so Thomas answered his mother's question. "A drop is when information is passed between two parties, clandestinely. The drop can occur at any location, but the method of pickup is predetermined beforehand."

"Oh." Betsy folded her hands nervously.

"As I was saying, dad made a drop in Washington, discovered he'd been followed, and that the drop had been compromised. Long story short, dad ended up nabbing a soviet spy."

Betsy turned to Michael in disbelief. "Is this...true?"

"I...I..."

"It was a shock to me when I heard it the first time," Thomas said, "believe me."

Michael's face had turned white. "How...how do you know any of this?"

Betsy was shocked. "Wait. You mean to tell me that you do work for the CIA?"

Michael methodically nodded, not taking his eyes off his son. "I do."

"And you caught a soviet spy?" she pressed.

"I did."

"Aside from the blatant fact that our son somehow just exposed you, what else have you been hiding from me?"

"Dad has been running the San Francisco division for the past four years. He's going places."

Michael practically collapsed into the folds of the couch. "How the hell do you know ANY of this?" he pressed his son.

"Because you explained everything to me."

"Like hell I did!"

Thomas held up his hand. "You're right, I didn't clarify that very well. In another lifetime you told me everything, including your desire to take down Yuri."

"Who's Yuri?" Betsy asked.

"Yeah," Michael added, "who's Yuri?"

It was Thomas' turn to be confused. "You know, Yuri. Frank Russell. The mole within the CIA you've been after for years."

Michael shook his head back and forth. "No, I haven't been. Frank Russell used to work for the CIA, but back in fifty-two he was killed while on a mission in Moscow."

"What?" Thomas asked as he leaned forward in his chair. "Are you absolutely sure we're talking about the same man?"

Michael nodded.

"Shit," Thomas said.

"Language," Betsy warned.

"Sorry," he said with a grin but then turned serious again. "So if Yuri doesn't exist anymore then who have you been after? Pinnacle?"

"Jesus Christ, Tommy, how the fuck do you know these things?"

"Language!"

"Oh, we're well past that now, dear. Our son here has me bent over a barrel, and for the life of me I can't figure out how he's done it."

"So, by your reaction dad, Pinnacle is still out there I take it?"

Michael took his time before he responded. "Yes."

"Would you like to know who he is?"

"No fucking way. How could you possibly…"

"It's your partner, Kevin King. He's Pinnacle, and he's been playing you for years."

The couch fully embraced Michael's figure as his brain processed this new information. "How…? Shit. Could it really be him?"

Betsy, on the other hand, was distressed. "Who are you, Tommy? You're not acting like our son. You're somehow…different…older."

Tommy nodded. "You're right, I am older, but I assure you I am and have always been your son. For example, and I'm sorry to bring this up, but I know that your parents, Thomas and Alice, were killed during a bank robbery when you were only eighteen. You never told me that, did you?"

Betsy was stunned and it took a few seconds for her to recover. "Then how do you know these things about your father and I?"

"I want to tell you about it, I really do, but neither of you would believe me even if I tried. Hell, look at me. I'm stuck in my five year old self, and trust me, this isn't easy."

"Stuck?" Betsy inquired. "I don't understand. What does that even mean?"

"Neither do I, mom, but all I do know is that you're still alive."

"Yes, what about that? Why did you try and frighten me earlier about dying? That wasn't very nice."

"I've lived through the moment of your death more than I care to admit because it happened today, during my birthday party."

"But I'm quite well," she insisted.

Thomas nodded. "And for that I'm truly grateful. However, I believe dad can shed some light on this."

Michael snapped out of his internalization about Kevin King, his partner at the CIA, being the notorious Pinnacle. "What?"

"I'll be blunt," Thomas directed at his father. "You've been following Nikolay Dmitriev's work. He's a member of the Soviet Politburo and has been involved with off the books small arms shipments for years."

Michael shook his head. "No, I haven't. Wait, what was the last name again?"

"Dmitriev. Nikolay Dmitriev."

"The only member of the Politburo with that last name is Mikhail Dmitriev. If memory serves me right his son, Nikolay, was murdered over a decade again."

Thomas was floored. *No way.* "You're telling me that both Frank Russell and Nikolay Dmitriev are dead, and have been for over a decade?"

"Yes, that's what I'm saying, son? Why?"

Thomas stood up and paced, lost in thought, while his parents watched. He eventually stopped and addressed them.

"Pinnacle used to work with Yuri and they both reported to Nikolay. If that's no longer a reality then that explains why mom's assassination never took place today."

"Assassination?" his parents both exclaimed.

Betsy shuddered. "What is he talking about?"

"I have a feeling our son is going to tell us," Michael told her.

"Without the pressure you were putting on Nikolay or Yuri, in another reality, there's been no reason to come after you yet. With everything changed well, I mean, at this point all I can assume is that you still stopped the Kennedy assassination, right?"

"Shit, son. Is there anything you don't know? It's like my entire life is being laid out here in front of me and there's nothing I can do about it."

Betsy stared at Michael. "You prevented the President of the United States from being assassinated and never told me about it?"

"Well...I..."

Thomas spoke up. "In his defense, mom, that's his job in a nutshell. Keeping secrets. But you can't hold any of it against him. He started working for the Agency long before he met you, and believe me when I tell you that he has always wanted to tell you the truth. And yes, he prevented JFK's assassination, at least the first one, and met the President in the Oval Office."

"Seriously?" Betsy voiced with awe.

"Yeah," Michael replied sheepishly.

"Tell her about sitting in the President's chair. Or maybe about the codename they assigned you, Wolverine."

"Wolverine?" Betsy tested. "Wolverine." She giggled. "I like it."

"So do I, but that's not the point." Michael had had enough. "Son. Tommy. Seriously, you're freaking me out. How do you know any of this?"

Betsy, like Michael, leaned forward and awaited their son's answer.

"I want to talk to you in depth about what's happened to me and how I know so much. But right now I have no idea how long I'm going to be here."

His mother became alarmed. "What do you mean? Where would you go?"

"It's hard to explain, and I'm sorry for that. What I do need is a pen, paper and some privacy. Can you give me that?"

"Son, that doesn't answer my...."

Thomas interrupted. "Please, dad, it's important. And the analytical side of you knows that all the truths I laid out today I had to have learned from you, whether your brain wants to make that connection at the moment or not."

Michael took everything his son had said and mulled it over. He then stood up as Betsy and Thomas looked at him.

"Michael?" his wife asked.

"I'm inclined to agree with Tommy."

"Why?"

"For two reasons. One, everything he's said is true. I do work for the CIA and I wish I had told you years ago. I'm sorry, but going forward I won't have any secrets."

Betsy smiled. "Thank you. And the second reason?"

It was Michael's turn to smile. "Because the birthday boy gets whatever he wishes."

*   *   *

An hour later Thomas approached his parents. He handed his father a thick, but sealed envelope.

"What's this?"

"All I can tell you is that with Nikolay out of the picture the future, as I remember, may not exist."

"The future?" his mother asked. "What do you mean the future?"

Thomas ignored her question. "Dad, it's your choice whether you want to open that envelope or not."

"Why wouldn't I?"

Thomas shrugged. "That's not for me to say."

Michael put the envelope down on the counter. "Tommy, we need you to be straight with us. What happened today?"

Thomas began to feel a pull deep within his body, the same pull he felt going through the vortex.

"I don't have a lot of time left," he told them, "and that means I don't know who I'll be to you in the next minute."

"Who you'll be?" Betsy replied. "What do you mean? You'll always be our son."

Thomas smiled. "I know, and maybe I'm wrong, but you'll know what I'm talking about very soon." He looked at both of his parents and then gave them each a huge hug. "I love you guys and I'm glad the truth is out on the table now."

"We love you too," Michael told him.

The pull on Thomas' body became stronger and he knew he only had seconds left before something happened. He used those seconds wisely.

"Mom, maybe it's time you told dad your secret. The secret that you're two months pregnant."

His mother's face blushed.

Michael turned to his wife with excitement. "Are you? I mean, are we having another child?"

She nodded as tears raced down her face. Michael pulled Betsy close and smothered her.

"You have no idea how happy that makes me."

Thomas floated out of his body and watched himself, and his parents, rejoicing below him. As he continued to ascend he wondered what was going to happen next.

* * *

Wednesday February 13, 1963

"Push, Mrs. Clark! I can see her head! Push!"

Michael stood by Betsy's side as their baby girl was born. Out in the waiting room Ed and Claire kept Tommy occupied. The doctor completed the delivery and smacked the newborn's bottom. A cry emanated from the baby girl and, with a smile, he handed her off to a nurse who expertly swabbed her down. Seconds later she placed the baby on Betsy's chest and stepped away.

"She's so cute," Betsy said, clearly exhausted.

"Yeah she is," Michael replied. "She even has her mother's eyes."

"Aww."

The doctor stepped in. "Any idea of what you'd like to name her?"

Betsy and Michael looked at each other, nodded, and then turned back to the doctor.

"Abby," Betsy told him. "Her name is Abby."

38
Friday December 8, 1967

Thomas opened his eyes and blinked a few times. On either side of him he heard voices, but they sounded far away, as if choked by a thick fog.

What's happening?

Thomas looked skyward, his eyes still unfocused, at the filtered sunlight that shone through the trees above him. Thomas realized his body was in motion and stopped.

Where am I?

The voices grew louder; closer. The confused look on his face was very apparent.

"Hey, Tommy, what's up?"

"Yeah, are you okay?"

Thomas blinked a few more times and the world around him finally came into focus. A hand grasped his shoulder and shook him.

"Tommy?"

Thomas looked into the eyes of Sammy who couldn't have been more than ten years old. Thomas shifted his gaze to the left and there was Billy.

"Uh…hey guys," Thomas said as he continued to look around the woods they were walking through.

"What's up?" Sammy asked. "Out of nowhere you spaced out on us."

"Yeah," Billy added with a grin, "just like the spaz he is."

Sammy let go of Thomas' shoulder, stepped over and gave Billy a playful punch. "No, you're a spaz."

"No, you are!"

Billy and Sammy laughed and began to tussle. Their antics quickly deteriorated into wrestling and they ended up on the forest floor. As the two scrambled to pin the other Thomas's question caused their playfulness to immediately come to a screeching halt.

"What's the date and year?"

"Are you shitting me?" Billy asked and then looked over at Sammy. "Is he for real?"

"I don't know."

The two picked themselves up off the ground and approached their friend, who still retained an air of confusion around him.

Sam waved his hand in front of Thomas' face. "Umm, Earth to Tommy, come in Tommy."

"Dude," Billy said, "he's out of it."

"No shit."

Before Sammy or Billy could make another comment a new voice entered the fray.

"Well, well, well. What do we have here?"

That voice. It's THAT day, the day he threw me into traffic. Sonofabitch.

Thomas snapped out of his haze as Sammy and Billy turned around to face their nemesis, Nigel Clemmings. His imposing stature seemed to block out the sun as he stepped towards them.

"So you thought you could continue to avoid me, but I figured out your trick about walking home through the woods, and now here we are. It's time for you to take your medicine," Nigel threatened as he pounded one fist into the other.

"We're not afraid of you," Billy countered.

Nigel laughed. "Right. That's why you're slowly backing away from me. You know I always enjoy the chase."

This isn't happening again.

Nigel kept coming at them until Thomas stepped forward. When he did Nigel paused and his smile faltered a bit.

"Oh, Tommy," he taunted, "what do you think you're going to do? Fight me? You're pathetic and weak and everyone knows it, especially your two butt buddies."

But Thomas didn't falter, his forty-four years of experience now stuffed into his ten year old form stood firm against Nigel's intimidations.

"You're weak, Nigel, but you already know that because your drunken father reminds you of it every day."

Nigel's face twisted as Thomas continued.

"He blames you for your mother's death, isn't that right?"

Nigel's fists tightened.

"But let's not forget about your twin brother, Albert, your brother that's locked away in the basement. That family secret, if it got out, would follow you for the rest of your life."

Sammy and Billy shared a confused glance for a split second before Nigel's bellow scared the birds out of the surrounding trees.

"I'm going to FUCKING kill you, Tommy!"

"Bring it asshole," Thomas retorted.

Nigel ran at Thomas, ten feet away, as Sammy and Bill scooted out of the way. Thomas raised his arms towards the lumbering behemoth, so he could propel him away with his powers, but Nigel kept coming.

What the…?

A split second later Nigel's fist split Thomas' lip open and sent him sprawling onto the ground, blood oozing down his chin. Thomas brought a hand to his mouth and pulled it back to look at it.

He hit me. The fucker hit me. What happened to my powers?

Nigel's imposing form stood over him. "You think you're so smart. We'll see how smart you are when you're dead!"

Nigel coked his arm back for another blow just as Sammy swung a fallen tree branch across the bully's back. Nigel roared and turned towards Sammy.

"I'm going to kill you too."

Billy took the opportunity and jumped on Nigel's back, wrapping both his arms around his neck. Nigel wasted no time and tossed Billy off like a ragdoll, who landed hard on the ground, somewhat dazed.

"Leave him alone!" Sammy yelled.

"And let me guess," Nigel jeered, "you're going to make me?"

Thomas stood back up. "No. I am."

Nigel twisted his body to face Thomas once again.

"Tommy, run!" Sammy cried out as he headed to Billy's side and helped him up.

"You should listen to your friend, Tommy, because when I get my hands on you I'm going to break every bone in your body."

Thomas stood there and faced Nigel down. "I used to be afraid of you, Nigel, but that was a long time ago. Hell, I think my entire life started down this specific path because of your family. But that sickness ends today, right now." Thomas changed his stance in one fluid motion as he brought his right leg back and both hands up in fists. "Show me what you've got, motherfucker."

"Oh shit," Sammy and Billy said in unison as Nigel came at Thomas.

Nigel swung his right arm around in a powerful haymaker that Thomas easily ducked under. In the same motion Thomas brought his right fist up, punched Nigel in his kidney and reset his stance as Nigel doubled over.

258

"What the fuck…" Billy managed to express as Nigel righted himself and turned to face Thomas once again.

Nigel's rage doubled and he ran straight at Thomas. As Nigel enveloped Thomas he suddenly found himself flying head over heels. Thomas, having used Nigel's tackle against him, had grabbed hold of his shirt, brought both feet up and tossed Nigel over his body, using his back as the fulcrum. Nigel landed hard on his back next to Thomas who swiftly proceeded to crush Nigel's nose with his elbow.

"OUCH!!" Nigel screamed out as his hands flew to his battered face.

Thomas scrambled to his feet but Nigel managed to grab his right foot in the process. Thomas lashed out with his left foot and connected with Nigel's jaw, dislocating it and knocking Nigel out cold in the same motion.

Sammy and Billy slowly blinked as they watched their friend circle Nigel's inert form, knowing what they'd seen but unclear about how any of it had just happened. Thomas relaxed his fighting pose and looked over at his friends.

"Are you guys okay?"

Sammy and Billy kept shifting their view from Thomas to Nigel and back again. It took a few seconds for them to respond.

"What…? How…?" Sammy tried to articulate.

"Holy crap, man, you KO'd him!" Billy yelled. "Way to fucking go!"

The two ran over to Thomas, patted him on the back and exchanged high-fives.

"Where did you learn how to do that?" Sammy pressed.

"But more importantly," Billy interjected, "why didn't you teach it to us? You cleaned his clock!"

The trio looked down at the unconscious bully, blood trickling out of his nose and his jaw that was misaligned. But none of their gazes held an ounce of remorse. They'd suffered at the hands of this monster and his comeuppance was long overdue.

"Well?" Sammy pressed. "How did you do that?"

I can't tell them the truth, because it was the two of them that taught me how to fight at SANDBOX.

Thomas shrugged. "I guess I've been watching too many Bruce Lee and war movies or something."

Billy was ecstatic. "Well, if you learned that from war movies then I definitely want to join the military when I'm older. I can't believe you just took Nigel down. Holy shit, this is incredible."

Sammy took his time to look at his friend as he eyeballed him. "There's something different about you, Tommy. Something I can't put my finger on."

If only you knew, my friend, if only you knew.

Thomas smiled. "It's me, Sammy." He took one last look at Nigel, laid out on the forest floor and took it in. *You're finished.* He looked back up at his friends. "We should really make like a tree and leave."

As the three left Nigel behind, replaying the event over and over in greater detail each time, Thomas felt the inner pull begin to happen within him.

Here we go again.

Thomas smiled as his soul ascended once again. He watched himself, along with his two best friends, as they continued down the wooded path, a new spring in each of their steps.

* * *

Two days later Harold Clemmings died in a shootout with the police. A neighbor had reported hearing cries for help coming from the Clemmings' residence and called the police. When they arrived, and made entry, they discovered the bodies of two boys who'd been badly beaten to death. Harold, a bloody two-by-four in his hand, stared at them as the two officers raised their pistols and ordered him to drop his weapon. Harold, who had reached the final straw with Nigel and Albert, had snapped after a night of heavy drinking. He stood there as the officers continued to yell at him…and finally lunged. His pathetic life ended before he took his second step.

39
Friday June 6, 1975

Thomas blinked a few times and looked around at his surroundings as he endeavored to ascertain his new location.

I'm back at Miramonte High School.

The outskirts of the school were teeming with parents while the students busily put the final touches on their outfits before the commencement got under way. He looked down at himself and realized he wore a gown.

It's graduation day.

Just then Sam and Bill walked over to him, all smiles.

"Hey brother," Bill joked. "You look a little lost."

"Yeah," Sam added. "I think the last time I saw you with that spaced-out look was when we were ten."

"I think you have a point," Bill said in agreement. "Our boy Tom here does look a little out of it. Maybe it's the fact that we'll be leaving him at the end of summer."

"More like he's leaving to go to college down south," Sam stated.

Thomas snapped out of his new reality and focused on his two best friends. "You'll both enjoy the Army, I'm sure of it."

Sam and Bill exchanged a look and then turned back to Thomas.

"How did you know?" Sam asked.

"Yeah, what the hell, who told you?"

Thomas smiled. "It was just a guess. But let me counter with a question of my own. Are you sure you want to go?"

Sam and Bill didn't hesitate with their replies and voiced them together.

"Yes."

"Okay then," Thomas said. "I just wanted to make sure. I know you'll both make me and our country proud."

"Fuck yeah we will," Bill announced. "But that's beside the point."

"What my esteemed colleague is trying to spit out," Sam interjected, "is that if anyone's going to be proud it'll be us of you."

Bill nodded. "What he said."

Sam continued. "We're headed off to the military because that's our calling. You're headed off to college because, out of three of us, you're the smart one."

"That's not true," Thomas challenged. "I know you'll both be very successful in the military."

"You know?" Sam questioned. "What do you mean, you know?"

"He's just being modest," Bill said. "Thomas knows he's going to become a professional and well respected writer, he's just playing it cool."

Sam eyed his friend closely. "Maybe. Or maybe there's something else going on. As I recall you never did come clean about how you took Nigel down."

Oh shit, here we go. "You taught me everything I knew…I mean know."

A puzzled look washed over both Sam and Bill's faces, but they were short lived as the announcement buzzed over the loud speakers that the ceremony would start in five minutes.

"Saved by the bell," Thomas said.

"Apparently so," Sam said in agreement. But then he lightened the mood considerably. "We're going to miss you brother."

"Totally," Bill added.

"Bill's right. You're a rock star and we know you're going to kick ass."

"Thanks guys," Thomas responded. "You have no idea how much that means to me."

The three friends leaned in and hugged each other. For Thomas it was a wonderful and treasured moment, far better than his scarred memory of what had happened to them in the Vegas suite.

After the ceremony Thomas's grandparents were the first ones to locate him.

"Hey kiddo," Ed said. "Congratulations."

Claire rushed in and gave her grandson a huge hug. "Your parents and sister are so proud of you, and so are we." She pulled back. "I wonder where they've wondered off to. Ed, they were right behind us. Can you find them please?"

My parents? I never had the chance to consider they'd be alive.

Thomas asked his grandmother a question. "Do I live with you guys or at my parents' house?"

Claire scrunched up her face and then lifted a hand up and felt his forehead. "Are you feeling okay? Perhaps sitting out in this sun for so long has dehydrated you?"

I live with my parents. Holy shit, they are alive. This isn't how I remember any of this. What's going on? And my sister? Oh boy.

Ed led Michael, Betsy and Abby through the crowd over to them. Thomas caught a lump in his throat as his mother and father each took a turn giving him a congratulatory hug. Those hugs meant the world to him.

"Way to go spaz," Abby teased.

Thomas squatted down a bit so he was eye to eye with his fourteen year old sister he'd never seen before.

"What are you looking at?" she demanded. "You're weirding me out."

Thomas smiled, stood and pulled her close. "Hey Abby, nice to finally meet you."

She pulled back and gave him an odd look. "Meet me? You sleep in the next room."

"Right, right. What I meant to say was, thanks for coming to my graduation."

"I didn't want to. Mom and dad made me come."

"That's enough, Ab," Betsy said to her daughter. "Be nice."

Michael changed the subject. "So, it won't be long until you're off on your own,"

"Oh shush," Betsy scolded. "He still has the summer before he heads off to college and I plan on enjoying every minute I can with my baby boy."

Thomas stood there and soaked in the hilarious exchange between his parents.

"He's a man now, sweetheart," Michael gently reminded his wife.

"Not to his mother he's not. Anyway, what's the plan for the day? I know we have a special dinner planned, but the rest of the afternoon is still wide open."

The last time I graduated it was just me and my grandparents. Ed took me to Loard's and that's when he handed me my father's letter. But my father's alive.

"Why don't Michael and I," Ed broached, "take Tom out for some ice-cream while you two head back to the house. We have some 'man stuff' to go over with our graduate."

266

Twenty minutes later Ed, Michael and Thomas walked into the Loard's ice cream parlor in downtown Orinda. Surprisingly they all ordered Rocky Road cones and then sat down together at one of the few tables the establishment provided.

Thomas looked back and forth between the two men. *I'm freaking out.*

"This is the day," his father said as he pulled out a worn envelope from his coat pocket and placed it on the table. Thomas recognized it immediately. It was the same envelope he'd given to his father on his fifth birthday. "This is the day, and the location, you wrote to me about in your letter thirteen years ago. In it you described that only now, and never before, should I bring this topic up. Do you know what I'm talking about?"

Thomas slowly acknowledged what his father had asked. "I do, and it's difficult for me to fathom that this is actually happening right now. This is all new to me."

"I don't see how it couldn't be anything but new to you," Ed stated. "We all live in the present, do we not?"

"This letter," Michael said, "would seem to contradict that completely. Isn't that right, son?"

Thomas swallowed hard and nodded.

"Then explain how you knew the things that you wrote to me. Because I'll tell you, when I decided to open and read it, I was absolutely flabbergasted. I showed it to your grandfather and…"

Ed finished the sentence. "And I barely believed anything you had written as well, and from a five year old no less."

"So what's really going on, Tom? By your own admission it's the time and place to explain things to us."

I'm really here and this is really happening. I never thought that would be possible which is why I wrote that letter in the first place.

267

Thomas looked at his father. "I have a few questions I'd like answered first."

"Go ahead."

"Do you still work for the CIA?"

"I do."

"And Nikolay Dmitriev and Frank Russell are dead?"

"Nothing's changed in that aspect."

"And you and mom are alive and well, obviously." It came out as more of a statement than a question.

"That's an awfully strange thing to say to your father," Ed indicated.

"Obviously," Michael answered.

Thomas waved his hand back and forth as to dismiss what he'd said out loud. "Sorry, I'm just having some difficulty."

"With what?" his father asked.

"Honestly?"

"It's the best policy."

Thomas sighed. "Conflicting memories. I've been here before, at this exact moment, but it was only with grandpa, and he was the one slipping an envelope over the table to me. And that letter was from you, when you died...or rather were killed over Christmas when I was ten."

Michael and Ed didn't know how to respond to Thomas' unbecoming history lesson. But the CIA agent part of him was inquisitive.

"I was killed? How?"

Thomas didn't answer.

"I asked you how."

Thomas relented. "Alright. You were killed by a kid named Albert Clemmings, in your bedroom, with your own shotgun."

Ed didn't like what he'd just heard and shifted in his chair.

268

Michael sat back as his brain worked the issue. "Clemmings. Clemmings. The name's familiar."

"The father's name was Harold and Albert had a twin brother, Nigel, who used to torment Sam, Bill and I in grade school."

Michael snapped his fingers. "Of course, Harold Clemmings. He was shot dead by police during a domestic dispute."

Thomas was shocked and it visibly showed. "Wait. What? He's dead?"

Michael nodded. "A neighbor heard screams coming from next door and alerted the police. When they arrived, and made entry, they caught Harold with a bloodied piece of wood in his hand because he'd beaten his two sons to death. Harold wouldn't cooperate and attacked the two officers. That didn't end well for him."

It was Thomas' turn to sit back in his chair. *What the hell? Nigel and Albert are dead? No wonder my father's alive. Un-fucking-believable.*

"You mentioned before," Michael said, "about a letter I wrote to you."

Thomas nodded. "Yeah."

"What was in it?"

"It was a bank statement."

"I don't understand. Did I leave you some money or something?"

"You could say that," Thomas replied. "It was for twenty-two point seven million dollars."

Michael's eyes opened wide. "What? How?"

"You appropriated illegally obtained funds from Nikolay Dmitriev, who in turn was skimming off the profits of his own small arms sales he'd been negotiating for the Soviet government."

His father was enthralled. "Go on."

269

"Long story short, you stole microfilm from Pinnacle, which contained the bank accounts Nikolay had the money stashed in, and decided to screw him over by taking it for yourself. You can imagine he wasn't pleased and wanted his money back. But when you turned up dead there was nothing more he could do about it."

"Intriguing."

"Intriguing?" Ed interjected. "This sounds like a bad episode of the Twilight Zone, if you ask me."

Michael smiled. "I'm enjoying it, strangely enough. How much did I take?"

"Apparently five-hundred and fifty-three million, but by the time you told me about the microfilm the interest alone had doubled that amount to a billion dollars."

Michael whistled. "That's a lot of money."

"You can't be seriously listening to this," Ed said. "You know your son is just messing with you. Have you forgotten that he wants to be a writer for Christ's sake?"

Michael ignored his father's remark and continued his conversation with his son. "So, if I'm putting the timeline together properly and, since Nikolay is dead, he never skimmed that money which means nothing was there for me to take and then give to you."

"Correct," Thomas answered.

"You're buying into this?" Ed pressed.

Michael smiled. "Somewhat actually. There are things that I just can't explain."

"Like what?"

"Tom was absolutely right about Kevin King, or Pinnacle, as he went by. I didn't want to believe it myself but I started investigating my partner and it turns out he was a Russian mole. I took him down myself."

Ed stared at his son. "You never told me about that."

"Dad, I work for the CIA. I don't tell you anything about my job. And, for your information, if you repeat what I just said to anyone you could go to jail."

Ed closed his mouth and decided just to listen as Michael resumed his story.

"To say that I was stunned, that my five year old son was right on the money, prompted me to finally open the letter four months after he'd given it to me."

"You waited that long?" Thomas asked.

"In all honesty your mother and I didn't know what to make of that strange conversation. You knew everything about my work and it made me feel vulnerable. I had no idea what was in your letter and was in no hurry to feel that way again."

"Sorry," Thomas said. "I didn't mean to…"

Michael brought his hand up. "You did me a great service, son. You made me look within myself and realize that I was wrong to keep those secrets from your mother." He paused to collect his thoughts. "Anyway, back to your letter. You had some ideas in there that seem farfetched."

"Very farfetched," Ed announced.

"Daddd."

"Well, they were."

"Nevertheless," Michael said, "I had no reason to, especially after taking down Pinnacle, that those ideas were bullshit."

"And…" Thomas urged.

Michael smiled and pulled out a second envelope from his coat pocket. He placed it on the table and slid is slowly towards his son.

"This is your share."

Thomas hesitantly picked up the envelope and opened it. Inside was a bank statement with a balance of five million dollars.

Holy shit. It worked.

"It might not be twenty-two point seven million dollars, son, but your grandfather and I, along with your grandmother and mother, wanted to thank you from the bottom of our hearts. The right property to purchase, combined with the insight on specific stocks to follow, have turned a sizeable profit over the years."

"And it doesn't appear to be slowing down," Ed added, allowing a smile to finally cross his face. "That being said, your father and I still don't know how you did it."

"That's for damn sure," Michael said. "But whatever the reason, it happened and we want to thank you. You changed our lives."

Thomas relaxed and placed the statement in his own pocket. He looked back and forth between both his father and grandfather a few times, and then smiled at them.

"You're welcome."

"No," his father replied, "thank you, son."

"Good," Ed announced. "Now that that's over with we wanted to talk to you about USC."

*   *   *

Friday September 12, 1975

Thomas slowly opened his eyes and took a minute to adjust to his new surroundings. Once he felt grounded again he scrutinized the situation. He looked around and then it dawned on him.

I'm in a house. Wait, I remember this place.

Thomas thought back to the first time he'd driven down Interstate 5 to USC located just outside Los Angeles. He now stood in the house he'd rented a few miles away from campus, for four consecutive years, in the exact same entryway. The front door, behind him, stood wide open. Thomas glanced down at the keys he clutched in his right hand and then noticed the suitcases he'd brought were stacked next to him.

I moved into this place a week before class started. He paused. I don't know what's happening to me but I seriously don't want to relive all four years of college.

Thomas put the keys in his pocket and turned to close the door. In the pit of his stomach he felt the tug start up once again. This time he let it happen and wondered where in time he'd end up next.

* * *

Tuesday September 21, 1976

Thomas materialized on the steps of a building, his legs a bit wobbly. He kept his eyes shut and immediately focused on his breathing.

In and out. In and out.

Once he felt grounded Thomas opened his eyes and discovered he stood outside the entrance to a lecture hall. A puzzled look washed over his face.

I'm…I'm still at college?

Just then a young woman rushed outside through one of the lecture hall doors. There was no time to step out of her way and they collided. The books she carried tumbled onto the stairs.

"Shit!" she exclaimed. She stooped down to pick them up. "I'm sorry. That was completely my fault."

Thomas froze as soon as he had bumped into her because he knew exactly who she was.

Why now? Why this moment?

Thomas shook his head to clear it, bent down and opened his mouth. "It's okay, Samantha."

Samantha McDermott had been Thomas' first love and lover. They'd met at this exact moment when she bumped into him, dropped her books and, during the ensuing conversation, had asked him out. They'd begun dating, Thomas clearly enthralled with her, until she had broken his heart when she surprised Thomas by bringing another couple in to their bed eight months later.

She picked up her books and they stood up together. Samantha gave Thomas an inquisitive look. "It's the first day of class and I'm pretty sure we've never met. How do you know my name?"

Ancient and distant memories began to surge through Thomas' head as their eyes met. Her shoulder length hair, soft blues eyes and the scent of jasmine all held keys to those locked away recollections.

You were the first woman I ever loved and you took what we had and threw it all away.

"I asked you a question. How do you know who I am?"

Thomas stood in front of her and just stared at her, unsure of how to properly answer her question at first. He then realized it didn't matter; none of this did. Long ago, back when he was nineteen, he'd had his heart crushed and it had felt like the world had ended. But the memories he'd collected in his head, over the forty-four years he'd been alive, coalesced and Thomas realized that at some point he'd already let her betrayal go.

Samantha doesn't matter. Only Laura does and she's not part of my life until much later. But I can wait. She's worth it.

Thomas smiled at Samantha, turned around and calmly walked away. "Have a nice day," he called over his shoulder.

She wasn't used to being dismissed so effortlessly and shouted after him. "That's right. Keep walking you freak."

Thomas didn't look back as the transition, as he had begun to describe it, started to occur once again.

* * *

Saturday June 14, 1980

"Please place your seats and tray tables in their full and upright positions. Flight attendants will be coming through the aisles to pick up any trash you have for them. Thank you for your cooperation and, as always, thank you for flying British Airways."

Thomas kept his eyes closed as he heard the announcement. He regulated his breathing to ensure he'd be completely cognizant when he did open them. He knew where he was this time.

I'll be landing in London. It's the first stop during my travel that starts in Europe.

A smile crept over his face as he thought back to new memories that he'd experienced just two weeks prior. After the incident with Samantha, Thomas had appeared at his college graduation. But this time around it wasn't just his grandparents that had been there for him. No, much to Thomas' relief, both his parents and seventeen year old sister had also been in attendance.

That evening, after the ceremony, the six of them went out to dinner and had a fantastic time. Thomas soaked in the encounter and treasured every moment. As the evening progressed both his family inquired what his future plans consisted of. Thomas, without hesitation, told them that he was going to take some time and travel the world. His grandparents, and parents, nodded in agreement as they too, since acquiring money, had partaken in many out of country adventures already.

As they finished dessert, Thomas silently wished he had more time to spend with his family, but somehow knew that's not how this strange 'walk down memory lane' functioned. He had caught himself, a few times, staring at Abby wondering what her life was like. He knew he'd physically grown up with her, but he didn't have access to those memories and that saddened him. Abby, when he caught him, had stuck her tongue out and given him a weird look that only brothers and sisters shared.

Thomas, as the conversation meandered, had also thought about his parents and how their life had turned out now that they were alive. But in a strange way Thomas had already made peace with their absence as a child due to his frequent interactions with them later on in life, thanks to Emily's gift. But, as he looked on, Thomas could tell they were happy and allowed himself a moment of introspective joy.

I don't know if any of this is real or not, or whether my actions directly influenced the fact that at this moment I'm sitting here with my entire family. Nevertheless, this is one special moment in time that I will treasure forever.

Thomas felt the transition coming and closed his eyes.

*   *   *

His plane landed in London and after he collected his luggage he took a taxi to his hotel. Instead of becoming overwhelmed and sequestering himself inside for two days, Thomas began to reexplore the same sights and sounds he'd traveled through all over again. But this time he made sure to add some twists and turns into the mix because he was no longer the same twenty-two year old who had embarked on this adventure before.

Keeping to the same circuit he'd randomly come up with his first time around, Thomas thoroughly explored the United Kingdom expecting the transition to whisk him away at any moment. But the transition never came and eventually Thomas began to think less and less about it as his adventures took him through Scotland, Ireland, Paris, Belgium and the Netherlands.

In Amsterdam Thomas made sure to eat in the same steak house restaurant he'd enjoyed before and then ambled through the Red Light District for the hell of it. During his walk his mind wandered and continued to grind on his newest concerns.

Am I dreaming? Why am I still here? What's the point to reliving all of this again?

Scantily clad women beckoned to him from behind floor to ceiling glass doors, using their bodies and facial expressions to lure prospective clients inside. Thomas ignored their advances, perplexed on what his true purpose was. But, in the back of his mind, he knew he'd partaken of the flesh the last time he was here, but now he didn't care to because someone else was on his mind as well.

Laura.

The next morning, after a fitful sleep, Thomas flew to Barcelona. He traveled throughout Spain before he crossed into Portugal on his way to Lisbon and beyond.

His next flight touched down in Athens, followed by a boat ride to the southern tip of Italy. He finally made his way to Venice. His elongated adventure took him into Switzerland and then Zurich. Afterwards he found himself in Frankfurt and then Cologne before he made his way to Copenhagen.

Chennai, India was where the next plane came to rest and from there he made his way down the coast until he took yet another plane to Manila. Bangkok, followed by South Korea, and then Nagasaki, is where he traveled next. He finished up with Asia-Pacific journeys in Tokyo before flying to Brisbane, Australia, working his way from there down to Newcastle, Sydney and Melbourne. A month later Thomas landed in Invercargill, New Zealand. Afterwards he traveled north through Christchurch, Wellington and ended up in Auckland.

As he boarded the plane back to Los Angeles Thomas realized it'd been nine months since he'd made a transition. Every day had been an adventure, and one that he'd been through before, but he'd thoroughly enjoyed that opportunity to relive it. He sat down in his seat, put on the seatbelt and closed his eyes.

Nine months of adventure. And now what?

But Thomas knew what lay ahead.

My book. I wrote my first book.

The twenty-three year old tried to get comfortable for the long flight ahead of him.

And I still have another nine years to wait before I see Laura for the first time. I miss her.

Thomas was unprepared as the knot is his stomach indicated his transition was starting. But he smiled nevertheless knowing that this next jump would bring him that much closer to seeing the love of his life.

<u>40</u>
March, 1975

Thirty-six year old Lt. Colonel Robert Aleman, the man known as Raven to his drug-running conglomerates, drove his car out the front security gate of Ft. Benning and headed towards his home located just outside Columbus, Georgia. It'd been a long day and he was tired. As he merged onto I-185 North he noticed how few cars were on the road with him. He looked out his window at the full moon and grumbled to himself.

These late nights are killing me. I've been working my ass off to maintain the drug enterprise to keep it running smoothly. And at the same time I'm in charge of an entire military base and all of it is definitely taking its toll on me.

Robert drove as if on autopilot while his thoughts continued to hammer him.

So if I'm doing the majority of the legwork, why aren't I getting the biggest cut of the pie? Robert sneered. *Because that portion is handed over to my father, the Serpent. Perhaps it's time for a change.*

Robert smiled as a plan began to form on how to wrest control of the business and eliminate his father in the process. As his mind wandered he failed to notice the intoxicated male driver who, while traveling at an exceptionally high rate of speed heading south, veered off the freeway. The car slammed into the barrier and propelled itself into the air. It wasn't until the headlights of the incoming car washed over Robert's face, on its return trajectory towards the ground that he snapped out of his train of thought. But it was too late as the two vehicles became one.

* * *

Six year old Anna Garland, the future assassin employed by Raven, left the playground when she saw a female classmate push open the door to the girl's bathroom. Anna dropped down off the monkey bars and calmly sauntered over to the bathroom door herself. She paused to take a drink of water, the faucet just outside the bathroom doors, and used that moment to survey her surroundings.

Good. No one else is coming.

Anna smiled and let herself into the restroom. Her mark, a girl named Cindy, had been one of the classmates she'd targeted before for their lunch money. Inside Anna waited in front of the circular washbasin for Cindy to finish, effectively blocking off any chance for the girl to escape without a confrontation. The toilet flushed and when Cindy exited the stall, and saw Anna, her face fell.

"I don't have any money on me," Cindy immediately declared.

Anna angled her head to one side and visibly clenched her fists. Cindy's eyes widened.

"Are you sure?" Anna taunted. "I would hate to find out that you're lying, and so would your face."

Cindy cowered as Anna lifted her right arm, fist cocked back.

"Fine, take it," Cindy whimpered as she pulled a few dollar bills out of her pocket.

Anna smiled triumphantly. "That's much better," she said and took Cindy's money. "But you still need to be punished for lying to me."

Anna stepped forward to hit Cindy but, at that instance, something snapped inside Cindy. She'd had enough and wasn't going to take it anymore.

"No!" Cindy yelled and pushed Anna backwards with as much force as the young girl could muster.

Anna, unprepared for her prey to fight back, slipped on a patch of water as she was shoved and lost her balance. Her head thumped solidly against the edge of the water basin and her body collapsed to the restroom floor. Cindy, clearly afraid, ran past Anna and out the door.

It wasn't until after the recess bell sounded, and during the headcount, that Anna's absence was discovered. Shortly after that Anna's inert form was found after Cindy fessed up to the bathroom confrontation.

The blood, from Anna's mortal head wound, mixed with the water on the floor and slowly whirled down the drain.

* * *

Forty-one year old Victor Bannon, the future director of the CIA who'd betrayed Thomas, tailed his suspect down Via dei SS. Quattro Street in Rome, Italy. The man he'd been following had just picked up a drop from a concealed location within the Colosseum, and was a known Soviet KGB agent. Victor hurried up as he lost sight of the man who'd just turned right on Via Celimontana.

Come on Victor, I have to know where this KGB agent's final destination is, so get your shit together.

Victor reached the corner and paused. The new street, aside from numerous parked cars, was devoid of any human traffic.

Shit! He must have made me.

Victor tried to appear casual as he continued down Via Celimontana, but his eyes darted back and forth in an attempt to locate the Soviet agent.

Where the fuck did you go? There wasn't enough time for you to run aw...

A six-inch blade buried itself in Victor's left side, just below the rib cage. Victor glanced at his assailant while his body, no longer following his commands to stay upright, fell sideways and landed on the cobblestoned walkway.

What's happening?

His attacker ransacked his clothes until he found Victor's wallet, and took it.

Why can't I fight him off?

As the KBG agent walked away, and left him behind, Victor finally felt the sharp pain that permeated his entire being.

It...hurts...

Victor's body was finally discovered seven minutes later. To the local police it was an open and shut case of a robbery that had gone bad. But to the CIA it was something else entirely, but they never found his killer.

* * *

Thirteen year old Alexei Vorobyrov, the ex-Spetsnaz soldier, who would eventually go to work for Nikolay Dmitriev as a hitman, struggled to keep the young boy beneath him pinned to the ground. A crowd of school children had gathered around them, some of them urging Alexi on while others yelled at the other kid to fight back.

"Get off me!" the boy cried out in vain as the immovable and heavier Alexei continued to remain dominate.

"Or what?" Alexei snickered. "Are you going to go home and cry to your daddy?"

The weaker boy, accustomed to being bullied, finally relented and stopped struggling. Alexei picked up on this right away.

"What's the matter? Too chicken to fight?"

His comment made some of his classmates chuckle, but their giggles faded as a teacher broke through the crowd.

"What's going on here?" She then saw Alexei on top of another boy. "Get off him this instant!"

Alexei slowly disengaged himself, stood up and turned towards the female teacher. Behind him the other boy collected himself and began to get on his own feet.

"What do you think you're doing?" the teacher pointedly asked. "Were you fighting?"

"He started it," Alexei lamely explained.

"I highly doubt that, Alexei," she responded. "Your reputation precedes you."

A smile formed on his lips just as the teacher's face changed to one of horror at something behind him.

"Don't!" she cried out.

Alexei barely had time to turn his head before the piece of concrete the other boy held in his hands, connected with the back of Alexei's neck.

Is that all he's got because that didn't hurt at all.

Alexei buckled as the weight of his body pulled him to the ground.

What's happening?

Alexei, his head turned to one side, glanced up at the boy who'd hit him as the teacher struggled to remove the concrete from his hands.

Time to get up.

Alexei's body didn't react to his commands.

Get up!

Once again, nothing, and he began to panic. He concentrated harder but the only thing he could move was his mouth and his eyes.

I can't move!

The teacher, having disarmed the other student, turned back and knelt down beside Alexei.

"Get up," she commanded.

When Alexi didn't comply she tried to pull him up on her own, but his entire body remained limp. She stopped trying and quickly turned to leave.

"I'll be right back."

As the teacher left the students reformed their circle around Alexei, then laughed and pointed at him. It wouldn't be until later that day when doctors would diagnose him with a broken spinal cord, severed at the neck. Alexei had become paralyzed from the neck down and would remain so for the rest of his life.

41
The Other Place

Where…where am I now?

Warm water lapped around Thomas' face and encompassed his entire body.

What is that?

Something repeatedly licked the side of his face. Thomas forced his eyes open and came face to face with a pair of red eyes mere inches away from his face. He instinctively recoiled away from the terror that had been trying to eat his face, splashing water in all directions in his haste to retreat. A chuckle emanated behind him.

"What, you didn't like the friendly greeting?"

Thomas looked over his left shoulder, saw the Caretaker standing over him, hand extended and breathed a sigh of relief.

"Here, let me help you up."

Thomas offered his right hand and froze as he realized his right arm was completely intact. A confused look washed over Thomas' face as he finally looked around at his surroundings and realized he sat in shallow waters.

Gavin's island…sunlight…no creatures…no skeleton…no bodies…and what was that licking me. Thomas focused his eyes on the red-eyed creature. *Holy shit, that's Stir.*

"Stir? Is that really you buddy?"

The tail, on the small black form, excitedly wagged back and forth. Stir bounded over to the sandy edge and waited as Thomas, still somewhat in a haze, picked himself up. The water drained down his soaked jeans and waterlogged shoes as he exited the ocean to join the Caretaker and Stir. Just to make sure Thomas placed his left hand over his right shoulder to verify his right arm was indeed there.

"Are you alright?" the Caretaker asked.

"I...I have no idea."

The Caretaker smiled. "I expected as much. Take your time and start to dry off. I'll be here when you're ready. Besides, it appears an old friend is craving some attention."

Thomas nodded that he understood and sat down on the inviting sand. Stir wasted no time and immediately jumped on Thomas' lap, thrilled to see him again. Thomas couldn't help but smile and began to pet Stir as he fended off the energetic creatures need to lick his face.

"Easy there, Stir. I'm happy to see you too."

You have no idea.

As Thomas sat there and continued to stroke Stir a wave of emotions, seemingly out of nowhere, welled up inside him and spilled out. He stared out over the vast Ocean of Time, with a strange animal in his arms and in the presence of a man he could never fathom. Thomas began to cry. Years of anguish and fear poured out of him as uncontrollable sobs as the huge ever flowing tears coursed down his face. He cried for his wife. He cried for his children. He cried for his best friends, and in turn their families. He wept until he couldn't anymore; Stir faithfully comforting him the entire time as the Caretaker silently stood watch.

"It's...it's all my fault," he eventually whispered. "They're dead because of me."

Stir snuggled against Thomas' wet shirt and rolled over to expose his belly for Thomas to rub. Thomas' head was still in a fog and he was unsure of absolutely everything.

Am I alive? Am I dead? Is any of this actually real?

Thomas slowly turned his head and looked up at the Caretaker. "Who are you and what's been happening to me?"

"It's okay. You're safe now, Thomas, and I know you have more than your fair share of questions. When it comes down to it you and I have much to discuss."

Stir uncurled himself, placed his paws on Thomas' chest and gave his cheek a few licks.

"Alright," Thomas replied. "Let's start with Stir then. If Gavin is dead then how is Stir even here?"

"Stir, as your son so aptly named him, is not from your world. He's actually a piece of the Ancient."

Thomas shifted uncomfortably. "A piece? But isn't the Ancient evil incarnate?"

The Caretaker nodded. "The Ancient is that, but Stir is unique. Although he shares similar characteristics of the Ancient you're well aware of his loyalty to both your son and the rest of your family. He's protected you on many occasions but has never turned on you, has he?"

Thomas agreed. "No, Stir's never shown any aggression towards us."

"And he never will because Stir cares for you." The Caretaker continued. "But Stir's absence from this place, was noticed by the Ancient, and that act alone gave the Ancient hope; hope that it too could escape."

Thomas pondered for a bit. "So where did this Ancient come from?"

"I mean you no offense, Thomas, but I couldn't begin to explain the unfathomable complexity that makes up the universe, and everything in it, because you just wouldn't understand."

Thomas nodded. "None taken, but where does that leave me in the overall equation? It was like I jumped from one portion of

287

my life to the next, but it was instantaneous. I have no recollection of what happened in-between. Was any of it even real?"

"Did you want it to be?" the Caretaker countered.

"I…I don't know. Maybe. Yes. There were significant differences I noticed as I progressed through my life."

"Tell me about them."

"Well, it felt like I was living a double life. I knew things about my life and I was able to express them. I used that knowledge to warn my parents, and I think because of it they never were killed."

"Go on."

Thomas tried to concentrate. "I have a sister now."

"Do you?"

"I…I think so. If she's real her name is Abby."

Thomas looked around at the beach and suddenly remembered the last image he remembered about this place.

"My family, they were all here. They stood silently by and watched me die." Stir jumped off his lap as Thomas made his way to his feet. He paced around a bit and finally asked the question he'd been dreading. "Am I dead?"

"A fair question, but one I'm not willing to answer quite yet."

"Why not?"

"Well, let me put it this way, what if you are. How would that make you feel?"

Thomas hadn't considered that. "I don't know. Sad, maybe."

"Why sad?"

"Because I feel responsible for the death of my planet, and all the people that died on it. A nuclear bomb detonated in Las Vegas and I imagine that was only the start." Thomas' face contorted. "I watched Sam and Bill get ripped to shreds right in front of my eyes and had to endure my children falling to their deaths."

"And what did you do?"

"I…I told my wife I loved her…and…and then I escaped through the portal." The painful recollections shot through Thomas' body and he staggered. "I escaped…only to be tormented…pulled apart by the Ancient. It hurt so badly…all of it. I couldn't take it anymore."

"And then you drowned."

"Then I drowned," Thomas consented as he looked out over the ocean. "So, it's true, I am dead."

The Caretaker remained silent as Thomas mulled over this revelation. Thomas' shoulders slumped as he contemplated his new reality, his eyes darting back and forth until they focused on Stir running around on the other side of the tiny island.

What's Stir doing?

Thomas fixated on Stir and followed his every move.

Something's missing. What the hell?

He turned and addressed the Caretaker. "Victor's skeleton isn't on this beach anymore."

"Well, so it isn't. I guess you're right."

"You guess? Where the hell is it unless…"

The Caretaker watched Thomas' brain kick in as missing pieces of the puzzle shifted around in his head.

"Why isn't his skeleton here?"

"You tell me."

"It's not here because we never sent Victor through in the first place, right?"

"But how's that possible? Of course you did."

Thomas shook his head and worked logically through the problem. "My mother wasn't killed because Nikolay never killed his father and took his seat on the Politburo. And my father confirmed that Frank Russell was dead and never became Yuri, the

CIA's deepest Russian mole. And because of those particular set of circumstances my father never pursued Nikolay or Yuri, thus saving my mother on my fifth birthday. And with my mother alive my sister was able to be born."

Thomas kept going.

"And then there's the instance of Nigel. If what happened in the forest that day actually occurred then I really beat the shit out of him. And somehow, because of that, his brother Albert never came to my house to murder my father. The question I have now is what happened to Nigel, Albert and their father?"

"In what timeline?" the Caretaker asked.

Thomas was taken aback. "What the hell do you mean what timeline?"

"In what timeline?" he asked again without wavering.

Thomas didn't know how to respond at first, but he eventually tried to wrap his head around what the Caretaker had just said. "You're saying there's more than one timeline?"

"The truth is, Thomas, I see all timelines."

"That's not an answer."

"Then ask me a more specific question."

Thomas thought for a few seconds. "What happened to Nigel, and his family, in the timeline where I beat Nigel up?"

"Better. In that timeline Harold Clemmings killed his two sons and then was shot by police."

"Holy shit, so that really happened?"

"It's a matter of perspective, at least from my point of view."

"Your point of view. What about my point of view?"

"What about it?" the Caretaker asked.

"What's real and what isn't? Did my parents die when I was a child or didn't they?"

"Exactly."

Thomas was frustrated and it showed. "You're speaking in riddles."

"No. I am merely presenting you with all options. It's up to you to figure this out."

"But my brain is on fire and I can't think straight."

"That's too bad, Thomas, you were so close."

Thomas opened his mouth to complain but decided against it.

I was close? What was I close too? The truth? Okay, what's the truth? Wait, I was talking about Victor and that his skeleton isn't here anymore. Where did that lead to? Concentrate, dammit.

"Okay. If Albert's dead then he never could have invented the serum that I would pass on to my children, giving them their special abilities."

The Caretaker smiled. "Go on."

"And because my parents are alive, and Emily doesn't have her powers…, which means my father never took money from Nikolay, then…then our entire lives changed."

"Correct."

"But how? Why?"

"You have the answer to that question already."

Thomas racked his brain and thought back to all those instances he briefly was able to rewind time. That realization hit him like a ton of bricks and it showed.

"I did this?" Thomas asked.

"Did you?"

"When I came through the portal…they ripped my arm out of its socket." He looked out towards the ocean. "You've called this the Ocean of Time more than once. Did I…did use my ability to turn back…time?"

291

"And there it is. Glaring realization. And in terms that you'll understand, Thomas, and from your point of view, you effectively pressed the reset button on the universe itself."

Holy fucking shit.

"But…but why…was it you that sent me back to relive those moments in my life?"

"Yes, it was."

"But why? Why would I remember what happened the first time I experienced those specific moments?"

"Because, Thomas, you chose to save the universe, whether you realize it or not without my interference or guidance. And because of your sacrifice, and your ability, you saved everything you've ever loved with just a little help from me."

"Help?"

"I was grateful, and making a few alterations to your new timeline was the least I could do, not to mention I had already promised to banish those six individuals from all past, present and future timelines."

"I don't understand. What are you talking about?"

The Caretaker explained. "Those moments in time defined who you were; who you are. I chose them for you, but ultimately you made your own choices within each moment. Your destiny, as it always has been and will be, is of your own making."

"But, you let me remember my past as I interacted with my current present. Why?"

"That was my gift to you."

"But none of that makes any sense. It was as if I was interacting with each moment, but only with the knowledge I possessed from my original history. I have no memory of my new timeline and the years of time between each jump I made."

"No, not yet," the Caretaker replied. "But you will, now that you're no longer traveling under my care."

"Under your care?"

"Your destiny I now place in your hands. You will choose which moments you want to visit."

"I can do that?"

The Caretaker nodded. "I am officially stepping away, Thomas. These moments I chose for you to participate in again I believed were life changing, or had life lesson implications. That chore is up to you now."

Thomas paced around the beach as Stir followed behind him.

"Why did you allow this to happen?" Thomas asked.

"As I said, it was my gift to you."

"But you only chose a few moments in my time, except for the nine months I traveled the world. Why?"

"Truth be told, I couldn't let you grow up, again, with all the knowledge you possessed in your head. You could have changed too much of the world, and quite frankly you would have been singled out for your predictions. Alternatively, I figured you'd be bored reliving your entire life all over again, day after day. However, as I stated, your life memories, as you know them, will combine with your new timeline."

"My head already feels cluttered, as if I have conflicting memories."

"That's exactly what you have. You'll soon have two lifetimes of memories to contend with."

Thomas slowly nodded. "I guess that's going to be both a blessing and a curse."

"Perhaps."

"So you changed the timeline I take it? You made sure Nikolay and Frank were dead?"

"Yes."

"Were they part of the 'six' you were referring to?"

"Yes."

"Who were the other four?"

"Robert Aleman, Anna Garland, Victor Bannon and Alexei Vorobyrov."

Thomas whistled. "Wow."

"Those six played a significant role in your original timeline. But they also chose their own destiny by interfering with mine. They have paid the price, and will continue to do so."

"I hate to ask this, but you didn't mention Dr. Matsushita. What happened to him?"

"When the American plane dropped the bomb, during World War Two, Yamato died alongside his parents and sister as he should have. It was a minor change to the timeline."

Thomas just stood there and gawked at the Caretaker.

"You're really blowing my mind right now. I mean, if you can make these changes why not kill Hitler, or better yet, send me back to kill Hitler and change the world for the better."

The Caretaker shook his head. "You are restricted by your own existence. You couldn't go back to the early nineteen hundreds because you never existed during that period of time."

"Seriously?"

"Time is linear, in your mind, but to me, Thomas, it's a constant flow, much like a river. At any point in that river I may stick my toe in and access it, so to speak."

Thomas paced some more. "This is difficult for me, and the memories of my new timeline are flooding back now. I have so many conflicting thoughts now."

"And you will for the rest of your life. That is my gift to you, aside from the fact that I looked the other way when you gave your father insight on profiting from the future."

Thomas cocked his head to one side and smiled. "You caught that, did you?"

The Caretaker returned the grin. "I have much to thank you for, and I have done so already. But for now, as you step back into your new life, you are at the reins. It'll be up to you to decide when to stop jumping from one meaningful crossroad to the next."

"So what happens now?"

"That's up to you."

Thomas squatted down and gave Stir one last belly rub somehow knowing he'd never see him again. Then he stood back up.

"I'm ready."

"Good," the Caretaker told him. "I hope not to see you again for quite some time, Thomas. Thank you for your sacrifice. Go and enjoy your new life. Goodbye."

42
Saturday December 1, 1984

The cool breeze sent a brief shiver down Thomas' spine as he opened his eyes and looked around.

Where am I now?

Thomas saw the playground in the distance, across from the tennis courts and the great lawn, and knew he sat at a picnic table in the Orinda Community Center.

Strange. The last time I was here was when...

"Hey brother," a very familiar voice quipped behind Thomas a second before Bill's hand slapped his back. "How's it going?"

"How in the hell are you Tom?" Sam asked as the two of them exchanged hugs with Thomas before they sat down across from him. "I can't believe it's been nine years since we've seen you. Where has all the time gone?"

Thomas smiled. *Time indeed.* "It's Thomas now, you sonsofbitches. And look how cute you both are, sporting muscles now and everything."

"Fuck you too," Bill said as he laughed. "It's really good to see you."

"You have no idea," Thomas replied. "I'm glad you made it through both Ranger and Special Ops training, not to mention all those secret missions you must have partaken in."

Sam and Bill's faces froze, and the two of them just stared at Thomas, who in turn just stared right back. The mood had drastically changed.

"Missions?" Bill asked. "What are you talking about?"

"Like the training you gave the Afghan rebels in their fight against the Soviets. The village you were initially stationed in was strafed by a Hind gunship."

"Fuck me," Bill whispered.

"What the hell is going on?" Sam demanded. "I've got that tingling feeling all over again; the same feeling I got when you somehow took down Nigel in front of us."

"Yeah," Bill added. "Something's still not kosher; neither then or now. Spill it Thomas because you're freaking me out right now. There's no way you could know what Sam and I have been through, no way at all."

"You're right," Thomas responded with all seriousness. "That is unless you already told me all about the shit you've experienced."

"Bullshit," Sam said. "We haven't seen you in nine years. We've never told you a damn thing."

"Not a word," Bill added. "He's just fucking with us; he has to be."

"That's impossible. This information is too detailed. What's this all about, Thomas?" Sam asked. "What's really going on? How could you possibly know about Afghanistan?"

Thomas leaned back. "I could try and explain it to you but you're just going to think I'm crazy."

"At this point," Sam countered, "I'm inclined listen to anything you have to tell us."

"Trust me," Bill added, "I'm all ears."

Thomas looked at both of his friends and then started in. "I'm not from this timeline."

"What?" Sam asked bluntly, his face indicating disbelief.

"See, I told you he was fucking with us."

Thomas repeated his statement. "I'm not from this timeline."

Sam abruptly stood up from the picnic table and pointed his finger at Thomas. "You don't get to make up shit like that and throw it in our faces like we're a pair of dumb shits who'd somehow swallow that line of crap."

"You've known me my entire life," Thomas insisted. "I'm not lying."

Sam made a face as Bill spoke up. "Oh come on, Thomas. You come to us with classified information and then try to cover up how you know it with some science-fiction nonsense. I know you're a writer and have one hell of an imagination, but you're full of shit."

Thomas kept his composure. He'd known this wasn't going to be easy as soon as he'd started down the path, but it was too late to stop now.

"Alright. If you think I'm full of shit then test me."

"Test you?" Bill asked.

"Yes. Ask me anything you think I wouldn't or shouldn't know."

Sam slowly sat back down, untrusting. "What's your game, Thomas? Who do you work for now, the CIA?"

"No, that's who my father works for."

Shock washed over Sam and Bill's faces. "Seriously?" Bill asked. "The Agency?"

Thomas nodded. "It's true. Ask him yourself if you don't believe me."

"And that's how you know what you know?" Sam inquired. "Through your father?"

"No," Thomas assured them. "I told you, I'm not from this timeline."

"But..." Bill began. But Sam put his hand up to cut him off.

"Thomas is right. We have been friends since childhood. Whatever his game is we have an obligation to hear him out. Now, with that said, what the FUCK do you mean when you say you're not from this timeline?"

"Sam, you're listening to this shit?" Bill probed. "Seriously?"

"For the moment, until I'm satisfied one way or another with how Thomas knows what he knows."

"But why listen to his timeline bullshit?" Bill persisted. "It's not like he knows what the future holds. No one does."

"Are you sure about that?" Thomas insinuated.

Sam and Bill stopped arguing and turned towards their friend, somewhat apprehensively.

"Okay," Sam began, "if that's how you want to play this, what have Bill and I been up to for the past year?"

"That's an easy one," Thomas replied. "The two of you retired from the Army and came up with a plan to start your own VIP protection business based out of San Francisco. For the past year you've been laying the groundwork, scouting locations, drawing up architectural plans and greasing the wheels for upcoming permits."

Sam and Bill's jaws dropped.

"The issue at hand, of course, is locating funding from investors."

"How could you possibly…" Bill tried to say as Thomas continued.

"And that's where I come in, or came in. It depends on how I remember it."

"Holy crap," Sam said. "How…"

"We've been down this road before, Sam," Thomas stated. "I'm sorry, but this encounter between us is old history to me. But, at the same time, it's very important."

Sam had somewhat recovered from his initial shock. "Why is it important?"

"Because the two of you are my best friends and I want you to succeed."

"Succeed, how?" Bill asked skeptically.

"I'm going to be one of your investors."

Sam smiled. "Right. You, Thomas Clark, are going to invest in us? What'd you do, sell a book or something?"

"Something like that," Thomas answered.

"No," Bill said. "No, we need full disclosure at this point goddammit. You can't drop a bombshell on us like this and just hope we swallow it. Tell us everything."

"Everything?" Thomas questioned.

"Yes," Sam said. "Everything. Make us believers."

So for the rest of the afternoon Thomas weaved an unbelievable tale of Russian spies, superpowers and heroic endeavors that kept their families safe over the years. Sam and Bill listened, interrupting with a question now and then as the afternoon sun dropped lower and lower. Thomas finally finished as he talked about his own jumps through time and how they led up to this exact moment.

"That's one hell of a story," Bill admitted.

"Yeah," Sam said, "and I can't argue with any of it, especially the part about how he knew about Nigel and his family."

"Or the fact," Bill added, "that Thomas wasn't bullshitting when he told us we taught him how to fight."

"This is a lot to take in."

"Take your time," Thomas said. "It took me quite a bit to wrap my head around it all."

Bill stared at Thomas and grinned. "I can't believe my best friend is a fucking time traveler."

"I wouldn't go that far."

"Why not?" Bill asked. "You turned back time with your ability, and then you turned back the entire universe to save the planet. It's fucking unreal."

"Tell me something I don't know."

Sam cleared his throat. "I hate to be forward but right here, right now, in 'your' other timeline you offered us fourteen million dollars to help us start up our company, is that right?"

Thomas nodded. "Correct."

"But I'm guessing that's not possible now because your father didn't skim off of Nikolay Dmitriev's small arms fund in this timeline?"

"Right again."

"So what's going to happen? I mean, you know our futures, right? How does any of this work?"

"All you have to do is live your lives normally," Thomas told them.

"Right," Bill quipped. "We're supposed to pretend that everything you just told us doesn't happen. Holy shit, bro, that's going to be impossible."

"Perhaps," Thomas told them. "But I haven't told you everything. In fact, far from it. I know I'm not done jumping which means our conversation here today has to remain absolutely between us."

"Why?" Sam asked.

"Well, for one, no one's going to believe you. And two, events that occurred in my other timeline can't repeat themselves in this one, mainly because those individuals are already dead. With that said I want to apologize. Maybe I shouldn't have told you but I just needed to share my life with my two best friends, and maybe that was selfish of me."

Sam nodded. "We understand what it means to keep secrets, to hold them close to the vest."

"Yeah we do," Bill expressed.

"So your secret is safe with us."

"Thank you," Thomas said.

"So what happens now?" Bill asked. "I mean, are you going to disappear right in front of us or something?"

Thomas smiled. "I don't think it works that way, but I see what you're getting at. Where do we go from here, right?"

Sam and Bill nodded.

"You start your business and then fall in love."

"One of us or both of us?"

"Both," Thomas assured them.

"Who do we fall in love with?" Bill questioned.

Thomas shook his head. "I'm not going to ruin that for you. I won't give you a head's up. That's all on you guys."

"Shit. Well, you can't blame a guy for asking."

"Then what?" Sam pressed.

"Then you live your lives. But, I have a favor to ask, and it's a huge one."

"Go on," Sam told Thomas.

"One day, years from now, I'm going to ask you to stop doing what you love doing and step back from your business."

Sam and Bill shared an inquisitorial look.

"Why?" they asked in unison.

"For the betterment of your family," Thomas said matter-of-factly. "Can you, or will you, be able to do that?"

"It's that important to you?"

Thomas shook his head. "No. It's going to be that important to both of you and that's all I will say about it."

"Are you saying you won't give us the startup money if we don't agree?"

"No, Sam," Thomas replied, "I'm still planning on giving you two million dollars either way. In the meantime just be prepared for my request in the future."

Depending on how this future plays itself out.

"However, aside from that, I wanted to say good luck with SANDBOX, but I know you won't need any. You two are going to kick some serious ass."

"Just as much as you will with your books."

* * *

Saturday July 5, 1986

Thomas entered the Spinnaker and immediately ran into Sam and Bill.

"Holy shit, Thomas, we didn't think you were going to make it," said Bill as he gave his best friend a hug.

"No shit," Sam added. "We missed you last night. A few of us went to the Hustler club for our last free night."

"And," Bill warned with a grin, "if you mention that to our future wives I'm afraid no one will ever find your body."

"Speaking of our future wives," Sam said, "I don't believe you've met ours."

Thomas gave them an odd look. "I might not have, if their names don't happen to be Julie and Kim Roads."

Sam and Bill opened their mouths in amazement and then smiled.

"You sly sonofabitch," Sam said. "You're back, aren't you?"

304

"Damn Thomas," Bill whispered, "you could have given us a heads up on these two sisters we're marrying. What if we had missed meeting them at the bar?"

Thomas smiled. "And yet here we are anyway, aren't we?"

* * *

The wedding was amazing. The sunlight was perfect and backlit the ceremony. Both Kim and Julie glowed.

"I now pronounce you man and wife. You may kiss the bride." Sam and Bill did just that.

Monday morning, the newlyweds, after spending a good portion of Sunday catching up with Thomas, headed out on their honeymoon to Hawaii. They spent two weeks island hopping and having the time of their lives.

The four of them couldn't have been happier.

* * *

Friday August 1, 1986

Sam and Bill had spent the past week installing furniture in their new office building as well as setting up the motor pool, armory and a million other things on their to do list. They were busy and desperately needed help meaning it was time to hire some much needed assistance as well as add some operators to SANDBOX's roster. They'd already hired a few, one of them being Christopher "Kit" Jones, a squad-mate that had helped Sam and Bill train Mujahideen rebels five years earlier in Afghanistan. Kit had survived the Soviet Hind attack and had eagerly come on board to work at SANDBOX.

Sam and Bill had met with a few perspective candidates to fill the executive admin role, which they had agreed was the initial position that had to be filled immediately. The first two applicants had been young, ambitious and well out of their depth because neither of them had experience in actually running a business before. Although Sam and Bill were desperate, to a degree, they knew they absolutely needed the right individual to be the forefront of their company. Kit suggested to his mother that she should apply for the job and she did.

"Thank you for coming in today, Mrs. Constance-Jones," Sam said. She was older, perhaps in her late fifties, and seemed very at ease.

She smiled. "I haven't gone by Misses in years. I'd love it if you'd just call me Roberta."

"You got it, Roberta," Bill replied. "Now, before we begin, we wanted to clarify that you're aware of the exact position you're applying for."

Roberta raised her hand slightly and politely cut Bill off. "I come from a family that's been in the military, Mr. Nicholson."

"Bill."

Roberta nodded. "My husband retired from the service with the rank of Major. I traveled the world with him from station to station, raising our two boys along the way. As life would have it, our sons ended up joining the Army.

"To answer your question more directly, Bill, this position requires both front and back end management, organization and attention to detail. You offer VIP protection to high-end clientele, both to individuals and groups; although at this time you've been limiting yourself to individual jobs. To bolster your bottom line you're going to need headcount, and from the looks of this building alone you're ready to start that process immediately.

"Let me assure you that I can and will provide you with the utmost professionalism, soft or tough as nails attitude that each particular situation requires. I am well versed in organization and will keep both of you focused on what you need this business to grow in to."

Roberta's words hung out there for a few moments before Sam spoke up.

"I see that your work history is limited to the past six or seven years."

"That's correct. My husband retired seven years ago and has been milling around the house, effectively driving me crazy."

"I'm sorry to hear that," Sam said with a grin.

"I love him to death, but I need to get out of the house. The age differences between our two boys had been significant. More to the point, our second, Christopher or Kit, hadn't been a planned pregnancy. Anyway, our oldest, Mike, didn't come back from Vietnam and it was tough on all of us for a long time. When Christopher decided to enlist my husband and I were furious, but he wanted to honor his older brother's memory. There was nothing we could do about it. He's told me all about you two and speaks highly of both of you. He tells me you're men of honor and that goes a long way in our family. I wanted to personally thank you for giving him this job."

"Roberta, it's our pleasure. Kit is a fine soldier and a great addition to our growing team."

"Thank you. But, Mr. Paige, Mr. Nicholson, I have been through hell and high water because of the military. But I'm still here, stronger than ever. When Kit told me about your executive admin position I knew I had to have it. From what I've seen so far you're going to need a firm hand as you continue to negotiate the ups and downs of growing your business. You're going to hire quite a number of personnel and you'll need someone to not only mother them, but keep them in line at the same time.

"I can help run and expand your business. More importantly I need to. Let me demonstrate that I have what it takes. I owe it to you, I owe it to myself and I owe it to my boys."

Sam leaned forward. "You realize this job isn't for the faint of heart."

"I do."

"Our plans are to ramp up very quickly, hiring approximately twelve to eighteen operators. That means a ton of paperwork, from hiring packages, medical coverage, paychecks and anything else that comes along."

"I look forward to it."

"Our job requires us to work long and impractical hours, seven days a week, depending on our client's needs."

"I'm at your disposal. I want to be an integral part of your business and I know I won't let you down."

Bill smiled. "You don't frighten very easily."

She looked them both in the eyes. "Try me."

Sam and Bill exchanged a quick glance and their eyes said it all. They turned back and they both extended their right hands.

"Roberta, welcome to SANDBOX."

"Tomorrow," Bill said, "we'll get you situated. Sam and I have some solid leads on personnel we'd like to pursue, along with a growing list of potential operators that have responded to our ad already."

"If it's all the same to you, I'd like to get started right away. Just show me to my desk and I'll organize everything you need from there with my own system. I'll have this place running like a well-oiled machine in less than a week."

It was Sam's turn to smile. "Roberta, I think we're going to get along just fine."

Roberta smiled as she followed them out of the room. "You two remind me of my boys."

"I hope that's a good thing." Bill said.

"It's comforting. But remember, you give me any sass and I won't hesitate to put you over my knee," she said with a grin.

Bill started to chuckle.

"And as for you," she said pointing a finger at Sam, "I'm watching you like a hawk. Don't think you're safe from me either."

Sam put up his hands as he gave up. "Okay okay. Truce."

* * *

Kit caught up with Sam and Bill in the hallway as Roberta began to organize her desk.

"You gave her the job?" he asked them.

"You'd better believe we did," Sam told him. "She's a firecracker."

Bill nodded and grinned. "I think I'm a little scared of her too."

Kit smiled. "I'm sure she won't mind looking after me now that we work for the same company."

"And that's on you," Sam joked.

"Tell me about it. Anyway, thanks for giving her a shot. You won't regret it."

"No," Bill said, "I don't think we will this time around."

43
December, 1988

"And who should I make this out to?"

"Rose. And thank you, Mr. Clark. I'm one of your biggest fans. My daughter just loves your books."

Thomas smiled as he inscribed his latest children's book, *The Haunted Trees*, for Rose. He handed it to her as she reluctantly departed so he could greet the next person in the long line who'd been waiting patiently to meet Thomas Clark, the famous author. An hour later, during a quick break from his autographing session, Nick Raynes pulled Thomas into a back room of the book store for an update.

"How's it going out there?"

"Busy," Thomas replied. "Really busy. Thanks for setting this all up."

Nick had been Thomas' publishing agent ever since he wrote his first children's book, *The Sandbox*. Thomas, of course, had followed that up with *The World to Tom*, *The Little Brown Chair* and *Make Me* before coming out with *The Haunted Trees*. They'd all been hits and Nick couldn't have been happier for Thomas.

"You're welcome," Nick said, "but I hardly did anything. You're the one with the wicked imagination which apparently leads to you landing on the best sellers list time and time again. How do you do it?"

This wasn't the first time I wrote them. "Just luck, I guess."

Nick grinned. "Well, whatever the case may be, keep up the good work. The agency is very pleased and wanted me to convey that to you. Please, let me take you out to dinner tonight. Susan would love to catch up with you."

"That sounds lovely. Thank you."

"Great," Nick exclaimed. "When this is all over you can follow me to the restaurant. I hear it's pretty swank."

"Doesn't every restaurant in Los Angeles claim to be swank?" Thomas joked.

"Touché. Oh, and before I forget, there's something else you should know before you see Susan tonight."

"What? Is everything alright?"

"Better than alright, my friend." Nick paused. "She's four months pregnant. We're going to have a baby girl. Can you believe that shit?"

Thomas smiled and shook Nick's hand. "Congratulations. I know you'll make a great father. Being a father is very rewarding."

Nick seemed relieved to have gotten that off his chest. "I hope so." He then got a puzzled look. "Wait, I didn't think you had any children."

Shit. "It's just from what I hear. I hope to have some of my own one day."

"Ah, gotcha. Well, Susan's not due for another five months, so I have some time to get used to the notion. To be honest I'm a nervous wreck. I mean I might know how to handle a boy, you know what I mean?"

Thomas reassured his friend. "You're going to be the best father to little Lisa, you'll see."

"Lisa? Why'd you call my future daughter, Lisa?"

Dammit, I did it again. "I don't know. I was just making up a name. Why? Is there something wrong with the name Lisa?"

Nick relaxed. "No, nothing at all actually. It's just that Susan brought up that name and currently it tops her list of favorite names."

"Strange but lucky coincidence, I guess."

"No doubt."

You have no idea. Thomas looked at his watch. "It's time for me to get back out there."

"Right, right. Your adoring fans are eagerly awaiting your return. I'll see you later for dinner."

"Absolutely."

Thomas left Nick and walked back out to the table, much to the delight of the long line of people that had come out to meet him. He sat back down, somewhat lost in his own thoughts.

Laura. In a year and a half we finally meet. I miss you so much but you don't even know me yet. How do I even approach you this time around?

Thomas signed another book, smiled and welcomed the next individual.

I'll figure it out, somehow. At least I know where my next jump in time will take me.

44
Wednesday July 4, 1990

Thomas locked the front door to his San Bernardino condo and walked to his carport. Less than a minute later he was on the road, his stomach in knots. The last time he'd seen Laura was when he'd left her behind at NORAD, and that felt like an entire lifetime ago. He was excited to see her again, but had to constantly remind himself that she didn't share his memories. To her he was a complete stranger.

What if she doesn't like me? What if this goes horribly wrong? What if I blow my only chance to be with her?

Thomas tried to relax but the butterflies and his unrelenting questions wouldn't settle down. He'd decided to make the appointment for the same time, on the same day he'd done it before, in the hope that somehow that would help the situation.

As he continued to drive Thomas was finally able to focus on the changes he'd made in his life and how they'd added up to place him in the position he was today, at this very moment. He's chosen not to buy a house in Running Springs, selecting instead a small condo in San Bernardino. Both his parents and grandparents didn't understand why he'd chosen to live there, nor had Nick, his agent. But Thomas assured all of them that he'd move out of his condo, and back to the Bay Area, when the time was right.

And I hope that starts sooner than later. At least I'm not going to see Laura because I think I murdered someone this time. But that begs the question, what's my reasoning for making this appointment? Shit. Oh well, I don't have any other choice but to make this up as I go along.

315

Thomas pulled into the parking lot and killed the engine. As he removed his hands from the steering wheel he realized they were sweaty.

Come on Thomas, get your shit together. This very moment; it's not like it's the entire ball game or anything.

Thomas nervously laughed out loud in the confines of his vehicle.

Yeah, no pressure whatsoever. Now get out of the car and get moving. You've got this.

Leaving his car behind Thomas made his way into the lobby and took the elevator to the second floor. He verified her office was still number 232 and headed down the hall towards it. He paused outside the door, took a deep breath, and pushed it open. The waiting room was empty and, as before, a number of psychological journals, pamphlets and assorted magazines littered the waiting room table.

"You're right on time, Mr. Clark," the receptionist told him as he entered. "Dr. Bond will see you now."

"Thank you," he stammered.

He walked a few paces and opened the interior door that led to Laura's office. As he closed the door behind him he knew he was nervous.

Be cool dammit.

"Hello, Mr. Clark. I'm Dr. Bond."

Thomas slowly, almost agonizingly, turned towards Laura's voice. When she came into view he practically fainted, but he caught himself.

As beautiful as ever.

"Are you alright?" she asked.

You have no idea. Thomas put his hand up and smiled. "I'm fine. Nervous, but fine."

She returned his smile with her own. "Well, you have nothing to be nervous about. Won't you please come in and sit down."

Thomas surveyed her office, as if looking at it for the first time, while he glanced at her Harvard diploma, degrees and her notorious bookshelf that housed numerous novels and books about murder. She caught the grin that appeared on his face as he took a seat.

"Something amusing catch your eye, Mr. Clark?"

He directed his gaze at her. "Please, call me Thomas. And no, nothing amusing, Dr. Bond. I'm just enjoying an old memory."

"And old memory? Anything you'd like to share? And you can call me Laura if you prefer, if that makes you feel less nervous and more at ease."

Like I've been calling you since the day I fell in love with you. "Alright, Laura it is. And the memory is silly, certainly nothing to bother you with."

Laura let it slip and moved on with the session. "Then perhaps you'd satisfy my curiosity and tell me who referred you to my office?"

Crap. Oh well, a little white lie isn't going to hurt. "Nick Raynes gave me your card. Apparently you helped him and his wife, Susan, out with an issue. He wasn't very forthcoming about the circumstances."

"I see." She made a notation. "And how do you know Mr. Raynes?"

"He's my agent."

"So you're an actor then?"

Thomas grinned. "No, nothing like that. He's my publishing agent."

Thomas could tell her curiosity was perked. "And what do you write about. Is it fiction or non-fiction?"

317

"I write children's books, Laura."

"That must be rewarding."

Thomas got a little more comfortable. "It is."

She cocked her head to one side. "Wait a minute. Are you THE Thomas Clark, the one that wrote The Little Brown Chair?"

"Guilty as charged."

She smiled. "Good for you. I don't mean to make a fuss; it's just that some of the pediatric doctors I interact with rave about that book."

"I'm glad they like it."

"So how long have you been writing, Thomas?"

"Technically since I was a kid, but professionally I began after college. More specifically, I wrote my first book after I came back from an extensive bought of traveling."

"Anywhere in particular?" she asked.

"Pretty much everywhere. I took nine months and stepped foot in a myriad of locations across the globe."

"I'm jealous," she said sincerely. "That must have been absolutely breathtaking. And you did this all on your own?"

Thomas nodded. "I did it to push myself. As a child I was bullied for a short time and that led to me pulling back from humanity, so to speak. I needed to prove to myself that I could venture out on my own in an effort to conquer those fears."

"And did that work?"

Shit. I'm mixing up my past life with my new one. They're intertwining. Chatting to her is more challenging than I thought it'd be. But, at the same time, it's so easy; just like it's always been.

"Thomas?"

He re-focused. "Yeah?"

"I tried to ask you if traveling the world helped you conquer being alone, but you zoned out for a bit."

"Sorry about that. I was tripping over another memory again. Sorry."

"There's no need to apologize. Would you like to share what you were thinking about with me?"

Wow. That's a loaded question. "Maybe in a bit."

"Fair enough. So, Thomas, what brings you to my office? What can I help you with?"

Alright, how do I play this? "I've been having nightmares."

She jotted down something else in her notebook.

"Nightmares? What kind of nightmares?"

No you haven't. You had those in an entirely different life. Just be honest with her. You can't bullshit your way through this.

"I'm sorry, Laura. That was a lie."

"A lie?"

"Well, kind of a lie actually. I used to have nightmares a long time ago, in another lifetime, but not anymore."

A puzzled looked appeared on her face. "I don't understand."

Shit, no time like the present. "This is weird for me."

"Weird, how?"

"It's weird because I'm used to you knowing when I'm telling the truth or not."

It was Laura's turn to look uncomfortable. "Thomas, I can't even begin to understand what you mean by that statement."

He put his hands up. "I know. But I'd like to ask your permission to explain it to you by sharing my life story."

"You're what, in your early thirties? What do you mean your life story?"

Thomas tried to reassure her. "I'm sorry, I don't mean to alarm or frighten you, but I know everything there is to know about you."

Laura's eyes darted towards her office door as she calculated her chances of escaping before Thomas could stop her. He caught on immediately.

"I swear I'm not here to hurt you."

His statement didn't relax her whatsoever so he tried a different tact.

"Here's the truth. I came through time to find you Laura, again, for the second time."

She stopped herself from bolting out of her chair as their eyes locked.

"What did you just say?" she tested.

"I said I came through time to be with you again."

"To be with me?"

Thomas nodded.

"What does that mean? Who am I to you?"

Shit, this isn't going well at all. "I'm hesitant to say."

"And why's that?"

"Because you'll think I'm bat-shit crazy."

"And who's to say I'm not thinking that already?"

Thomas grinned. "Fair enough. I did kind of just drop a bomb on you with an exceedingly farfetched statement. I'd naturally be more than happy to prove what I'm saying to you is true, if you'd give me the opportunity."

Laura was intrigued but wary. *Who is this man? Why does he think he knows me?*

"Alright, Thomas, I'll bite. Convince me, somehow, that you've traveled through time to find me."

"Okay." Thomas shifted in his chair. "I'll start with the easy ones. You were born on August eighth, nineteen-fifty-five to Henry and Helen Bond. When you were seventeen your mother died of cancer. That was on a Wednesday, August twenty-third, seventy-two."

Laura's eyes widened a bit but she didn't interrupt.

"Your father, heartbroken, died nearly a year later on Sunday, June seventeenth, seventy-three."

"That information could easily be obtained."

"True, but I've only started."

She leaned back. "Continue."

"When you were nearly out of med school you met a man by the name of Rick Surge. Your relationship lasted two and a half years before you caught him in bed with another woman."

"How could you possibly know that? I've never told anyone that."

"I know it because you told me."

"I've never met you before today."

"From your perspective you're absolutely right," Thomas said. "But from mine I've known you for eleven years."

"Eleven years?"

Thomas nodded.

"So who am I to you, from your perspective?"

Thomas gulped. *It's all or nothing.* "You're my wife."

Laura didn't run, she didn't scream, and she didn't flinch. She just stared at Thomas.

"You actually believe that, don't you?"

"I have so much more to tell you, if you'd like to hear it."

Laura pondered his question. *I'm not getting any creepy vibes from him, which is highly unusual. And the truth is I'm actually very curious to see where this is going.*

"You have my full attention," she told him.

"How much time to we have?"

"We have all afternoon."

* * *

Two hours later Thomas finished his abbreviated recounting of the past eleven years they'd spent together. During the history lesson Laura had only interrupted a few times for clarification, but overall had become thoroughly engrossed in his version of reality.

"That's quite a tale you've wove for me," she voiced. "But, here's the problem. You're a writer which means you obviously have a very active imagination. Who's to say you didn't make all of it up?"

"I can't, but you can."

"What do you mean?"

"Put me under. Previously we went through a number of hypnosis sessions. Put me under and ask me anything you want, absolutely anything at all."

Laura leaned in. "You're serious."

"I have nothing to lose. I'm here for you, and since my life has drastically changed from the first time I lived it I don't have any other choice about how to convince you. The question now is what do you think you have to lose?"

"Other than my sanity?"

Thomas chuckled. "There's always that. Sam and Bill, who I told you about, had a similar time swallowing what I just shoveled your way. But they came to see that I wasn't full of shit, and I hope that you do too."

"You do realize," Laura shot back, "that you, a complete stranger, just walked into my office and told me he's my husband, that we have two children, we all had super powers and were sought after by the Presidents of both the United States and Russia. That's aside from the notion the Director of the CIA built a secret bunker for us to work out of."

"You neglected to mention that…"

Laura held her hand up to stop him. "I get it. There's more, a lot more. The truth is my head's spinning."

"I'm sorry. That wasn't my intention. I'm sorry if that frustration is seeping out. I'm just so used to us talking I forgot that you actually don't know me at all."

Laura eased up. "You sound sincere, I'll give you that, so I'm going to give you the benefit of the doubt."

"Really?"

"Yes," Laura assured him. "I've gone this far down the rabbit hole so why stop now?"

* * *

Laura began. "Okay. Sit back and relax. Close your eyes and try to clear your mind."

Thomas shifted around in his chair and closed his eyes.

"With your mind free of cluttered thoughts your body starts to float. You only hear my voice talking while your body gently floats. You are weightless and don't have a care in the world. In the distance you see a bright light. You are drawn to it. Your body drifts towards it. The light is warm and inviting."

Thomas sat peacefully in the chair. Laura had just finished regressing Thomas. It had taken about five minutes of softly walking him through her process. He seemed to take to it very well.

"Thomas. Can you hear me?"

"I hear you," he replied.

"What do you see?"

"A bright light and it's warm," he said a little dreamily.

"Good Thomas. How do you feel?"

"Safe. Relaxed."

Perfect. "Thomas, I'd like to ask you a few questions."

"Okay."

"Who am I to you?"

"Laura Clark, my wife."

Sonofabitch, this is incredible. He thinks he's telling the truth.

"When and where did we get married?"

"On the island of St. Lucia, January eleventh, nineteen ninety-one."

But that's only six months from now. Is any of this real? I have to delve deeper.

"What was the name of your childhood bully?"

"Nigel Clemmings."

"What happened to Nigel?"

"I…I have conflicting memories. In one he was killed by his brother Albert. In the other he was killed by his father."

"Why are your memories conflicted?"

"Because they both occurred."

"How is that possible?"

"I died and reset the universe. The Caretaker sent me back to relive my life over, but this time without the complications that stood in my way the first time."

Laura didn't know how to respond, or even what question to ask next.

Is he psychotic? Is his mind that broken he's allowed this fantasy to override his actual memories? But even if that's true there's no way he could have known about my relationship with

324

*Rick, or my parents. I mean, why would he go through all that
trouble in the first place?*

Laura was torn but still very fascinated.

"You said you came back through time for me, is that right?"

"Yes," Thomas answered, still in the hypnotic state.

"Why?"

"Because you're the love of my life and we have two beautiful
children together."

"What were their names again?"

"Emily and Gavin."

*At least I know what to name them when the time comes. Wait,
am I getting drawn into his delusions? What's going on?*

"Would you ever hurt me?"

"No. Never. I love you."

*Goddammit. Who is this guy and could any of this really be
true?*

"What about your parents. Are they alive?"

"Yes."

"But you told me they were killed."

"In my other life they were. My mother was killed when I was
five. My father when I was ten. My grandparents raised me."

"And your father works for the CIA, in both timelines?"

"Yes."

This is so weird.

"And what about you? What have you changed from your
other life to this one?"

"I stood up to Nigel and beat the crap out of him. My parents
are alive and because of that I now have a younger sister. I
traveled the world all over again, for the second time, and it was
still amazing."

Let me try a different line of questioning.

"And what about the women in your life. How many girlfriends have you had?"

"None, in this timeline."

"None? Why not?"

"Because I'm saving myself for you."

Laura didn't know how to respond to his brazen honesty. It took her a few seconds to speak up again.

"Soooo, you're a virgin?"

Thomas unconsciously smiled while his eyes remained closed. "Technically."

Oh my god, that's sweet. He's saving himself for me. But shit, is he for real? Am I dreaming? Laura paused as she looked down at Thomas. *I mean, he is pretty cute. And whether anything he's saying is real, he does have one heck of an imagination. I don't think he'd be dull, especially since he's a successful writer; not to mention a world traveler. And he's already been forthcoming about where his money came from, if I'm to believe he gave his parents a heads-up when he was five. But here he is, in my office, and he sought me out. I could easily pass this up, but that begs the question, should I? The truth is I'm riveted by his story and he knows so much about me it's bizarre. Maybe he is telling the truth or maybe he isn't. In either case he believes he is and that might be enough for me to convince myself to give him a shot.*

* * *

"Three. The bright light is fading in the distance."

"Two. Your body is getting heavier."

"One. You are relaxed and awake."

Thomas slowly opened his eyes, blinked them a few times and looked up at Laura.

326

"How'd I do?"

"You've got balls," Laura told him as she sat back down in her chair.

Thomas straightened his and looked over at Laura expectantly. "And having balls is a good thing I take it?"

"Let's just say I'm not completely convinced."

Thomas looked dejected. "No?"

"No. However, I don't feel it's fair that you know so much about me while I know next to nothing about you."

Thomas caught a hint of a chance. "No, you're probably right, that's not fair at all. How can I rectify that?"

Laura wrote something on the back of a business card, stood up and handed it to Thomas. He looked down and saw her phone number, July 7th and eight-o'clock written on it.

"What's this?" he asked as he stood up.

"I expect a call sometime tomorrow to confirm our date for Saturday night."

Thomas beamed. "Why wait?" he proposed.

She returned his smile. "Why indeed."

45
Saturday January 11, 1991

"I now pronounce you man and wife. You may kiss the bride."

On the private beach of LeSPORT, located on the northwest tip of the island of Saint Lucia, Thomas and Laura Clark kissed each other as husband and wife for the very first time. Their officiant clasped his hands together, smiled broadly and enjoyed the moment. He sensed something very special about these two. Maybe it was how they looked at each other; held each other's hands; or maybe it was just the kiss. Whatever the reason he knew their lives would be anything but ordinary.

* * *

Thomas' two best friends, Sam Paige and Bill Nicholson, their wives, his agent Nick Raynes, his wife, his parents, grandparents and sister, Abby, had been invited along to witness and celebrate their wedding. They had all arrived on Wednesday, three days prior, at Hewanorra International Airport, on the southern end of the island. All thirteen had piled their luggage and themselves into a large party bus and thoroughly enjoyed the hour and twenty minute ride north to the resort. Along the way the view was absolutely breath taking. At every turn there was something else that caught their attention. Everything was heavenly, and the alcohol continued to flow. Samuel, their driver, was very energetic and answered their questions.

Thomas had done a great deal of traveling in his younger years, as had Sam and Bill, during their military careers, but none of them had experienced the raw beauty the Caribbean had to offer until now. Laura looked over at Thomas, smiled and squeezed his hand.

"This is amazing honey," she said. "Thank you."

"Anything for you. Especially since this is my second time marrying you," he tried to whisper.

"I think I'm going to be sick," said Bill next to them with a playful jab.

"Oh, ha ha," she joked.

It'd taken Laura some time, along with everyone else, to fully grasp the mind-boggling story that Thomas had laid out to them. But, over time, they'd come to truly believe him, as farfetched as the idea of time travel actually sounded. Thomas' 'previous' adventures had become an inside joke that only their core group would ever understand or hear about.

Bill made his way to the cooler and pulled out a few more beers. "Who needs a refresher?"

"I'll take one," Nick replied.

"I'd like one as well," Betsy announced.

"Me too," Ed declared.

"I don't think so," Claire, Ed's wife cautioned to him. "You have to look out for your blood pressure. You're not getting any younger."

"I'm only eighty-seven."

Chuckles erupted throughout the bus as the two continued. Bill handed out the beers and then offered one to Laura. She shook her head and put her hand on her belly.

"I will, however, have some of yours though," she said to Thomas with a wink. "I don't think one little sip will hurt."

"So Thomas," Sam's wife Julie interjected, "the only thing I've been told is that you dragged us all to paradise for your wedding. Care to let us in on the rest of the secret?"

Nick, Susan, Sam, Julie, Bill, Kim, Ed, Claire, Michael, Betsy and Abby all turned their attention away from the picturesque views and looked at Thomas. He took a long drink of beer before he proceeded.

"Ladies and gentlemen, and I use the word gentlemen very loosely in this company."

"Out with it you storytelling bastard!" Sam cried out. Everyone laughed.

"Fair enough. Fair enough. As you know, Laura and I have asked the eleven of you to witness and partake in our marriage here in the Caribbean. You're my family and I wouldn't want to share this moment with anyone else."

"You mean share it again," Bill joked knowing that Nick and Susan wouldn't get it.

Thomas raised his bottle. "Touché. My life, and yours, are intertwined; more so than I ever thought possible. And because of my unique perspective on life I believe we've developed a stronger bond. I reunited with my two best friends, my grandparents, my parents, and my sister I never had. I wrote some more children's books, and most importantly I convinced Laura, the love of my life, that I wasn't a stalker."

The group snickered and smiled as Thomas looked directly at Bill.

"Bill, if you say one word I'm going to punch you in the junk."

"Mums the word brother." Bill smiled.

Thomas continued. "Without going in to too much detail I want to personally thank each of you. Sam and Bill. We've been through the shitter and back since grade school. You two were always by my side. I'm indebted to you both. Thank you."

"Actually, Thomas," Sam said, "it's the other way around. So thank you."

Thomas nodded Sam's acknowledgement and turned to his friend's wives. "Kim and Julie, I know you've only started to get to know me, but because you can put up with the likes of these two," he said as he pointed towards Sam and Bill, "I believe you should both be awarded medals."

"Ha ha, very funny," said Bill and raised his bottle as a sign of affection.

"Grandma. Grandpa. Mom. Dad. Sis. You have no idea how much you being here, right here right now, means to me. I can't wait to see what happens in the years to come."

"Thank you for inviting us," Michael told his son. "We're sitting pretty because of you and enjoying every minute of it."

Thomas then turned to Laura. "And Laura. If it wasn't for you I wouldn't be the happiest and luckiest man in the world. Thank you for trusting me."

She smiled and said, "It wasn't easy. I could have easily called the psych ward and had you committed."

"I'm glad I wasn't the only one thinking that," Sam told everyone."

"No shit," Bill added as he made a circular motion by his ear. "Crraaazzzzyyy."

As the laughter died down Thomas gazed at everyone. "Laura and I wanted to bring you down here not only for our wedding, but as a small token of our appreciation for being an essential part of our lives. Ladies and gentlemen, we'll be staying at The Body Holiday. It's an all-inclusive private resort and spa. Everything's paid for. You can do absolutely anything or nothing at all. The sky's the limit."

"Oh my God! You're kidding?" Julie and Kim said at the same time.

"Thomas, if I weren't married to Nick I'd propose to you right now," Susan purred.

"For the next week all your needs will be catered to. Naturally, if you're not too busy, we'd love for you to actually pick yourself up off the beach, or out of your comas, and come to our wedding this Saturday."

"We wouldn't miss it for the world," his mother said. "Thank you."

"No mom, thank you."

Bill raised his bottle. "To Thomas and Laura."

"Here here," came the unanimous reply.

The excitement in the van was palpable. For the rest of the drive each couple planned what they wanted to do, if anything at all. There were so many options at their disposal. Spa treatments, tennis, scuba diving, fishing, drinking, eating and relaxing. The list of activities was endless.

Thomas squeezed Laura's hand and looked directly at her. "I love you."

"I love you too." They kissed as Samuel kept smiling, waving and honking.

* * *

"I now pronounce you man and wife. You may kiss the bride."

"I love you," Thomas whispered.

"I love you too," Laura whispered back. They both had huge smiles on their face.

"Congratulations, Thomas." Sam stepped in and gave each of them a big hug.

"I second that notion," Bill added and followed suit.

"Laura. You are so radiant," commented Kim. Susan and Julie both nodded their heads in agreement. "And what an amazing backdrop. I could move here in a second."

"Thanks Laura," Bill joked. "No pressure on us, right Sam?"

"None at all. What you think sweetie?"

Julie didn't hesitate. "My sister's right, in a damn second."

Sam and Bill could only roll their eyes as they moved away to make room for the rest of Thomas' family.

"That was a beautiful ceremony," Betsy told Laura and her son while she gave her new daughter-in-law a huge hug.

"It absolutely was," Claire agreed. "And you are stunning in that outfit, my dear."

"Thank you," Laura replied.

Ed and Michael pulled Thomas in close. "You did good, son. Thank you."

"Yes," Ed said in agreement, "very good."

Abby embraced Laura and whispered in here ear jokingly. "Are you sure my brother's not crazy?"

Laura smiled at her new sister-in-law. "Let's just say he keeps things interesting."

"I bet."

Thomas piped up and made an announcement. "That's it for the ceremony. Thank you all for coming. We'll see you at TAO at seven o'clock."

The group finished congratulating them and then moved off down the beach towards the resort. The weather had been perfect. The sun had begun to set during the ceremony as planned. The backdrop to their wedding couldn't have been more beautiful. Thomas and Laura slowly walked hand in hand up the beach as man and wife, for the second time.

"I love you, Dr. Laura Clark."

Laura smiled and tilted her head. "Say it again."

"I love you more than life itself, obviously. Without you everything I did would have been meaningless, well, aside from saving humanity."

"Oh, naturally."

"What I'm trying to say is…you're my everything."

She stopped and looked into his eyes. "I know, and you're mine. But, part of me still wonders what would have happened if I actually had called the psych ward."

He smiled. "I'm glad I didn't have to find out."

"Me too." Laura took his hand and placed it over her belly. "Emily will be here in six months."

"I can't wait. You're going to be a fantastic mother."

She grinned. "Excuse me. Spoiler alert. Maybe I'd be a bad mother."

He laughed. "Sorry."

The warm wind brushed their cheeks as the final rays of the day's sun retreated into the ocean.

46
Monday July 15, 1991

"Doctor Harper to the Delivery Room. Doctor Harper to the Delivery Room."

Laura was in her private delivery room at Marin General. Thomas held her hand as two nurses prepped her for the inevitable.

"Doctor Harper is on her way," one nurse told them.

"Thank you," replied Thomas.

Thomas and Laura had moved from San Bernardino up to Marin shortly before their wedding. And like before, at least from Thomas' point of view, they managed to secure a house next door to Sam and Bill's. Laura had become pregnant three months into their relationship, and with Thomas' endless stories milling around her head, she agreed to sell her practice and move north with his promise that she'd reopen her business whenever she wanted to. He readily agreed, much to the delight of Thomas' parents and grandparents who were thrilled to hear that a child was on the way. Sam and Bill were also glad to have the three musketeers reunited once again.

In the hospital Laura had just reached full dilation and her contractions had become closer to each other now.

"You're doing great sweetie."

"Then you get in this bed and give birth."

He smiled. "I would do just about anything else. You seem like you have this covered. I'm just going to step out into the hall." Thomas pretended to get up.

"Don't you even think about it mister!" Laura smiled back at him before her face contorted again. She squeezed his hand hard. Another contraction had hit. "Yeah, you owe me big time for this."

"You're going to do fine," Thomas assured her.

"Oh yeah? How do you know?"

"That's easy. I've done this with you before, remember?"

"So you've been saying since the day I met you."

"Well, it's true," he insisted.

She looked at him with probing eyes. "Alright then. Prove it."

Thomas was all too eager to play her game. "Okay. The heartbeat machine is currently showing you and the baby's rhythms, yes?"

Laura looked over at the machine and then back at him. "Yes. And?"

"Well, the machine is going to briefly display three heartbeats."

"Bullshit," Laura whispered as Doctor Anna Harper glided into the room.

The doctor had just scrubbed up and checked the machine's readouts. "Laura. How are your contractions?"

"They're more frequent, Anna."

"Thomas, glad to see you haven't passed out yet."

He could see her smile behind her mask. "Give it time doc."

"We have a pool going."

"Swell." He smirked at their banter.

"Hello?" Laura reminded them. "Mother giving birth here."

"And we're back," said Anna.

Thomas and Laura had gotten very close to Doctor Harper over the past six months of checkups and prep work. They had immediately bonded as their shit talk escalated during their initial meeting. Overall Dr. Harper made them feel at ease.

Anna checked Laura's dilation, pulse rate and both heartbeats. The machines beeped in the background. "I think we're ready to kick this off Laura. What do you say?"

"Get this kid out of me."

"That's the spirit." She turned to Thomas. "Now for the hard question. From what angle are you going to experience this miracle of birth?"

"I'm okay right where I am doc," he replied as he stood fast by Laura's side. "No need to traumatize me from your end. But sincerely, thanks for the invite."

Anna grinned, definitely having fun at his expense.

"Okay Laura. This is all you now. We're going to get you through this just fine. When the next contraction hits I want you to push."

Laura's nails bit in to Thomas's hand as the next wave hit. He gritted his teeth and bore the pain silently as his wife started giving birth to their baby girl.

"That was great Laura. A few more of those and you're going to have the easiest birth on record." She kept watch on Laura's pulse and both heartbeats. Both were nominal. She noticed that Thomas was holding his own.

A different beep started up on the heartbeat monitor. Anna glanced over at it and froze. A third heartbeat had appeared.

"What the hell?" she breathed.

"A third heartbeat, doc?" Thomas asked.

Dr. Harper looked over at him, an inquisitive look on her face. "How the hell do you know that?"

Thomas shrugged. "Lucky guess."

Laura's mouth hung open in shock as she stared at Thomas. He met her gaze and smile.

"Holy shit, it's all true, isn't it?"

Thomas nodded.

"What are you two talking about?" Dr. Harper inquired. "Because whatever it is it needs to wait. You've got a kid on the way."

Dr. Harper glanced back at the monitor again and only two heartbeats were displayed. Twenty minutes later Laura gave birth to a healthy baby girl. The cord was cut and then the nurse took her, cleaned her and brought her back. She placed the newborn in Laura's arms; who began to cry. Anna noticed that Thomas's face wasn't very dry either.

"Congratulations you two."

"Thank you, Anna."

"My pleasure. Do you have a name for her yet?"

Thomas and Laura looked at each other. "Emily," said Laura, conceding to Thomas' advanced knowledge. "Her name is Emily."

"That's a beautiful name."

Doctor Harper walked to the heartbeat machine and tore off the printed sheet that had accumulated during the procedure. She took it back to her office, closed the door and poured over it. There, in black and white, was a third heartbeat. For two seconds a third heartbeat had been recorded and then mysteriously disappeared. *What the hell does it mean?*

Back in the delivery room Thomas and Laura, along with Emily, were left alone. The two doted over Emily, but curiosity finally took over and Laura turned towards Thomas.

"Talk. The 'how' is irrelevant at this point because I'm left with having no other recourse but to believe that you've lived this life before."

Thomas nodded. "I have."

"And that's hard enough to wrap my head around, but it is what it is. However, with that being said, I want to know where that third heartbeat came from?"

"It was mine."

"Yours? I don't understand."

"The Caretaker took me on a journey through my life. Imagine, if you will, your entire life presented around you as floating pictures, depicting one moment in time from the next. During that expedition through time he showed me the birth of our two children. When that happened I merged with you and Emily for a fleeting instant."

"And that was the third heartbeat? It was you?"

"Yeah."

"Wow. I can't even begin to imagine anything you've been through. What a mind trip it must be."

Thomas took hold of Laura's hand and held it to his face. "Not anymore sweetheart, not anymore."

She smiled. "I love you."

"I love you too."

Laura went back to little Emily that laid on her chest as she mulled this new information over. "So, the same thing's going to happen when Gavin's born?"

"It will. You'll see."

"I can't wait."

"You and me both."

* * *

Saturday February 13, 1993

A year and a half after Emily was born they were back at Marin General. Laura's contractions had started earlier that evening so Thomas brought her in. Julie and Kim had offered to look after little Emily in the meantime.

Doctor Harper came in and met them in the delivery room.

"You two certainly know how to ruin a good night's sleep." She smiled.

"Exactly as planned…mhuahahaha," Thomas replied.

"Cute honey," said Laura. "Why don't you let the women work now?"

"Ouch." He grabbed her hand and made sure her nails couldn't dig in this time around.

Laura's contractions had peaked and the process began just like before while Anna kept one eye on the monitors. Since the day Emily Clark had been born she hadn't experienced the same system malfunction again. *It had to be a malfunction. It's the only obvious explanation.*

"Breath sweetie."

The machine beeped regularly and then made a distinctive new sound. Anna's eyes grew wider and both Thomas and Laura caught it.

"Is everything okay?"

Dr. Harper caught herself. "Everything's fine. Push for me Laura."

Thomas and Laura smiled at each other, clearly pleased with their inside joke.

The regular interval of machine beeps returned. Seven minutes later a healthy baby boy was delivered and placed in Laura's arms.

"Congratulations again you two."

"Thanks doc."

"You have a name for this little monster?"

Thomas spoke up this time. "Gavin. His name's Gavin."

* * *

Later that same morning, back at their house, they tucked Gavin in his crib. Little Emily watched, wide-eyed and full of wonder, stared down at her tiny brother from the comfort of her father's arms. Laura, tired but exuberant, leaned against Thomas.

"This is perfect," she whispered.

"Yes," Thomas agreed, "yes it is."

This is my life now; my new life and I'm completely happy with it. As we move forward, together as a family, I'm not going to have to worry about anyone targeting my family. And that sense of security gives me an enormous amount of relief.

He took the time to take in the scene. He'd found and somehow convinced Laura that they were meant to be together. Both his parents and grandparents were alive. His friends, Sam and Bill, lived next door and hadn't had to relive the awful and traumatic incidents that Albert Clemmings had previously imparted on all of them. No, life was going to be dull, and Thomas knew that was just what the doctor ordered. His days of placing himself in harm's way were over.

Thomas shuddered, ever so slightly, at his new realization. And at that moment the power the Caretaker had instilled in him, the ability to jump forward in time, dissipated. Thomas felt it leave his body, but he didn't give it a second thought because right now, in THIS moment, he knew his family was going to be happy; and that's all that he ever wanted.

343

47

Tuesday October 21, 1997

In Marin, California, a smartly dressed mid-twenties
Caucasian woman with shoulder length black hair opened the front
door of SANDBOX. Roberta, the executive admin, had followed
the young lady's approach from the parking lot via the CCT, the
closed circuit television cameras, from behind her desk. Roberta
raised her head as the young woman approached.

"May I help you?"

"Good morning. My name is Rebecca Cross. I have an
appointment at ten."

"Yes, of course, Ms. Cross."

"Rebecca, ma'am."

"It's hard to break those habits."

"Ma'am?"

Roberta smiled. "Rebecca, my name's Roberta and we've
been expecting you." She closed Rebecca's dossier that lay on her
desk, stood and extended her hand. "Welcome to SANDBOX."
Rebecca shook the offered hand firmly and let go. "Is there
anything I can get you while you wait? Coffee? Tea?"

"No, but thank you just the same, Roberta."

"Very well." She pushed a button on her desk's intercom.
"Alex, Rebecca Cross is here."

"I'll be down in ten minutes," came the reply.

"We've got a few minutes before they're ready for you."
Roberta gestured towards the plush couches that bracketed the
large coffee table adjacent to her desk. "Why don't we make
ourselves comfortable and get to know each other." They walked
thirty feet and then sat down across from each other.

"So Rebecca, why don't you tell me a little about yourself?"

"I'm twenty-seven and enlisted in the army right out of high school at eighteen. I thought about piloting helicopters but decided on becoming a combat medic instead. I was deployed and participated in Operation Desert Storm, back in ninety-one, as well as Operation Desert Strike last year."

Roberta nodded her head as if hearing it for the first time but she was already well versed with Rebecca Cross' entire military career. "And what brings you to our doorstep rather than re-enlisting?"

Rebecca shifted a little in her seat. "May I be direct with you?"

"That's one of the ways we run our business, dear."

Rebecca digested what she'd just heard and took it at face value. "I've seen combat and what it does to soldiers, both to their bodies and their minds. During my deployments I've patched up more combatants than I care to remember."

"Go on."

"What it comes down to is that there are no real winners on the battlefield."

"I see. And why do you think we should hire you?"

Oh God, did I just blow this interview? Crap, I might as well go for it. "There are quite a number of reasons SANDBOX needs me. I'm a seasoned combat medic for one. Two, I know how to handle a weapon. Three, my guess is that SANDBOX only has a few, if any, females on its staff, present company excluded. And four, the Army currently won't let me, or any other female, on the front lines. I'm as good as any man and I'm here to prove it."

Roberta grinned. "Do you really think playing the gender card is the best way to approach this?"

"Ma'am…, Roberta, I'll play whatever card I have to in an effort to procure this job. I want…I mean I need to be part of something I actually care about. Your PMC, or private military company, gives me control over my life and the jobs I accept. Being a female, in my opinion, actually gives me an edge over my male counterparts."

"Explain."

"What if SANDBOX gets an offer to protect a HVT, a high value target, but that target is female and requests an all-female protection detail? Not only could I fill that role, since who really expects a female bodyguard, but my skillset and background come in very handy in case something serious happens."

Roberta changed gears. "Are you married?"

"No."

"Boyfriend?"

"Maybe someday but not currently."

"Drugs?"

"No, ma'am."

"Are there any skeletons in your closet that we should be aware of?"

"I...I don't believe so. No." *What do I do? Do I keep answering her?*

They both heard the distinct sound of combat boots approaching. Roberta smiled and stood up, as Rebecca followed suit.

"Who do you have for me today, Roberta?" said Alex as he walked up to them. He was dressed in a black t-shirt with SANDBOX embroidered on it.

"Alex, this is Rebecca Cross. She'll be starting with us this week."

A stunned look came over Rebecca's face as she looked back at Roberta. "I don't understand."

"I'm a pretty good judge of character my dear. Alex runs our Human Resource department."

Rebecca caught herself and then smiled warmly at Roberta. "Tricky. Thank you."

"My pleasure; and you're right you know."

"Right?"

"We do need more women. However, more importantly, we need more forward thinking women like you. It's going to be a long time before the US military allows equality in the armed services. You're smart, level headed and know what you want. SANDBOX is a family and I think you're going to fit in nicely." She turned to Alex. "I'd appreciate it if you wouldn't mind running through all the paperwork with this young lady."

"Of course." He turned to Rebecca. "If you'd come with me please."

Rebecca hesitated and Roberta caught it.

"Is there something else, dear?"

"Am I the first?"

Roberta smiled and nodded. "That you are. Don't let us down."

Rebecca grinned. "Thank you very much, Roberta."

"You're welcome."

Alex walked Rebecca Cross towards the stairs that led to the second floor.

Roberta made her way back to her desk and sat down. "See, old habits can be changed."

She took Rebecca's dossier, made a notation in it, unlocked her file drawer and slipped it back into place.

* * *

Friday October 24, 1997

Sixty-six year old Betsy Clark put her hands on her hips as she walked up to Michael. He was on the couch enjoying his daily newspaper. The two of them still lived in the same house in Orinda, the same house they'd raised Thomas and Abby in, although it had been long since vacated except for the two of them. Abby, now thirty-four, had left the Bay Area for Portland a few years prior to pursue her career as an art dealer. She often came down to visit with her parents and grandparents, but not as often as Michael and Betsy would have preferred.

Michael's parents, Ed and Claire now in their early nineties, had moved to Rossmore in Walnut Creek twenty years previously. Michael and Betsy had tossed around the idea of moving, but Michael was unsure of the prospect due to his parent's ages. With Abby up in Oregon the two wanted to live closer to Thomas, Laura, Emily and Gavin, but the driving distance from Marin, to Ed and Claire's house in Walnut Creek, was a blatant challenge. On top of that Michael had recently retired from the CIA and was having difficulties getting used to the transition.

"You need to stop moping around," Betsy told him.

"I'm fine," he replied as he rustled his paper.

"You're not and we both know it. So I've invited Thomas over for lunch so the two of you can talk. We need to figure something out because this house is too big for just the two of us."

Michael grumbled something under his breath as Betsy departed. He knew it wasn't fair for Betsy to feel isolated, their daughter in Oregon and Thomas across the bay in Marin.

And now, with me home, I haven't exactly been a model husband. I miss the Agency, but I need to realize that part of my life is behind me.

349

The doorbell rang thirty minutes later and Betsy rushed to open it. When she did Thomas leaned in and gave his mother a big hug.

"Hey ma. It's good to see you. How're things?"

She closed the door behind him.

"I'm fine, but things could be better. Your father's in the family room."

Thomas nodded and made his way through the house.

"Hey pop."

Michael twisted in his seat on the couch. "Hey son. How goes it?"

Michael stood up to greet Thomas and they briefly embraced each other.

"Soooo," Thomas began, "shall we get out of here and take a drive?"

"Apparently that's what your mother wants."

Betsy called out from an adjacent room. "Don't think I didn't hear that."

Thomas chuckled. "Come on, let's go before she kicks us both out."

Thomas drove into downtown Orinda and stopped at Nations, a local hamburger joint. Inside they placed their orders and then sat down in an open booth. Thomas looked at his father from across the table.

"So what's new? How's retirement?"

"You tell me," Michael shot back.

Thomas sighed. He knew his father was used to being in control, but ever since he left the Agency he'd become grumpy and somewhat unhappy. Michael no longer felt needed and that new sensation was anything but comfortable. Betsy, naturally, had said as much over the phone when she'd invited Thomas over, but he wanted to hear a reason directly from his father.

"Pop, what's eating you?"

"What, you didn't see this in your other life already?"

Thomas took the barb in stride but responded firmly to let his father know he wasn't going to take any shit from him. "You were killed when I was ten and I walked in on your body. Your parents raised me after that. So no, this is all new to me, just like retirement is new to you."

Michael met his son's eyes for a few seconds and then softened his voice. "Sorry."

"I get it, or at least I think I do. Shit changes. You used to run an entire division of the CIA, and now you don't. It takes some getting used to, and that feeling I completely understand."

Michael conceded that point. "I bet you do. Still, anytime I think about your story it troubles me."

"Why's that?" Thomas asked.

"To think what you went through, always looking over your shoulder as you tried to protect your family. I just can't imagine what you went through, aside from the glaring fact that," as Michael lowered his voice, "you're a time traveler."

Thomas grinned. "Yeah, that's a weird one for me too. And I should admit, while we're on the subject, that I miss my telekinetic ability as well. I had some serious power at my disposal."

"But at what cost to you and your family?"

Thomas nodded. "Exactly. And now I've been given a second chance so I'm going to make the most of it, and that includes you and mom, grandpa and grandma."

Michael cocked his head to one side. "What are you talking about?"

"I've got an idea that I want to run by you, especially now that Em is six, Gav is four, and your folks are both ninety-three."

"Okay. What is it?"

"Family is important to all of us, and dare I say, exceptionally important to me. With that said I want us all to move to Hawaii."

"Hawaii? All of us, together?"

"Yes. I know mom wants to spend more time with the kids and you're worried about your folks. If we move we can live practically next door to each other. The warm weather would do us all some good and the kids would absolutely love it."

Michael pondered his son's idea for a little while. "I know I've been a royal pain in the ass to your mother ever since I retired. Maybe a change of scenery would be good for all of us."

"So you'll talk to mom about it?"

Michael smiled. "I will, but I don't think it'll take too much convincing."

"Neither do I."

"And I think my folks will be a push over. They'd love to spend time with your kids."

"And Laura and I would welcome that."

One of the cooks spoke up loudly from behind the counter. "Order eighty-six! Order eighty-six!"

Thomas exited the booth, retrieved their food and brought it back to the table. As they began to devour their fries and burgers Thomas brought up the sore subject of his father's retirement once again.

"I know the transition you're in isn't going to be easy, and I'll help you through that if you let me. But, in the meantime, I'm assuming you still have contacts within the CIA you can utilize?"

Michaels' demeanor perked up. "What's on your mind?"

"I have two people I was hoping you could track down for me."

"Two people?"

"Yes. And as far as I know, from my previous timeline, they both worked for the Agency and they're family."

"Interesting. They must be important to you."

"They are. They played major roles in protecting my family."

Michael was all business. "Who are they?"

"The first is a guy named Hobbes?"

His father gave him a strange look. "Hobbes?"

"Sorry. That's what we all called him. His real name is Charles Hillburg and I believe he works in Information Technology. He most likely works in conjunction with a man who goes by the handle of Calvin."

"Calvin and Hobbes. Seriously, Thomas?"

"Yeah. Seriously. But I'm only interested in Hobbes."

His father shrugged. "Alright. And the second person?"

"Her name is Gabbi and she was part of the R&D division."

"Does she have a last name?"

"I'm sure she does but I never knew it. But, she has a huge dragon tattoo down her arm, and when I knew her she had purple hair."

"Unique, to say the least, but that'll help me locate her that must faster."

"So, you can do this for me?"

Michael nodded. "Absolutely. It'll give me something to do so I should really be thanking you for the task. Now for the million dollar question. What happens when I locate them?"

Thomas picked up a fry and popped it into his mouth as he contemplated the right course of action.

"I'm working on that, but in the meantime let me know if you find them."

"I can do that."

"Thanks, pop."

* * *

On the way back to Marin, from lunch with his father, Thomas stopped off at SANDBOX. He parked and exchanged waves with a few of the contractors that were onsite as he entered the lobby. Thomas was well known for outshooting a number of the operators SANDBOX employed. He often left the shooting range pocketing the money of experienced soldiers, leaving them questioning how a children's book writer had just taken them to school.

"Hello, Thomas," Roberta greeted. "What brings you here today? More time on the range?"

"Not today, Roberta. I was hoping to catch Sam and Bill. Are they in?"

"That they are, and…," she said as she checked their schedule, "they should be free. Go on and head on up."

"Thanks."

"You're welcome. Say hi to Laura and your kids for me. They're really sprouting up."

Thomas smiled. "The life of a father. I love it. I'll tell her you said hi. Cya."

I'm glad Roberta doesn't have an ulterior motive for working here, especially since her son's alive and Raven couldn't exploit his death to use her. She's been the kindest person I've known and has dedicated herself to SANDBOX over the past eleven years. Some stories do have a happy ending.

Thomas took the stairs up to Sam and Bill's office rather than using the elevator. Ever since SANDBOX broke ground in eighty-five, twelve years prior, the business had taken off like gangbusters. Within six years Sam and Bill had expanded to international contracts and that had immediately brought more money to the table. Now, with over a hundred operators on the books, SANDBOX had become a pioneer in the industry and showed no signs of slowing down anytime soon.

Thomas approached their office and knocked on the door. Sam and Bill, deep in a serious conversation, turned to see who it was. They did not have happy expressions on their faces.

"Hey guys," Thomas said. "Sorry to just drop by like this. Busy?"

Sam waved him in. "Come on in. We need a break anyway."

"Yeah we do," Bill said sullenly.

Thomas took a seat. "What's going on? Anything I can help with?"

"I don't know," Bill quipped. "Does your wife constantly bitch about what you do for a living?"

Thomas tried to keep a straight face. He knew this day had been coming for a long time. "I guess Laura WOULD might have something to complain about, but the last time I wrote a book I wasn't being shot at." He put his hands up to emphasize his point. "But that's just me."

"Goddammit," Sam said. "You KNEW this was coming…but to us this shit isn't as humorous as you make it out to be."

"Sorry," Thomas said. "But I've been down this road with both of you before."

Bill jumped in. "Oh yeah? Well if you're so smart, what the hell are we supposed to do?"

355

Sam and Bill stared at Thomas and waited for him to answer. They became confused when he didn't open his mouth.

"What?" Sam finally asked. "What is it?"

"Oh shit," Bill added. "Is it something bad?"

Thomas put a hand up to ward off their immediate concerns. "Do you want the truth or do you need to hear what you want to hear instead?"

Sam and Bill deflated a bit.

"Give it to us straight," Sam finally told Thomas.

Thomas cleared his throat and began. "Julie and Kim have stood by your sides while you built up your business. You've gotten married and you both have two children, ages nine and five. But their patience has been worn down, time and time again, because you've both put your personal and business needs ahead of your family."

"Bullsh.."

Thomas cut Bill off. "Stop. I know you're soldiers and you want to protect people. But you're also my friends which means I get to tell you the hard truth, whether I've experienced it with you before or not. The time has come, as I told you fifteen years ago when I offered you two-million dollars, to step away. I told also said you wouldn't like it but the choice isn't up to me. However, let me break it down for you. IF you ignore your wives, and continue to place yourselves in harm's way, you will lose them."

Sam and Bill jolted back as if he'd struck them in the face.

Thomas continued. "I can't say it any plainer. They will divorce you."

"This…this happened?" Sam tentatively asked.

Thomas nodded. "I'm not shitting you, alright. I'm telling you this because I give a shit about your well-being, both as my friends and as a cohesive family unit. Julie and Kim need you home; to be husbands and fathers. It's that simple."

"But what about our business we built?" Bill inquired. "We can't just leave it behind."

"And that's where they're willing to compromise with you, whether you know it yet or not. They don't want you to sell or walk away from SANDBOX. All they want is for the two of you to stop going out on missions, period. They want you safe, to be husbands and fathers, not soldiers."

Sam and Bill leaned back in their chairs as if they'd been hit by a train.

"Shit," Sam let out. "I only knew the tip of this iceberg you've just unveiled to us. I had no idea it was this bad."

"Me either," Bill said.

Thomas let his words sink in as the three of them sat in silence. A minute later Thomas broke it.

"I have a proposal that I'd like you both to consider, if you decide to side with your wives on this."

"Proposal?" Sam asked. "Well, I guess whatever you're about to say can't be any worse than knowing what the future holds for us. Lay it on us."

"Laura, my parents and grandparents are moving to Hawaii."

"What the fuck?" Bill exclaimed. "When did you decide this shit?"

"I just came from talking with my father about it. Anyway, my point is, IF you're going to withdraw a bit from SANDBOX, why not move with us? Think about it. Your kids would love the sand, sun and water, not to mention Julie and Kim would too."

Sam gave Thomas an odd look. "Wait a minute. All of us already lived there. I remember when you were telling us your story. I'm right, aren't I?"

Thomas nodded. "We did, before it all went to hell. But that's not going to happen this time, and we both know it. Come to Hawaii with us and indulge your family. We all deserve it."

Sam and Bill looked at each.

"As much as I hate to admit it," Bill expressed, "the sonofabitch has got a point."

"More than I'd like to admit myself," Sam tagged on.

"I'll tell you what," Thomas said. "Let's all plan a huge family vacation to Hawaii in a couple of weeks, and we'll go from there. Once you see the smiles on your kid's faces you'll be sold, and may I add, if something requires your attention back here at SANDBOX you're only a five hour flight away." Thomas got up to leave. "All I'm asking is that you think about it. It's time to step away before it's too late."

48
Wednesday November 5, 1997

Two weeks later the contingent of families, made up of the Paige's, Nicholson's and multiple generations of the Clark's, landed at Oahu, Hawaii. They disembarked and made their way down to baggage to wait for their luggage. Michael helped his parents, Ed and Claire, who weren't quite as nimble anymore flag down an electric cart so they wouldn't have to walk and the three of them eventually joined the rest of family.

"I have to hand it to you, Thomas," Sam said as he pulled his friend aside. "This was a great idea." He lowered his voice so only Thomas could hear. "And thanks again for the heads up. You should have seen Julie's face when I told her I was going to start phasing out of the actual contracts SANDBOX handles and concentrate on just the day to day activities instead. And then I tell the family that we're all going to Hawaii for vacation. I found myself at the bottom of a dogpile when the three of them tackled me."

Thomas smiled. "You're welcome."

"Yeah, that was a fantastic feeling, one that I'd practically neglected in pursuit of building up my company. Life's really about the little things."

Bill walked over to join them and left the gaggle of family milling in front of the carousal.

"I'm being bombarded with questions about what's next on the agenda," he told Thomas. "So what's the plan now that we're all here?"

* * *

The large transport bus drove east out of the airport. The six children were glued to the windows, as were the adults, as they took in the beautiful lush mountains, the blue sea and the inviting warm air. They were headed to the southeast side of Oahu, and the bus eventually stopped on North Kalaheo Ave in front of a house, with a minivan parked in the driveway. Emily, Gavin, Sarah, Edward, Amanda and Craig disembarked as quickly as they could, followed by everyone else. The driver began to unload the luggage as everyone migrated towards Thomas, excited for the next step of their Hawaiian vacation. Thomas grinned as he held his hands up to quiet his family down.

"Alright everyone, I know you're all wondering what's going on because I've kept you in the dark about where we're all staying. Behind us as you can see is a house and, because I know you can all hear it, has direct access to the beach. It also has a pool, for those of you who desire extra options when it comes to relaxing."

Betsy poised a question. "What about everyone's sleeping arrangements?"

"Inside there are four bedrooms which should give everyone plenty of space."

Confused looks appeared on a number of their faces. Even the children didn't understand and immediately voiced their option.

"Um, dad," Emily said. "That's not enough room for everyone."

"Yeah," Sarah added. "Only four rooms?"

"I don't want to share with my sister," Edward stated. "I'd rather sleep on the beach instead."

More grumbling commenced but Thomas remained steadfast.

"What are you talking about?" Thomas asked everyone with a sly smirk. "Four bedrooms happen to be more than enough for all of us."

Sam and Bill rolled their eyes, along with Julie, Kim and Laura. Michael and Betsy also smelled a rat.

"You're so full of shit." Laura playfully announced. "What's really going on?"

"And all along you can still tell when I'm lying," he replied. "I knew it."

Laura punched him in the shoulder and smiled. "Out with it, mister."

"Okay, okay." He readdressed the entire family. "Perhaps I forgot one minor detail."

"Here it comes," Bill good-humoredly jabbed.

Thomas raised both arms and pointed in each direction. "I rented four houses and vehicles for us. Everyone gets their own, and they each have pools."

Collectively everyone looked left and right and quickly realized that three other identical mini-vans adorned the three adjacent driveways.

"No way!" Amanda yelled.

"This is awesome!" Craig added.

"Seriously brother," Bill said, "you've really outdone yourself this time."

"Wow," Sam mouthed. "I did not see that coming."

"You should be used to that by now," Laura told them with a smile. "We've all had to adjust to Thomas' previous adventures over the years."

The children were hopping with excitement and couldn't contain themselves any longer.

"I want to see my room!"

"I want to go in the pool!"

"I want to build a sandcastle!"

"I need to pee!"

"I'm hungry!"

The adults smiled as Thomas handed out keys to the other houses to Bill, Sam and his parents, who would bunk with his grandparents.

"Enjoy," Thomas called out to all of them as they departed, "and dinner at our place tonight. See you all on the beach!"

Thomas turned to Emily and Gav. "You guys ready to go inside and check it out or what!?"

"Yeah!" they cried out in unison and raced towards the front door.

Laura hugged Thomas. "You're full of surprises. I love you."

"I love you too."

* * *

In the early evening hours everyone wandered over to Thomas' rental and rapidly were handed drinks as they congregated outside together. Since their arrival that afternoon it hadn't taken everyone very long, especially the children, began to unwind. In fact, as each family came by for the inaugural dinner, they all wore smiles on their faces whether they realized it or not.

As the kids played, and the adults drank and indulged in conversation, Thomas fired up the outside grill. It didn't take long before the savory scent of hamburgers, hotdogs and chicken made everyone's stomach grumble. Laura had made potato and green salads and placed them on the buffet table along with paper plates and plastic utensils in preparation for the feast. Shortly thereafter the other tables were filled by hungry individuals as they all devoured the delicious feast Thomas and Laura had prepared.

Michael stood up and raised his glass. "May I have everyone's attention please?" He waited a few seconds and then continued.

362

"I'd like to propose a toast to my son, Thomas, and my daughter-in-law, Laura. Thank you for inviting all of us, your family, on this remarkable escape. Betsy and I needed it more than you know."

"I second that," Sam said as he stood up.

"As do I," Bill added and joined them.

"Yes," Julie gratefully declared, "this is amazing."

"Our kids and I couldn't be happier," Kim acknowledged.

"Even our old bones," Ed announced referring to himself and Claire, "are as happy as could be. Thank you."

Thomas lifted his own glass alongside Laura. "You're welcome. Anything for my family."

They all drank and retook their seats. The kids started to squirm.

"Can we be excused?" Emily asked.

"Sure, sweetie," Laura replied. "Go on inside and play."

"But we want to play on the beach."

Laura shook her head. "Not without adult supervision. There will be plenty of time for all of you to do that tomorrow, okay?"

The six kids slipped out of their seats and headed inside. They all watched them leave before Sam spoke up.

"So Thomas, I have a question."

"Alright," Thomas replied. "Shoot."

"Well, it's more of an observation that could lead to a question."

Bill gave Sam a funny look. "Out with it already."

"So you rented us four houses."

Thomas nodded. "Yup."

"And you rented us four mini-vans."

"You're two for two, Sam."

"Then riddle me this…the mini-vans don't have rental stickers nor are they registered to a rental company. On top of that I find it difficult to believe you were able to locate four houses, all for rent, that are located right next door to each other; certainly not in the two weeks since you mentioned we should go on vacation together to Hawaii."

Thomas didn't reply so Sam continued.

"In fact, during that conversation you told Bill and me that you, your parents and grandparents were moving to Hawaii."

Laura turned her head towards Thomas. "You said that? We hadn't even decided that yet. What's going on?"

Thomas smiled at his wife but Betsy piped up before he could say anything.

"I thought that was just an idea and that this vacation would give us the opportunity to decide whether or not that was something Michael and I wanted to pursue." She addressed her son directly. "Thomas, what's Sam getting at?"

Thomas took a sip of his beer and dived in. "Due to Sam's keen powers of observation I believe I'm left with little choice than to move my time table up."

"Time table?" Laura asked with some hesitancy. "Seriously, what are you talking about?"

"I was hoping we could enjoy our week of vacation here before anyone actually caught on, but it appears that ship has sailed. Sam's right, the probability that I found four houses on the beach next to each other is impractical. In fact, the truth is, all four of these houses belong to me."

"I fricking knew it," Sam stated.

"What?" Laura stammered.

"How…why…when?" Michael asked.

Thomas put his hand up. "As you all know this hasn't been my first journey through life, whether you subscribe to that notion or not. In my previous existence we lived here, although not all of us had that privilege," he said as he glanced at this parents and grandparents. "But our time here was cut short, and all of our lives were turned upside down, to put it mildly.

"These houses were the same ones we owned previously, plus one, this go around. I wanted to find a way to express my thanks to each and every one of you, and to show you in no uncertain terms how much you mean to me. So yes, I quietly began to make inquires a few years ago on these properties so that I could gift them to each of your families because I wanted us all to be together. I lost you all before, one way or another, and that's not going to happen again. So the bottom line is, welcome to your new homes. They're yours if you want them."

Julie and Kim put their hands over their mouths in shock as tears welled up in their eyes.

"Oh my god," the sisters murmured as one.

"Damn, brother," Bill uttered in awe, "you really don't play around."

Michael and Betsy stood up, walked over to their son and embraced him. Laura joined in and before long all the adults had united in one enormous hug. Tears were wiped away as each of them eventually retook their seats.

"I had no idea you were going to go to such lengths," Laura told Thomas. She smiled at him. "But I'm really happy that you did. Now I have to convince everyone else to stay."

"That's not going to take very much from me," Kim assured her, "I can tell you that much. Thank you, Thomas. Thank you, Laura. But this is way too much to accept."

Julie mirrored her sister's sentiment. "I'm just glad the kids weren't out here to hear this, not that they don't feel at home already. But Kim's right, we can't accept this."

Sam interjected. "Yes, we will."

All faces turned to Sam as Julie broached the obvious question. "What? We will? I mean, you'd seriously consider moving here. You weren't kidding about your work at SANDBOX, were you?"

Sam took Julie's hand in his. "Thomas has opened my eyes and ears; eyes and ears that should have listened to you years ago. And he's absolutely right. Family is the most important thing and I don't want to waste another moment missing out on you or our kids growing up with an absentee father. So yes, I'm serious. We're moving here, and don't you worry about this house being a gift because I'll work something out with our time traveling host about that."

Julie wasted no time and wrapped her arms around Sam. "Thankyouthankyouthankyou! You have no idea how relieved I am to hear those words come out of your mouth."

Bill turned to Kim. "Say, I have a crazy idea. Do you want to move to Hawaii?"

She punched him in the shoulder. "You dummy. I thought you'd never ask."

Everyone laughed as Bill and Kim embraced.

Ten minutes later, with the excitement of moving to Hawaii the topic of conversation, Emily opened the back patio door and called out.

"Moooommmm. Gavin opened the front door and went outside because he heard something."

Laura abruptly got to her feet, her smile gone. "You let your four-year old brother walk out the front door?"

"He'll be just fine," Thomas assured everyone.

Laura shot him a dirty look as she started towards the house. "How can you say that?"

"Please," he said. "Trust me. Come back and sit down."

Laura hesitated, unsure of her next move until Thomas spoke the next words.

"This has happened before. He's going to be just fine, you'll see. Come back and sit down. Gav will come to us soon enough."

All the other adults stayed quiet.

"Why?" Laura asked. "What's he doing?"

"He's getting Stickers."

"Stickers? I don't understand."

Thomas held up his hand towards his wife, enticing her to come back to the table, which she reluctantly did.

"What's a Stickers?" Betsy asked.

Thomas chuckled. "Stickers happens to be a cat; a long haired tabby that's orange with a white belly. And he's a member of this family."

Laura stopped panicking. "A cat?"

Just then Gavin appeared in the doorway, the other children behind him, his arms full with the same cat Thomas had just described. Some of its fur was matted and they could all hear its loud purr.

"Mom," Gavin said softly, "this is Stickers. Can I keep him?"

49
Wednesday December 24, 1997

Five weeks later, in mid-December, Thomas and the rest of the Clark family had made the plunge to Hawaii. Their furniture had arrived, by way of cargo ship, on the seventeenth. Thomas and Michael wasted no time unpacking and setting up both houses so his grandparents, Ed and Claire, would feel right at home as soon as possible. Laura, Emily and Gavin had never left the island and remained behind to watch over all four houses while everyone else headed back to the mainland. However, it hadn't taken long before Julie and Kim, along with their kids, made the return trip leaving Sam and Bill behind to work out some business details before they joined everyone.

Everyone's life slowed down the moment they finally moved in. New daily rituals soon cropped up with included more and more time both on the beach and in the water. Some of the older kids experimented with snorkeling and took to it quickly. That led to boogie boarding and endless smiles. And with so many water activities at their disposal, ranging from the pool to the ocean, it didn't take long for all six kids to quickly become aquatic experts.

With everyone living in their new houses, and with Christmas only a week away, the six children had become doubly excited. This would be their first time celebrating the holiday in Hawaii and in their new houses that they loved. Questions began to arise on how Santa would deliver their presents due to the fact that none of the houses had fireplaces. The parents chuckled and explained that Santa would find a way and reminded them that Santa always knew who had been naughty or nice.

Stickers had readily taken to his new home and had become a mutual pet between all the children but, naturally, considered

Gavin his owner and only slept with him on his bed at night. Julie and Kim's kids, not wanting to be left out, begin to drop hints that they wanted a pet of their own, much to the chagrin of their mothers. Their answer was always to deflect and told their kids to ask their fathers, who were still back in Marin.

The afternoon before Christmas the rest of the clan finally arrived in Hawaii, along with some additional guests that Thomas had personally invited to join them. Julie and Kim charged Sam and Bill as they walked through Thomas' front door, clearly happy to see their husbands and fathers. Behind them walked in Abby followed by Nick, Susan and their eight-year old daughter Lisa.

"Hey sis," Thomas said as he embraced Abby. "Good to see you. I'm glad you could make it."

Abby smiled. "And miss spending the holidays with my family in paradise? I mean, it has nothing to do with all the snow in Portland I'm happy to get away from. Nope, absolutely nothing at all."

"I'll bet," Thomas replied with a grin. "Well come on in and say hi to everyone. I think you're going to be bunking over at mom and dad's house next door, right mom?"

Betsy and Michael walked over to their daughter and they all hugged.

"Yes," Betsy replied. "The guest room is ready for you whenever you are. Your father and I are so happy that you're here."

"So am I." Abby turned to the kids in the room. "Maaayyyybe someone can help me take my bags over to my room. I have all these presents to carry and I wouldn't want to lose any of them…"

"PRESENTS!" the kids exclaimed followed by a mad dash to grab Abby's luggage and drag it towards the front door.

Everyone chuckled as Abby led the procession next door with her mother. As they exited Thomas stepped out and welcomed Nick and his family.

"Hey brother," Thomas said as he hugged his friend and agent. "How're you doing?"

"Good. Better now. You remember Susan and Lisa."

Thomas smiled and greeted them. "I most certainly do. Thanks for flying out."

"Are you kidding me?" Susan replied with a smile. "I've been bugging Nick to take us on vacation for years and you beat him to the punch. If you ask me my husband's going to have a tough time getting off the s-h-i-t list for not coming up with this first, if you know what I mean."

"Mommm," Lisa warned her mother. "I know what that spells."

The adults snorted at Nick's expense, which he took in stride, at Lisa's remark.

"What can I say," Nick explained, "we all can't be as successful as Thomas here has been. Your latest books have been killing it."

Thomas blushed somewhat but kept his answer neutral because Nick and Susan, along with all the children, had never heard of Thomas' previous timeline adventures. That secret was held and would remain close to the vest.

"What can I say," Thomas said in response, "I guess the children of this world like what I write."

"Apparently. Just last week your numbers were…"

Laura politely cut Nick off. "Perhaps I could get the two of you a glass of wine and show you to our guestroom?"

"That would be lovely," Susan told Laura with a thankful grin.

"And you, little Lisa," Laura said, "will be staying with Emily in her room. Is that okay?"

Lisa nodded and smiled her approval.

"Great. Let's get you settled in then."

As Laura led Nick and his family away a polite knock was heard at the front door. Thomas glanced around at Sam, Bill, Julie, Kim, Ed, Claire and Michael with a questioning look.

"Are we expecting someone else?"

Sam spoke up. "Sorry. Yes. I took the liberty of inviting a few SANDBOX employees to join us. They were reluctant to come but I insisted. Apparently, according to you, you know them pretty well."

"Try not to scare them away with your knowledge of their past," Bill added with a grin.

Thomas gave Sam and Bill the finger and then walked to the front door to open it. As he did he was assaulted with familiar faces. There, on his doorstep, were Roberta, Rebecca, Hobbes and Gabbi. Thomas practically fainted but managed to recover. Instantly a huge smile spread across his face and he eagerly welcomed the four inside.

"Please, come on in."

He greeted them individually as they entered.

"Roberta. I'm so happy you could be here," and pulled her in close.

She smiled. "Thank you for having me. This is amazing."

"It's my pleasure. You're family."

Rebecca stepped in next and Thomas gave her a hug. "Hi Rebecca."

"Um…hi, Mr. Clark. I had no idea you were a hugger."

Sam and Bill snickered as Thomas, once again, mixed his past and present up in front of them.

Thomas pulled back when he realized his mistake. Nevertheless he moved forward. "Call me Thomas. And you have no idea how happy I am that you're spending the holidays with all of us."

Rebecca gave Sam and Bill an odd look as she walked past Thomas and joined them.

"Don't worry about our buddy, Thomas," Bill whispered to her. "He's good people and he's going to treat you like family, no doubt about it."

Rebecca quickly reminded herself she was in Hawaii over Christmas with her bosses. *What's happening?* But it didn't take her long to start to relax and feel right at home.

Two more people came through the door and Thomas couldn't contain the grin on his face. Before the man, or woman with the purple hair, could open their mouths Thomas opened his.

"Hey Hobbes. Hello Gabbi. You're both a sight for sore eyes."

"Umm, okay," Hobbes replied somewhat confused. "I was going to introduce us, but apparently you already know who we are."

Thomas fibbed. "Sam let me know you both were coming and I'm happy you're both here. Please, come in and make yourselves at home."

* * *

Christmas Eve dinner was a huge spectacle featuring a large adult table and a separate one for the kids. The food, the drinks, the company and the conversation were all fantastic as Thomas, and the people he considered his family, reacquainted themselves with one another. From Thomas' perspective he considered himself the luckiest man in the world because he, finally, had his entire family under one roof. As everyone laughed and enjoyed the evening Thomas took a moment and soaked it all in.

No more running. No more hiding. No more being shot at; and no more dying.

Thomas swiveled his gaze around the huge table.

My parents and grandparents are alive and they're in my life.

His eyes moved to the next person.

I have a brilliant sister that never had a chance at life before.

Sam and Bill, and their wives, are destined to be happy.

Nick, Susan and Lisa are out of harm's way and unhurt.

Rebecca and Roberta are alive and thriving at SANDBOX.

And Hobbes and Gabbi are now working for Sam and Bill as well now, and apparently have started seeing each other. Good for them.

Thomas leaned back a bit and let out a sigh of relief.

This is what life is all about.

"..omas. Hey, Earth to Thomas."

Thomas snapped back to reality. "What?"

The entire table stared at him. "Where were you just now?" Sam asked.

"I guess I was just enjoying the moment. Why, did I miss something?"

Nick spoke up. "I'll say. I'm being probed down here about being your publishing agent and was trying to get your attention."

"Sorry about that," Thomas replied. "What's your question?"

"Well," Nick continued, "I know that your latest children's book hits, such as *Trial and Error*, *Messy Room* and *Do Bunnies Rabbit?* have topped the best-selling charts."

"If you say so. I don't pay attention to that stuff like you do, Nick."

"Well, that IS my job," Nick joked. "But my point is…, what's coming next? Care to give us a preview of what's rattling around in that brain of yours? You know, maybe an early Christmas present for your dedicated agent."

Thomas had been thinking about his next endeavor, amongst the millions of other memories that resided in his head, from both timelines. The problem was that they conflicted more often than naught, and that had become difficult for him. But he had an idea about how to rectify that and he'd planned on pursuing it as soon as the holidays had come and gone.

"I have an idea," Thomas told the table.

"What are the children of the world going to read about this time?" Nick eagerly asked.

Thomas shook his head slightly. "Actually, I might try my hand at writing a novel."

"Wait, what? A novel? Really?"

Thomas nodded as Laura took his hand under the table. She knew where this was going because he'd confided in her about it already.

"I think it's time to give it shot," Thomas said.

Nick was supportive. "That's great. Knowing you it'll be something I'll definitely be looking forward to. Do you have an idea about what you want to write about?"

"Yes."

His family waited for Thomas to continue as he drifted off again.

"Care to share your thoughts?" Sam probed.

Laura squeezed his hand and Thomas pulled himself back.

"Right. Yes. Um, something in the suspense genre, I think."

Nick nodded his approval as Thomas clarified his statement.

"As it turns out, I have an idea for a series actually."

"I know this might be asking a lot," Nick pressed, "but do you have an idea of what you're going to call them?"

Thomas squeezed Laura's hand back and smiled at everyone. "I'm going to entitle the first one, *Shadows of the Mind.*"

A glimpse into the Author's head

Hello everyone and congratulations on reaching the end of my Shadow series!

When I began to pen Shadows of the Mind, at the inconceivable age of nineteen, I had no idea it would develop into a ten book marathon. Even after I rediscovered my initial conceptions of that novel, at the ripe old age of forty and somehow miraculously finished that book, I had zero thought that it'd turn into a series. None whatsoever. But here I am, five years and ten books later, knocking out the final touches on an endeavor that has been one of the most grueling, and rewarding, phases of my life.

See, what you may not understand is that Thomas, Sam and Bill are derived from my personality; of me. Shocker! So you can imagine how easy it was for me to jump back and forth during their banter, shit-talking and general closeness you read about. But those characters, in and of themselves, transcended their friendship with one another when they found themselves in one horrible situation after another.

And why's that? How could their friendship possibly survive the countless atrocities they prevailed against? Because they worked together to overcome them, as friends and as family; the two things I hold dear to me and the two things that I believe affect me the most in this life. And yet the idea of family is somewhat peculiar to me, nearly abnormal, because of my interactions, or lack thereof, with immediate family. Perhaps, as I look back over the course of this entire series, I authored a happy ending for my own edification than Thomas'.

The old saying is that you should write about what you know, so that's what I back when I was nineteen because it was easy to remember the years of being bullied, both on and off the playground. It was easy to remember the few close friends I managed to hold on to as I grew up, only to lose touch with them as life progressed. It was easy to incorporate those feelings into my characters, somehow cathartically intertwining and expressing myself through their eyes and actions. Two decades worth of real-life experience later, when I took up the writing bug a second time to finish Shadows of the Mind, I was able to take those layers of backstory I had created, combined with my own experiences, and being to weave a tale of intrigue through each and every novel in the series. And, as you're all aware, Thomas' journey culminated ten books later, and I'm very pleased with the results.

Thank you for joining me and I hope whatever creations I come up with in the near future hold as much importance to me as the comradery that Thomas, Sam and Bill shared during their adventures. Moving on to new characters, and new ideas, will be a difficult transition but one I'm ultimately looking forward to. Thank you.

D.W. Neuman

Recorded 3/7/2016 at the fledgling age of 45, which is reasonable if you equate it to the age of the Caretaker...

Visit my website at

http://www.dwneuman.com

If you enjoyed this novel please consider
taking a moment and writing a quick review
about it (on Amazon). It helps me out more
than you know and fuels my motivation!
Of course, word of mouth
works wonders too! ;)

Thank you!

www.ingramcontent.com/pod-product-compliance
Lightning Source LLC
Chambersburg PA
CBHW072339020726
47506CB00004B/935